LT-Med

# A Whisper of Black

ALSO BY CLAY HARVEY
A Flash of Red

# A WHISPER OF BLACK

## Clay Harvey

G. P. PUTNAM'S SONS
NEW YORK

G. P. Putnam's Sons
*Publishers Since 1838*
200 Madison Avenue
New York, NY 10016

Library of Congress Cataloging-in-Publication Data

Harvey, Clay.
  A whisper of black / by Clay Harvey.
     p.     cm.
   ISBN 0-399-14232-0
   I. Title.
PS3558.A71824W48   1997                96-46252 CIP
813'.54—dc21

Printed in the United States of America
10  9  8  7  6  5  4  3  2  1

BOOK DESIGN BY KATE NICHOLS

*This book*
*is dedicated to my elder sister,*
*Anne Tyler,*
*who endured the sounds of grinding sand,*
*though not exactly gracefully.*
*I love you, dear.*

I'd like to acknowledge the following:

My son, Christopher, whose loving support is unquenchable, non-judgmental, freely given, from the heart, humbling.

Dr. Barbara H. Harvey, ever exuberant deadline watcher. Yes, she got the sofa.

Ruby Hawks, mother-in-law of the year, gran'ma of the decade, my most enthusiastic reader.

Dale Hawks, who tried to run the sneak on me—role-playing the bad guys, of course—and nearly succeeded.

As always, Mike Holloway, gentle giant, whose patience and buttressing never, ever flags.

Longtime friend Andy Riedell, who read and critiqued even when he had better things to do. Like mow the grass.

Ed Humburg, martial artist, law enforcement officer, voracious reader, close friend, and a remarkable griot.

Faithful Debbie Ortiz, who never allows herself to be left out of the middle of things, health problems or no, and who always laughs in the right spots.

Cynthia and Don Adams, new friends, and dear ones. How did I ever get along before?

Ms. Emma Laine, for starting it all . . .

David Hale Smith, for his assistance in keeping it going . . .

And Neil Nyren, for patience, patience, patience.

God bless you all.

# Prologue

"Tell me again why I'm way up here in this tree," I yelled down. Forty feet down, each of those feet a full twelve inches in length.

From far, far below me, Dave Michaels yelled back, his voice harsh in the chill December air, "What's the matter? Scared of heights?"

"Not really." My voice sounded an octave or two higher than intended.

"Then why're you clinging to that branch with your teeth?"

"Drop dead."

"Shut up and cut the last clump loose," he yelled again, his voice quaking from suppressed mirth.

I did, with my Spyderco, letting the mistletoe drop, hoping it would find a tender portion of Dave's anatomy.

"Hey!" he yelped, dodging the descent. "You tried to hit me!"

"Aren't you a quick study," I answered, loudly, so he could hear me all the way down there, then shinnied groundward carefully, mindful of pointy branches and protuberances.

When my grateful feet were once again planted solidly amidst the western North Carolina bracken, we loaded up our festive gather—a bushel-basketful—and went off to find my son, Cullen, five and a half and counting, and his grandfather, Odie, seventy-three and no longer counting, who had ventured afield in search of holly.

We like Christmas, we three Vances. Dave does too, so we usually invite him to come along. He shows his appreciation by badgering me into climbing trees of such lofty height as even eagles shun.

At least I'd never seen an eagle in one.

A possum once, but no eagles.

We toted our catch to the truck, voices raised in a seasonal medley including "God Rest Ye, Merry Gentlemen," among others, reveling in the crisp air full of fellowship and woodsmoke.

And, soon, terror.

**One**    I was poking a marshmallow onto the end of Cullen's freshly shaved laurel stick when the man materialized from the darkness outside the campfire's reach, a large, loose-jointed specimen, jowls darkened with heavy beard, inky hair drooping over a high forehead, thick ears, hooded brow. Black Adidas. Ebony Dockers. The bulge of a shoulder rig showed under his matching alpaca cardigan. It was too damn cold for just a sweater. Perhaps he was impervious, or tougher than me, hunkered there in my down jacket.

Or maybe he just wanted me to spot the gun.

Without preamble, he growled, "We want our money." Cullen's eyes were large and rimmed with fear, but he sat still as a statue. Good boy.

Casually, I removed the marshmallow from its pointed stick while judging the distance from me to our uninvited guest. Through the campfire, twenty feet. Going around it, farther. And slower. On the positive side, at least I wouldn't get burned.

Just shot.

I decided on tact, diplomacy, and ignorance. Only the latter is not hard for me.

"What money?" I said.

The big loose-jointed specimen bored a hole through me with his eyes. "Do not make me angry. Our two millions. Dollars."

Fear clawed its ugly way into my throat, constricting it. I'd been afraid I knew what money he was referring to. Now I was certain.

"Why do you think I can get it?"

"You kill Valentin Resovic. He stole our money."

"And now the police have it."

"No. Money was not recovered."

I hadn't known that. "You sure?"

He gave a curt nod.

"Well, I sure don't have your dough," I insisted.

"Dough?"

I decided to push a little, gauge the menace. "American for 'moolah.'"

"Moolah? I do not understand." His forehead furrowed; then he smiled unexpectedly, displaying many teeth, including a gold one. "You are pulling my rope, yes?"

"Chain."

"Chain, that is right." Bigger smile. Just a big ol' friendly guy.

With a gun under his sweater.

"No, Mr. Vance, I do not pull your chain. You will find our money because you killed Resovic," he went on. "You, uh . . ." He cast about for the proper phraseology. ". . . made an inconvenience for us. Now you will fix. Okay?"

"But why me, instead of the authorities?"

He shook his big head. "No authorities. You found Resovic, not authorities. You killed Resovic, not authorities. Is *your* problem, not authorities'."

Pushing a little more, but terrified of the answer, I said, "And why is it *my* problem?"

He looked a little uneasy. Not a lot, sort of like he had an unpleasant taste in his mouth. "Because we will make it so."

I stood and regarded his bulk across the campfire. "I don't respond well to threats."

"What will you do? You have no gun. Besides, I could easily have kill you, from out in the night. Instead, I come to talk, like a reasonable man. You too must be reasonable. Get us our money. We need it very badly. Many die in my country every day. What is one more death? Or two?"

He had me there.

But how in the hell was I going to find his two million bucks?

He came around the fire to stand close, very close, towering above me. At this range I could easily have prevented his reaching his gun, and he knew it. It was a gesture. He handed me a card with a phone number handwritten on the back.

"Call us there. Anytime," he said, then turned, walking to the edge of the light, where he stopped, glanced back over a massive shoulder. "We have no quarrel with your son, or your *tata* . . . your father . . . and do not wish to harm them."

"You won't," I said, and then he was gone, a whisper of black.

Cullen stirred beside me, hugged my leg. "I won't let him hurt you, Daddy," he comforted, body quivering, not all from the cold.

I smiled down at the earnest little face. "Thanks, babe."

He tried to smile back, but his smiler wasn't working so good.

Staring into the night, I thought, *Oh, God, here we go again.*

•  •  •

Cullen and I had originally planned to meet Dad and Dave for supper immediately following our marshmallow roast, but our mood was now irrevocably dampened by our surprise guest. So right after he took his leave, we packed up our new Subaru and moved the bivouac site two miles, making certain we weren't followed.

After erecting the tent, distributing our sleeping bags and cots and lanterns and Ritz emergency rations, and placing a jar near the bed of the least continent among us—never mind who—we sought the Good-all farmhouse in rural Wilkes County, not far from Virginia and even closer to Tennessee, where the two of them awaited us.

"What I wanta know," said my father, "is why this feller came to you about his money instead of going to the cops."

Cullen took a sip of cocoa, endowing the end of his nose with a Cool Whip snowcap.

"That's easy enough to figure," Dave figured. "As the guy said, your hell-on-wheels son here is the one responsible for finding Resovic and his pals, not the cops. And it wasn't the cops who settled Resovic's hash."

"No. It was me," said my hell-on-wheels father.

"But they don't know that," I said.

(For those of you coming in late, six months ago I had accidentally interrupted a bank robbery in progress, and had been forced to retire two of the robbers, permanently. One of them had a brother, Valentin Resovic, who viewed my slaying of his sibling dimly, to say the least. Resovic had embarked on a vendetta that endangered my entire family. With the local police being little help, I'd had no choice but to pull some strings with a former military liaison, who provided intel and then active assistance, enabling me to pursue my pursuers, despite my ignorance of exactly who I was dealing with. Valentin and his head arm-breaker, the awesome Hector Diaz, were no common felons, but were involved in a multimillion-dollar arms deal with Bosnian Muslim money they'd been liberating from the bank upon my arrival. I and my family had been most fortunate to get out of the whole mess alive, and we'd lost a good friend, Lawrence Goodall, who had owned this farm.

And now the Muslims wanted their money, and had decided that I was just the guy to get it for them. The alternative, they'd made clear, would be unpleasant.)

"Further," I continued, "since those Muslim millions had a murky past, having been routed through Switzerland from questionable origins elsewhere, any U.S. government official approached by the Muslim faction would have given them a hearty horse laugh."

"Can a horse laugh?" asked Cullen.

"Only at Dave," I replied.

"So here's our Bosnian friends," Dave continued, "far from home with no contacts, maybe low on money, and things back in their homeland not looking up. So what do they do? Likely flounder around for four or five months, tripping over one another's feet, maybe seek assistance from a private agent, only to draw a blank. In their situation, I'd do what they finally did. But I'd have done it sooner."

"Come talk to hisself?" Dad indicated me with a lift of his chin.

Dave nodded. "Sure. He found Resovic. Maybe he can find their money."

"Do I get a finder's fee?" I asked, wiping a glop of Cool Whip from my scion's beak, transferring it to a napkin.

"Thanks," from Cullen, as he took another heated sip, recrowning the pinnacle.

"You're welcome. Hold your head up a bit. You won't dip your nose in every time you take a swallow."

"Where's the fun in that?" said Dave. I shot him my withering don't-interfere-I'm-trying-to-guide-him-besides-you-don't-have-kids-anyway look.

Odd. He didn't wither.

"Yeah, Daddy, where's the—"

My stern look did stop Cullen. Would it still, five years hence?

I sighed. "I suppose these guys won't go away and leave me alone?"

"Oh, right. Sure they will," from Dave.

"You bet," concurred my father. "They followed you all the way up here on a long shot."

"The man gave you his phone number," Cullen reminded me, Cool Whip on his nose from disregarding my advice.

I sighed again. "I suspect you're all correct. Dammit."

"Don't cuss in front of him," Dad snapped.

"Sorry, Dave."

"Not him, dang it! The boy," hammered my father.

"Don't cuss in front of—" Dave began.

"You stay outa this," Dad fired back. "And 'dang' ain't cussin'."

Cullen smiled and dripped Cool Whip, enjoying the mock-heated exchange.

After things simmered down, Odie rubbed his hands together and said, "Say, do you really think they'd give us a finder's fee?"

"I was kidding, Dad," I objected.

Too late. The wheels were turning.

# TWO

Everyone was asleep, except me. And the mice. I could hear their intermittent scritch-scratching behind the walls in the parlor, where I sat in Lawrence Goodall's old rocker, God rest his soul. He'd died right there, on the linoleum floor of his own farmhouse, gunned down by men he'd never seen and didn't know, nor did they know him. They'd shot him simply because they were evil, ruthless bastards.

Lawrence had been trying to help me, by offering his home as a haven for Cullen, and my dad, and Heather Patterson—my lady of interest—and her young son, Web. For this blessed Samaritan streak, Lawrence had died.

I rocked, and thought, and remembered . . .

The bank robbery, when Resovic's brother, Mikhail, had tried to machine-gun me into shark food, instead winding up on a slab himself . . .

The retaliation, when Valentin Resovic and Hector Diaz—a malignant monster so large he completely filled a doorway, top to bottom, side to side—had made attempt after attempt on my life, and then on Cullen's . . .

The final confrontation, when to save my son—kidnapped and then tied to a tree in Lawrence's front yard—I'd wounded Valentin in this house, fought Hector from wall to wall, then watched the giant die, right over there, slumped in a pool of his own fluids, bloody intestines coiled in his lap, courtesy of my father and a twelve-bore shotgun . . .

Resovic, watching from the other room, where he sat, back to the wall, bleeding, and in spite of being racked with pain threatened us with even more horror . . .

Dad, who tends to take threats seriously, removing that one by splattering Resovic's face all over the wall.

No more threats.

No more Bosnians.

For six peaceful months.

Until now . . .

*Back to square one,* I thought, sitting there in the wee hours, coffee at hand, rocking and missing Lawrence and listening to the mice scamper. Planning.

In order for this not to get out of hand—like the last time—I'd need help. I knew where to get it.

This time Cullen would stay safe.

# Three

We traveled the hundred-odd miles to Greensboro next morning, Dave and Cullen in the back seat playing "checkerds" and doing aikido drills, at least as much as they could do sitting down. Dave and I had been teaching my son martial arts disciplines since he was two. When we arrived home, Dad stayed with Cullen while I went off for a close encounter with the local police, and Dave drove to his electronics store, The Lion's Din.

When I was uncomfortably seated in front of his familiar pockmarked desk, I told GPD Homicide lieutenant John T. Fanner all about my current Bosnian dilemma, all the while looking earnestly into his disinterested eyes—for a little help, you understand, something the police are not always known to provide, except on their own behalf.

As cops go, Fanner wasn't bad. Six feet two inches, 235 pounds of suet and blood dressed in a twelve-hundred-dollar Canali suit, bright Pancaldi knotted four-in-hand, highly polished Johnston and Murphy oxbloods; given to heavy gold wrist jewelry and a bluff manner. Mutual respect resided within us, but we weren't pals. After I finished my tale of woe, he said, "What is it you want from me?"

"What do I want? I want you to take care of this situation, Fanner, what do you think?"

"How?"

"Can't this big Muslim guy be arrested for making threats?"

He shook his head and held up three large fingers, ticking them off one by one with a digit from his other hand. "First, he did not do so in the presence of witnesses, other than your child, so it would be his word against yours. Second, simply threatening a citizen is not, of itself, illegal. Finally, the Goodall farm is outside my bailiwick."

"Then, you're not—" I began, but was interrupted by an underling with a handful of papers for Fanner, who took them, said, "Thanks, Ben," then tossed the pile onto his desk without a glance.

"Obviously," I continued, "you're telling me, once again, that there is nothing you can do for me."

Fanner tugged his ear, swiveled his chair to look out the window, then said, his back to me, "I suppose I can look into it. But since no money was recovered from Resovic, at least according to the FBI, who investigated the, ah, situation at the farm, then I have little to go on. If the Muslims do make a try at you, or anyone around you, I will intervene on your behalf, if you convince me they were the the ones."

Spinning his chair to catch my face, he said, "I do not, and I say again, *not* want a repeat of the situation last summer."

"Me neither," I agreed.

"Then may I suggest," Fanner continued, "that you enlist your friends at Bragg to enlist their friends in Virginia to find out what is known about the missing Muslim millions, since I have no clue. I would not be a bit surprised if the money had been, shall we say, appropriated."

I considered. "If that's a possibility, or worse, a probability, then I could be up the creek here. It's pretty certain they'd never admit it."

He concurred by arching his eyebrows.

"Hmm," I said.

"Hmm," he agreed.

After a brief hesitation, he said, "Actually, this comes at a more inopportune time than you know. I was about to call you, I am afraid with further unpleasant news."

"I don't want to hear it."

"About Hector Diaz."

"Late and unlamented."

"It appears that he is not so late as we thought."

"What do you mean?" I asked, sitting up straight in my chair.

"The FBI ran the prints from that big Mexican carted out of your friend's house in the mountains, identified by you and your military contacts as Hector Diaz, whom the newspapers claimed you killed."

"I did kill him, Lieutenant."

"So I read, and heard. I also heard another story . . ." He raised his hand when I started to object.

". . . which is of no consequence to me. That battle took place outside my jurisdiction. I do not care who killed whom. Nonetheless, shortly following that affair I requested of a friend in a nameless federal agency to be kept informed of any possible backlash resulting from the demise of Valentin Resovic and his Hispanic bodyguard, at least here in the States. A tidbit crossed my desk two days ago."

I waited; he'd get to the point. In due time. Fanner never let a good story suffer in the telling. He shot his cuffs, exposing an ornate gilt bracelet, tugged at an ear, and continued. "The fingerprints taken from the cadaver identified as Hector Diaz did not match prints Interpol had in their files under that name."

I waited some more, not patiently.

"They did, however, match those of one Emilio Diaz."

"Emilio?" Quick-witted, that's me.

"Apparently a younger, smaller, nicer cousin of Hector," Fanner elaborated.

"Smaller?" I said, remembering how the huge man I'd fought—more than a foot taller than my five eight, and roughly 130 pounds heavier than my 165—had tossed me around with relative ease despite my fighting skills, superior guile, fancy footwork, and strenuous objections.

"Shorter by an inch or two, I am told, and lighter by perhaps a stone and a half."

"What does a stone weigh?"

"Fourteen pounds."

"So a stone and a half is roughly twenty pounds," I said. He smiled pleasantly. "Did your sums as a lad, I see."

"That means the real Hector will go over three hundred," I mumbled to myself. "Dad'll need a bigger shotgun."

"Beg your pardon?"

"Nothing. So what happened to Hector Diaz if he isn't the one I traded licks with at the farm?"

"I do not know," answered the lieutenant. "I merely find it interesting that the dread Hector Diaz is not dead. I do not, however, wish for you to be alarmed unnecessarily. So far as I know, Señor Diaz has not rejoined us from Mexico."

"He's below the border?"

"According to my source, Hector left the United States two days before you terminated his cousin and Valentin Resovic."

"Two days *before*?"

"Bound for Juarez, I believe."

"And he's still there?"

"Mexico City of late."

"So why did you refer to this earlier as bad news?"

"Well, since your Bosnian brethren have materialized from the woodwork, I assumed you would not welcome the news that Hector Diaz is alive and well, even though distantly south of the border."

I thought about it. "Maybe I don't mind, at that. He might have taken the Muslim cash with him. If so, I could sic the Bosnians on old Hector, kill two birds with one rock."

"Assuming that your Muslim tormentors feel free to travel from country to country, and have the means."

"Right," I said, standing. As if in afterthought, I said, "Think he's nursing a grudge?"

"Who?" said Fanner.

"Diaz. You reckon he and Resovic were bosom buddies, or just business partners?"

"In the Latin heart, loyalty runs deep. And remember, Emilio was a cousin."

"Then this might work, Lieutenant."

"Good. The Muslims will be out of your hair, and you will be out of mine."

"I'll call the colonel," I said.

"Please keep me apprised," Fanner said, as I turned to depart. "If the money or the larger, meaner Mr. Diaz turns up nearby, I will be all ears." He smiled as benignly as a tiger as he leaned back in his swivel chair, big hands laced behind his closely cropped head.

"Of course."

" 'Of course,' you say, as if you were a font of information last summer."

"That's me, Ol' Blabbermouth," I said, and left. His chuckle followed me out the door.

• • •

Heather Patterson was stringing lights on the eight-foot Fraser fir in my sitting room, her kindergarten-age son Web very close by (too close?) placing figures into the crèche at the base of the tree. Heather was tall, beautiful, classy, with hair the color of honey. She had wit and charm and grace, and a Porsche she sometimes let me drive when I was good.

Web I was worried about. After the disastrous events of the past summer, which included his being taken hostage along with my son and mother-in-law, the boy had internalized his trauma. He was in therapy, but progress was slow. Heather, a children's magazine editor, had given up going to the office and was working out of her home in order to have Web near her. The result so far had not been encouraging; Web remained withdrawn and unresponsive, would respond verbally only to Heather; his father, Jason; my dad and mother-in-law, Ethyl Cullowee; and Cullen. I could touch Web without him recoiling, and talk to him, as could Dave, but he wouldn't reply. When anyone other than this tight-knit circle entered the room, Web would simply leave.

Heather was doing the best she could with the problem, though it tended to get her down. Her ex-husband Jason was gay, which was why they'd split, but of late the two had developed a reasonably comfortable friendship—good for them both, and especially so for Web. He depended on them for constancy in his life, stability, safety. For a few days last summer, his life had been seriously deficient in those factors.

I ruffled his cowlick as he carefully placed Baby Jesus in the manger. He looked up, a latent smile tugging determinedly at the corners of his mouth. "You're doing a fine job with that," I proffered.

He kept looking at me, politely waiting for me to finish, still doing his best to smile. Heather watched, a strand of lights leading from her hand. I hugged his head to my leg, tousled his hair again. "Keep up the good work, bud," I said, glancing at Heather. She shrugged and smiled ruefully: A for effort. Web went back to work and I went to check on

Dad, over in the corner spreading holly and whistling "Up On the Rooftop" with artificially dentured sibilance.

"Good berries on those."

"You think I can't pick holly?" he responded, flexing arthritic fingers.

"I'm going to make a pot of coffee. Any preference?"

"Got any of that African stuff you fixed Thanksgiving?"

"Kenya roast? You bet. Decaf?"

"Think I wanta stay up all night?"

"Decaf it is." I turned to leave him to his whistling.

"Son?"

"Yeah, Pop?"

"You make up your mind what to do about them Arabs?"

"Muslims."

"Whatever."

"I have some ideas."

"Well, keep me in suspense, why don't you?"

"I left a message for McElroy to call me. After I talk to him, I'll fill you in."

"I could sure use some of that money. What if I go after it?"

"I told you, leave it alone, Dad. The Muslims won't part with a dime of that bread. Besides, it's too dangerous. Stay out of it."

He puffed up like a pouter pigeon, but said nothing.

"Just be sensible," I said, and went to make some coffee.

*There's no way he'll follow through with this,* I thought.

What a fool I was.

•  •  •

Dave had been outside festooning with blue lights a pair of leafless maples in the front yard. "Cold," he said, as he stomped through the foyer into the kitchen, flapping his arms for warmth like a big, muscular penguin.

"Wuss," I said.

"Easy for you to say. You've been inside while I, a manly man, braved the bitter cold, tears streaming down my frozen cheeks, suffering silently to make the neighborhood a brighter, happier—"

"Coffee?"

"Sure." He withdrew his tattered brown outback-style hat, shoul-dered loose from his mackinaw, piled them atop the kitchen table. I filled the Garfield mug he kept in my cupboard, handed it to him, filled a Christmassy one for Pop, took it to him, asked Heather if she'd like some—declined with a smile—and returned to the kitchen to pour my own into a cup that said *Jultomten* on its side.

"Hot," Dave said.

"You saw me brewing it."

"Your machine is set on too high a temperature."

"Blow on it."

Heather came in with Web, made each of them a cup of warm tea, then joined us while Web went to help Dad finish up the lights.

The room smelled strongly of coffee and my sweetie. I inhaled deeply. Dave said, "So old Hector Diaz is not only alive, but hale and hearty and in his homeland."

"What?" said Heather.

"Yep. According to Lieutenant John T. Fanner," said Dave.

"Then who was that gigantic man at the farm with Resovic last June?" Heather asked, wide-eyed.

"According to Fanner," I said, "it's his smaller, nicer, younger cousin Emilio."

"Nicer?" said Heather. "The man who shot Lawrence Goodall, pistol-whipped your father, and turned you black-and-blue has a *mean* cousin?"

"So I'm told."

"But now he's back in Mexico?" Heather asked.

"So Fanner says."

"I hope he's right," she said, shuddering.

I didn't shudder, being a manly man and all. I just *felt* like shuddering.

Heather finished her drink and rejoined the pair in the living room. Strains from Mannheim Steamroller's *Christmas in the Aire* drifted back: "Angels We Have Heard on High," George Vosburg's brassy skill lofting the listener, Chip Davis and his drums keeping the frantic pace. *Nobody* does Christmas like Mannheim Steamroller.

"What you going to do about the Muslims?" Dave queried.

"Try to point them at Diaz," I said. "And keep Dad out of trouble. He wants to give them a hand finding their money."

"That's a hoot. He'd get exactly nowhere," Dave said.

What a fool he was.

# Four

Next morning, I called the number the big Bosnian had given me. No answer. Second priority: breakfast.

I was removing the seeds from three cardamom pods when Heather's Porsche slid into my driveway with a growl and a high-pitched squeal. *Dust on the rotors*, I thought, as I placed the seeds in a food processor for grinding. When she came through my door into the kitchen, I was beating a trio of eggs with a wire whip. I'm a traditionalist. She kissed my cheek, sat at the counter, and laid her emerald gaze upon me. *Zing!* went the strings.

"What are you preparing?"

"You'll see. What did Ethyl have to say this morning?" Since my wife, Tess, died almost a year ago, victim of a drunk driver, Ethyl Cullowee, my mother-in-law, and I were in partnership in a small publishing business. For years I'd been making a living as a free-lance outdoor writer—mostly stuff about guns and hunting—and Ethyl was in charge of the books I produced for my own imprint. She worked hard and long and testily, which is one reason my father avoided her like a dose of Epsom salts. Sometimes I did, too.

"That she'd keep Web and Cullen for a couple hours, but that we could . . ." She paused to dramatize her mimicry. ". . . *for Pete's sake* have taken them to Blandwood with us."

I grinned. "For Pete's sake" is one of Ethyl's favorites, for use when her dander's up. The eggs had attained a proper lemony color, so I dumped them into a blender with the finely ground cardamom seeds and one-quarter cup of two percent and turned the machine on, letting it run for a minute while I placed a nonstick frying pan over medium heat.

I said, "She knows I took Cullen to see the Blandwood decorations last week, so she was just being Ethyl. We could take Web, though, if he wants to come," meanwhile adding three-quarters cup of sifted flour, a tablespoon of sugar, and two tablespoons of melted butter to the mix.

Heather, standing closer than was absolutely necessary for conversational purposes, said, "I was planning on our having some time alone. I can take Web later. Besides, Jason is picking the boys up to take them to see the original *Miracle on 34th Street* at the Carolina Theatre."

"Time alone, huh?" said I, switching the blender on again and watching it swirl. "What do you have in mind?"

Small smile of promise. "A little hand-holding perhaps."

"Yeah?"

Bigger smile. "Maybe a kiss. Or two."

I held up a palm. "But no groping."

Smile so electric I felt its wattage behind my sternum. "Who knows? Maybe you'll get lucky."

"Or one of us."

Laugh lines in broad evidence, she began to sing, "You're so vain, you prob'ly think the world spins around you . . ."

"We're talking serious ego when you have the gall to paraphrase Carly Simon," I complained, while pouring into my now heated pan sufficient batter for a couple of medium-sized pancakes. She came around to my side of the counter and did several things with her anatomy that I won't describe because Cullen might read this someday.

Suffice to say that I burned my first pair of Swedish pancakes.

• • •

A couple hours later, filled with pancakes, and maple syrup brought back from Vermont, we climbed into Heather's 911 Turbo and pointed its nose toward the Blandwood mansion in downtown Greensboro. The former residence of John Motley Morehead, governor of North Carolina from 1841 until 1845, the place had begun life in the 1790s as a four-room, two-story frame number with no pretensions, and grown from there. Each year it's decorated for Christmas in period motif, and is the pride of Greensboro's cognoscenti, and those who fancy themselves such. Some of us peons like it too, but we don't put on airs when we go. Nor ties neither.

I eased the Porsche through the gears, keeping it tightly reined; traffic was thick as treacle.

"You're uncharacteristically light on the throttle," she observed.

"Basking in the afterglow."

Devilish smile. "Of a delightful breakfast?"

"Or something."

"Is your reproductive system rejuvenating itself?"

"So insistently I can feel it groaning."

"Did you say growing?"

"Fizgig," I said, as the sound of my cellular interrupted our foreplay, or afterplay.

"It's me," I said into the phone.

"And it's me," a voice came back. A familiar voice, one that I had not encountered in nearly six months. Before that, twenty years.

Unfortunately, whenever I heard it, trouble followed.

"How are you, Colonel McElroy?" I said.

"Right as rain. You?"

"Fine."

"Missed me?"

"Who is this again?"

He laughed. "Me too. So, what can I do for you?"

"I seem to have acquired another Bosnian thorn in my foot."

"What!"

"My sentiments exactly." For the next three minutes, I told him about my confrontation with the large Muslim.

"So that's why . . ." He paused thoughtfully.

"Why what?"

"Your dad called. I've no idea how he got my number here at the base."

"I have it in my Rolodex."

"You ain't supposed to."

"So what'd he allow?"

"That he needed to know how to find Feron Simmons."

Now there was a name I'd hoped never to hear again. "What did you tell him?"

"I gave him the name of that bait shop out on Lake Brandt Road. Why?"

"Oh, shit!" I said.

"What?" from Heather.

"What's the matter?" from Colonel Rufus Earl McElroy, United States Army, ninety miles away.

"Tell you later," I said into the cell phone. "Gotta go now, I need both hands for driving." I rang off.

Heather said, "What!"

I told her about the Muslims and their desires, and my father's professed intention of doing something on their fiscal behalf.

"I never thought about him calling McElroy, or even remembering about Feron Simmons."

"Why would he want to find this Simmons character?"

"Feron worked for Resovic, as a gofer. I got my first lead on him at a fishing tackle joint out near Lake Brandt."

"So your dad thinks Feron might know something about the missing money?"

"Apparently."

She held her breath. "You think he might be right?"

"I don't know, but I think that if he's gone out there looking for Feron, and finds him, he could be in deep shit."

As I motored on, dodging and weaving, honking and plunging, irritating people right and left, Heather asked, "Just how did you come to know Colonel McElroy, anyway?"

"We met in Korea in 1974."

"What was he to you?"

"Nothing at first. Later, he was my control officer."

She looked at me very oddly for a moment, then said, "What is a control officer?"

I drove some more, tapped the horn, the brakes, my creativity, looking for an explanation that might satisfy her curiosity, since I couldn't tell her the truth.

"Are you going to answer me?"

"A control officer is exactly what the name implies."

She sucked in her exquisite lower lip, said, "It makes you sound like an attack dog or something."

*Pretty close*, I thought. What I said was, "I can't be more specific."

"Why not?" she asked, a frustrated frown creasing her brow.

"Because it's classified."

"What's classified?"

"What I did in Korea."

"What you did in the service *two decades* ago is still classified?"

I nodded, spinning the wheel to avoid a postal truck parked halfway in the street, its driver hustling to deliver a package, not caring who was inconvenienced. She was a postal worker, by golly, so could park where she damn well pleased.

Heather was silent, absorbing what I'd told her. And not liking it very much, I suspected.

Well, neither did I. What I'd done for McElroy and good old Uncle Sam still gave me nightmares, which was fitting, since it had begun with a nightmare and ended with something worse. I shook my head to dislodge the memory.

And the Porsche rushed on.

We entered the parking lot of Bobby Tew's Bait and Tackle Shop four minutes later, the car's rear end slewing around on some loose gravel. Heather pointed toward the picnic tables at the side of the lot. "There's your dad's car."

And, twenty yards away from his car, was my dad . . .

On his knees, bleeding profusely from nose and mouth . . .

Surrounded by four men, none of whom was Feron Simmons. One of them held a tire iron, another a length of lead pipe.

Taking off my jacket, I got out of the car.

Heather said, "Do you have a gun?"

I shook my head.

"You'll need one."

"No, I won't," I responded, and went to get my father.

# Five

The quartet of assailants turned to face me as I approached, stringing out in a line. Dad was to their rear, wiping blood from his face with the back of a hand and sitting back on his heels, chest heaving from strain and exertion.

The guy with the pipe was obviously the head toughy. In that capacity, he addressed me formally: "What the fuck do you want?"

"You all right?" I said to my dad.

"Okay," from Odie. "Not as bad as it looks. My uppers cut the inside of my mouth. That's where most of the blood is coming from. That 'un with no ass in his britches," he continued, indicating my pipe-wielding friend, "hit me on the beezer with that pipe. Maybe broke it."

"Shut up, old man!" from Head Toughy.

I looked up into his eyes, high above mine—he was about six four, but roughly my heft—and asked, "That true? Did you hit my dad with a piece of pipe?"

"Dunno if he's your dad, and don't give a rat turd, but I sure as fuck popped him with this pipe. Want some of the same, asswipe?"

"Sure."

"Say what?"

"Sure. Hit me with the pipe."

He was long and lean and fast and mean, but he also telegraphed his intentions. His pupils dilated as he dipped his right shoulder slightly to get power in his swing. I caught the pipe by one end with my left hand when it was still about ten inches from my left jawline, and rotated it sharply counterclockwise. The head tough guy, macho man that he was, didn't have sense enough simply to let go and step back out of my reach. He resisted, clinging tightly to the lead-filled pipe as I rotated it nearly 180 degrees, twisting his wrist along with it, his elbow moving into his side from the torquing motion. I clamped his wrist with my right hand, squeezing hard, then jerked the pipe loose with my left, continuing the motion by reaching over his captive hand to smash him on the bridge of the nose with his own weapon. At the impact, he sagged to his knees, blood spurting from both nostrils, his twisted hand still held tightly in place by mine, as if in a vise. Again using the pipe, with one strike I broke all four fingers of his right hand, then rotated my body at the hips, still holding his wrist, causing him to spin toward the man on my left, now moving in. Head Toughy landed right in front of Tough Guy Number Two, who obligingly tripped over his pain-racked buddy to pile in a heap at my feet.

The tire iron specialist—250 pounds of blubber and bone, maybe 15 of muscle—made his move from my right, bludgeon raised over his head to strike downward, intent on pulping my scalp. I dissuaded him with a straight right to the larynx and a follow-up shot with the pipe that caught him above the ear. He dropped like a sack of compost, tire iron clattering to the pavement. His pal, filled with the urgency of the moment, charged straight in, windmilling his arms as if he had no fighting experience whatever. I felt a little sorry for him, until I remembered that he had stood there while his cronies beat up my father, so I sidestepped to let him go past, breaking his right elbow with the pipe as he went by and drawing a cry of pain. When he stopped to clutch the wounded wing to his bosom, I used a low side kick on the outside of his right knee, and felt bone yield. That sent him to the ground; applying the pipe to the side of his neck sent him to dreamland.

Three down.

Tough Guy Number Two had disentangled himself from his gangly obstruction, risen to his Reeboked feet, and produced a folding knife with a four-inch serrated blade.

He held it menacingly in front of himself, lip curled in a vicious sneer, or what he thought was vicious. I flashed to Korea, where an Army sergeant had once pulled a similar knife on me, long ago, but quickly cast the vision from me. I needed to focus on the danger before me, not one from the past.

"Put that down," I advised. "You might cut yourself."

"Gonna cut your balls off, man," he screamed at me with too much vehemence. Louder bark than bite? Possibly. Still, he had a blade; my underestimating his ability or resolve wouldn't do Dad much good.

He set his legs shoulder-width apart, the knife in his right hand held back against the hipbone, protected by his left arm, held horizontally in front of his chest. He'd shifted the knife in his hand and turned its

cutting edge inward, placing his thumb on top of the handle, not lock-
ing it onto his middle and index fingers. That grip is known as the modi-
fied saber, and I found it interesing. It implied that he'd used a knife for
cutting something other than a Christmas turkey.

Best finish this quick.

Tossing the pipe at his eyes for diversion, I moved into him. He deflected the pipe with his left forearm, then brought down the same arm
to ward me off, meanwhile starting a slash with the knife aimed at my
ribs. Placing my right leg between his spread ones and spinning
counterclockwise, I blocked his strike with my left forearm, extended
my right arm under his, continued to pivot as I captured his knife wrist
in my left hand, gripped his right upper arm with my right hand, bent
over at the waist and pulled, causing him to sail over my shoulder and
onto his back. The breath left him in a whoosh. Keeping his knife hand
under control, I continued the move, then straightened slightly and
stomped his right armpit with the heel of my shoe, very hard, feeling
tendons tear. Still applying upward pressure on the captive arm, I grabbed
the thumb of his knife hand and tried to wrench it off. He dropped the
knife and lay writhing and kicking, trying to get away from me. My response was to encircle his throat with my right arm, release his wrist
from my left hand, slip behind him while dragging him half upright,
then clamp my left hand onto my right arm. I squeezed and he
thrashed, pulse pounding in my temples, until Heather said, "You're
killing him!"

I kept the pressure on for a few more seconds, until his body went
completely limp, then released it. He slumped over.

"No. Just putting him to sleep."

Odie took Heather gently by the arm. "Honey, you don't need to see
this." Her eyes were huge with fright.

"Come with us," she pleaded of me, as Dad tried to lead her away.

"I'll be along."

"What are you going to do?" Terrified.

"Find out why these gents were pounding on my dad."

"What if they won't tell you?"

I looked down at the sad quartet on the ground, mired in misery.
"They'll tell me."

Nearing hysteria. "Don't hurt them anymore!"

That made me angry. I went to her, pointed at my father. "Don't *hurt* them, Heather? Look at Dad. You think he cut himself shaving? What would those assholes have done to him if I hadn't arrived? You worry about my father, not those sacks of shit. Now get him to Cone Hospital."

I looked at Odie. "The keys in your car?"

He shook his head, took them out of a pocket and tossed them to me.

"Son, all I did was go in that store and ask had anyone see Feron Simmons lately. Them boys gave me some lip, then started askin' me questions. I told 'em to go suck eggs, so they grabbed me, dragged me out here, and smacked me around some. I tagged one of 'em good, but there was too many for me."

"Ten years ago, you wouldn't have needed any help," I said.

He grinned a bloody grin. A toothless bloody grin; his plate was in his pocket. "Wonder why they were so protective of old Feron," he said.

"I plan to find out, right here in a minute."

"Please . . ." Heather began.

I looked into her eyes. "Just take care of him," I said gruffly, nodding at Pop.

"We better go," Dad offered. "One of 'em's stirrin'."

While they climbed into the Porsche to leave, I went to see who was stirrin'.

•  •  •

Tough Guy Number Three was stirring—but only a little, trying to minister to a severely damaged knee with his one good arm, and not faring well. His fellow troops were unconscious, or nearly so in the case of Head Toughy, still vaguely aware of his surroundings but not in a productive way. Blood streamed from his ruined nose.

I knelt beside Number Three, who paid me no mind whatever, so engrossed was he in his discomfort. I gained his attention by grabbing his left ear and jerking his head around, and his trust by saying: "Listen very carefully, because I won't say this twice. I'm going to ask a few questions, and you are going to answer them quickly and truthfully. If you do not, I will rip this ear off and stuff it in your shirt. Do you believe me?"

I released the ear so he could nod, petrified. Good that he was scared. Maybe I wouldn't have to hurt him any more.

"First question," I said. "Do you know Feron Simmons?"

Nod.

"Have you seen him lately, say in the past week?"

He thought, then shook his head.

"Know where he is?"

Nod.

"Where?"

He took a deep, shaky breath. "Right now, at his mama's in Engelhard. Day after tomorrow, he's going pig hunting at Royce Rucklin's place."

"In Taylorsville?"

Painful nod.

"Hunting at Rucklin's isn't cheap."

He concurred with a bob of his grungy goatee. "Feron come into some money here lately."

"Did he? Big money?"

"Dunno. I reckon. He's been hunting and fishing all over the state since last summer. Bought a new four-by, big Dodge Ram V-eight, and he ain't worked a lick."

"So why'd you boys decide to work my dad over?"

Breath coming in short painful gasps, he continued, "Feron tolt us someone might come asking after him someday. Said he'd make it worth our while to let him know about it."

"He say who?"

"Naw. Did say it might be a big greaser."

"My dad look Hispanic to you?"

Miserable, sitting there with likely more than one broken bone, he began to cry. "We was just after a little fun."

"Call this fun?"

Head shake, tears streaming. "Your dad got mouthy with Caplock. Cappy don't take that off nobody, not even a geezer." He cringed at his inadvertent insult, glancing sideways to see if I was going to box his ears or break his other elbow.

Instead, I pointed at Head Toughy. "That Caplock?"

Nod.

I watched Caplock, now slumped over and staining the tarmac with his fluids, then said, "Okay, listen up. Get to a hospital, get fixed up, then get the fuck out of Greensboro. If I see you again, it will upset me."

He nodded his full understanding and agreement.

I climbed to my feet. "Oh, one more thing."

He raised his eyebrows encouragingly, a willing audience.

"If I drive all the way to Taylorsville day after tomorrow and Feron's not there, I'll find you and rip out your adenoids, even if you move to Rwanda. Understood?"

Vehement nod.

"You know where Rwanda is?"

"No, but it don't matter. I ain't telling Feron, and they ain't neither," indicating his buddies.

"You promise?"

"Fuckin' A."

"I'll count on it," I said, and left him to his plight.

**Six** In the emergency room at Moses Cone, I paced and drank some really lousy coffee. Six cups had me as jittery as an armadillo on a swinging bridge. Heather was sitting on a bench against the wall, carefully avoiding eye contact. Okay. Let her play it that way.

A little girl came through on a gurney, one leg bandaged, holding her father's hand as he kept pace with the attendant doing the pushing, moving right along. To X ray, maybe.

Heather lit her second cigarette since I'd arrived, an occasional habit she'd acquired late in life and was striving mightily to resist. Unsuccessfully at present. She puffed away, lost in thought.

"Mr. Tyler Vance?" from a funereal nurse at my elbow.

"He hasn't died, has he?" I said.

Her demeanor was remonstrative; she didn't find me funny. I ran into that a lot.

"The cuts in his mouth and gum required fifteen stitches. He is coming down now."

I nodded my appreciation.

She started to turn, hesitated, thinned down her lips and added gravely, "Your father is a profane man."

With equal gravity, I nodded. "Gets it from his mother. She was a bos'n's mate on the USS *Maine*."

The look on her face would have cowed a lesser man.

Here came my dad riding a wheelchair propelled by the comeliest nurse in a three-county area. Last time he was here, unfortunately not too long ago, he'd had a similarly nubile caregiver. She brought him over, blessed me with a smile sufficient to put starch in any stamen, and took her leave with, "Don't go 'way, now, honey."

"Lech," I admonished, when she was gone.

Pop tried to smile, but the damage to his mouth precluded it. He beckoned me near; I bent close so he could whisper. "Find out anything about Feron?" he asked.

"Sure."

"Well?"

"He's running for mayor of Stumpy Point."

"Smart aleck."

"If I tell, you promise not to run off half-cocked?"

"I didn't run off half-cocked, just didn't expect to run into no trouble asking a few questions. Would you?"

"I suppose not. Still, you should've told me what you had planned."

"Okay, okay," from my dad, Mr. Contrite. "So what'd you find out?"

"My informant related that Feron's wallet runneth over. He's been playing Nimrod all over the state, in fact will be looking to waylay a wild pig at Rockytop Hunting Preserve two days from now."

"That's clear over in Taylorsville? You going up there?"

"Indeed I am."

"Me too, then."

I shook my head. "You're stove up."

"We'll see." He looked across the room to where Ms. Patterson was contributing to air pollution. "By the way, Heather's upset."

"No kidding."

"Very upset. You serious about her, long-term?"

"Probably."

"Then you need to tell her."

"What?"

"How you come to be like you come to be."

"Korea?"

"Uh-huh."

"Dad. That's classified. It would be a violation of—"

"Who you think gives a toot!" he hissed, grimacing from the pain. "That was years ago. And who do you think she'd tell, son? That gal loves you, but she saw something this afternoon she's trying to come to grips with and can't. Up to you to help her, if you care. If you don't, that's another story. But I'll tell you this, if you don't explain things to her, she's gonna cut you loose."

He was almost certainly right.

"It's your decision," he finished, dumping the problem back in my lap.

Where it belonged, I suppose.

"Take her home in her car. I'll drive myself," he said.

"You sure? What if you get groggy from the painkiller?"

He snorted. "What painkiller? Get on outa here." My dad's a tough old bird.

"Oh, shit! Here comes Ethyl," he expleted, grabbing one wheel and spinning his chair in panic.

Then again, maybe not so tough.

I left him to her.

# Seven

Sitting in the big maple rocker in the corner, I watched Heather pace the floor of her condo. From the fireplace to the couch; around the coffee table littered with children's magazines and a copy of Winston Groom's *Gump & Co.;* over to the blue floral-print chair that matched the couch; into the dining area.

Repeat.

On a heavy oak end table rested a lamp, assorted bric-a-brac, several photographs of Web—one in a cute sailor outfit—and a framed portrait of your obedient servant. There were no dart pricks in it. Yet. Her large-screen TV was on, sound muted, the late Audrey Meadows giving Jackie Gleason what-fer.

Cigarette smoke hung blue in the air, though Heather knew I hated it. She usually didn't light up inside her place, not only for me but in deference to Web's youthful lungs. Puff, pace; puff, pace. I could almost see her lungs blackening.

"Why don't I leave?" I said. "I don't want to be responsible for your getting lung cancer."

She angrily stabbed the butt into an ashtray, wrapped her arms around her slender torso for want of something to do with them, and resumed pacing. "Too late. You're already responsible."

"I didn't start you smoking."

"No, but you sure as hell compounded the habit this afternoon."

"Sorry, but it couldn't be helped. I needed to find my dad before he got himself into trouble, and I almost didn't manage, at that. Simply asking those boys to stop working him over didn't seem like the most effective course of action, but I thought I might as well try. They never gave me the chance. So I did what I had to."

She stopped her pacing to look at me. "You sure did, and it's what has me so upset. You did it so effortlessly." She sat on the couch, clear across the room from me.

I rocked and waited, sipping tepid tea.

She chewed on her thoughts, biting her lip. "I never saw anything like it, not even in a Chuck Norris film. When we arrived, I first thought you were being brazen, hoping to bluff those men into leaving your father alone. You didn't seem scared, but I figured that was an act. Who wouldn't be scared facing four men, two of them with weapons in plain sight? But then you . . ." She paused to shiver. "I mean, after all that happened last summer, you'd think I'd be impervious to a simple fist-fight, wouldn't you? But it wasn't the fight that upset me. It was how you went through those men like a bowling ball mowing down the pins. You showed not only a lack of fear, but a complete lack of emotion of any kind. None, not even anger. Even James Bond looks pissed when he trashes a bad guy. Not you, boy."

She stopped and stared at me. Obviously it was my turn to contribute, so I said, "James Bond's in the movies. This wasn't. In real life, you don't have the luxury of getting mad, not if you need to win. Not *want* to win, *need* to win. If I'd allowed myself to lose control, even a little, and it had cost me the battle, where would you and my dad have been, let alone me?"

"But how could you *know* that? How many fights have you endured? And how could you beat the hell out of four tough men in about three seconds?"

"Those weren't tough men, Heather. They were ruffians. Mean, and possibly dangerous if they had things under their control. But tough? Uh-uh. Dave is tough. And McElroy. My dad used to be pretty tough, but not professionally so."

"Could any of them have taken those men?"

"Dave, yes, and maybe McElroy, I'm not sure. He's tough enough, all right. But it isn't just that, it's being willing."

"Like you? Are you willing?"

I said nothing.

"How did you come to be like this, so tough, and so . . . willing?"

More nothing from me.

"Ty. I need to know."

"Why?"

"Why? *Why?* Because I saw a different man today, different from the one I had hoped my son might take as his role model, the one I see in my dreams, the one who takes my breath away when he walks into the room. This new man scares me. Maybe if I know why he's like he is, he won't."

I mulled it over, pro and con. On the one hand, she deserved an answer; on the other, Leavenworth did not appeal to me.

What a pickle.

"I could get in big trouble for telling you this."

"With the government?"

I nodded.

"Who would I tell? *Why* would I tell? How could anyone prove it was you who told me? And how recently did you perform classified work for the government?"

"Twenty years, more or less."

"In Korea?"

I nodded again.

"Are you sure something that old would still be classified?"

"You bet," I said. "What I did was not exactly legal, on an international level. Necessary, but frowned upon by civilized nations. Outcry from the citizenry would surely result should the media get hold of it."

"And you think News Two is hiding in the closet?"

"No. But what if you and I don't . . ."

"What?" She inclined her head. "Make it as a couple? You think I'm so petty that I'd try to have you sent to jail if we stopped dating?"

"When people feel slighted, they often do things they don't normally do."

"Oh. You *do* think I'm that petty."

I was most uncomfortable.

"Tyler." She shifted her weight on the couch. "I saved Cullen's life, remember? Do you think I would send his father to jail? If you do, then you don't know me at all."

I made my decision. "You can never tell a soul, for any reason."

She smiled, reassuring me that I could trust her.

So I took a deep breath and told her . . .

About the massacre of my squad, and seeing the survivors tortured, my decimation of the North Korean troops responsible . . .

About meeting McElroy during those bleak, bleak days, and my dark moods . . .

The subsequent intense training in Thailand . . .

And then the Korean DMZ . . .

All the solitary patrols . . .

The killing . . .

All the killing . . .

Oh, God . . .

I was so ashamed.

During the telling, Heather moved from the couch to the floor at my feet, then onto my lap, stroking my hair, my face. Tears and anger and angst and empathy and hurt and sorrow in turn played across her exquisite face. My pain was evident; during the recounting I'd been far, far away . . .

From her, this room, this life. From Cullen. She'd forced this plunge into the nether regions of my past, where I'd never wanted to be, ever again . . .

It fell to her to draw me out . . . bring me back.

When I fell silent, depleted, she kissed me gently on the cheek, an ear, my neck, drawing me back . . . taking my hand . . . caressing . . . kissing again, this time on my lips, startling me into the present.

She said, "I'm so sorry," eyes filled.

"You were entitled to know."

"No one should know that, or should have to live through it to begin with. One thing after another . . . How do you . . ."

"I often wonder. Without Cullen, I probably couldn't. And Tess helped."

"Did she ever ask?"

"No."

"I'm sorry."

"No matter."

"To have put you through it."

"Forget it."

She hugged me hard, pulling me to her, then inside, holding me there, loving me on the floor.

Making me whole again.

# Eight

Taylorsville's only a two-hour journey from Greensboro, going west on I-40 to Statesville, where you pick up NC90 and a little altitude along with your latitude. The terrain is rolling, though not gently, and with more deciduous trees than I prefer in my scenery. Not enough green. My little Subaru Impreza tooled along nicely; not so nicely as the Toyota Supra I'd had until it was shot full of holes last spring. The Supra'd had six cylinders, twin turbos, and a jillion horsepower; the Subaru was bereft of boost, boasted only four cylinders, and gorgeous women probably wouldn't faint when they rode in it, except from my driving. Still, the innocuous Japanese two-door was a half-ton lighter than the Toyota, had 135 horses to do its bidding, and was good in rain and snow and sand and stuff.

Why did I go from a fifty-thousand-dollar car to a fifteen-thousand-dollar job, you ask. Last spring I'd also had a faithful Toyota pickup, elderly but tough as an anvil and with a bulletproof engine. Well, not exactly bulletproof as it turned out, never mind the details. When I'd reported the foregoing to my insurance agent, Nellie, she'd thought I was joking. After a minute or two of persuasion on my part, she sat down and fanned herself with an old-fashioned handheld number like my mom used in church when Sis and I were kids. When most of her color had returned, Nellie went to work at her computer screen.

I said no, I didn't want a used Supra, and no, not one with an automatic transmission, either.

Then I was SOL, she said, because Toyota had ceased importation of the straight-drive turbo version.

Hell's bells.

So Cullen and I went to look at cars. Test-drove a mean Ford Mustang Cobra, five-speed and 305 horses—nearly as many as had lived under the Supra's bonnet. Alas, the Cobra's seating was a bit cramped, the fit of the body panels not up to Japanese standards, and the rear end would break loose with scant warning when you toed the throttle at nine tenths in a tight curve, a situation Cullen enjoyed but which our sales consultant emphatically did not.

The Greensboro Ford dealer I'd selected for a test drive also sold Subarus. As I helped the pallid salesperson into the building, Cullen spotted the little Impreza sitting off by itself.

"Hey," he said, "that's a neat car," and ran over to it.

"You bet," I concurred, without really looking. "Let's go test-drive a Trans Am." We'd borrowed Ethyl's Oldsmobile, which was big as a house, old as elephant jokes, and had a drippy crankcase. Beggars can't be choosers.

"Reckon it's fast?" from my budding hot-rodder over by the Impreza. Any moment he'd kick its tires.

"Not very, son. Let's . . ." Too late; he was through the door and into the back seat.

It turned out the car had a 2.2-liter engine, not the loss-leader 1.8, and despite its auto tranny, would pull a zero-to-sixty time of under ten seconds with only seven miles on its odometer, by my very own Camero stopwatch. The color was Caribbean-Green Metallic, more or less lime to us unimaginative folk.

Our current sales representative (a different one; the first had not recovered from our minor spinout) mentioned from the back seat— where he gamely gripped the headrest in front of him as if it were a flotation device—that the Impreza had All-Wheel Drive.

"Is that like four-wheel drive?" asked Cullen.

"You bet," advised the salesperson, leaning into the turn as the superior traction of AWD proved its mettle.

"Then it'll go in the snow?"

"Like a wolverine."

Cullen just smiled.

Like a wolverine.

And gave me the Look.

So I bought it. (Your child ever give you the Look?)

Just to satisfy my right foot, I called Garson Rice at the Toyota store and asked him to order up a Toyota Tacoma pickup: white, 4 × 2, Xtra-cab, five-speed, stereo that would deaden nerve endings. Best of all, with the four-cam, fuel-injected V-6 engine with nearly two hundred horsepower that the magazines claimed would run like a scalded weasel. Now I could have my male-identity-crisis hot rod plus a "responsi-ble" car in which to chauffeur Cullen. Ethyl would be so pleased.

Dad wasn't. "Two new vehicles is stupid. How many can you drive at once?"

"But they're paid for, Pop, and with insurance money. Besides, the pair didn't set me back what the Supra did by itself."

"Harrumph," he grumped, then held out a hand for the keys to the truck. He came back an hour later, body language one big grin.

"What'd you think?" I asked.

"Wow."

"Pretty quick, isn't she?"

"Wow."

"Time to get out, now."

His response was to spin gravel on my shoes.

So he had the Tacoma today while the Impreza and I—with Cullen curled up on the bucket seat beside me, its backrest fully reclined—headed west in search of Feron Simmons.

Taylorsville came and went as I wended my way to Rockytop Hunt-ing Preserve, which specialized in nasty-tempered feral boar—hawgs to good ol' country boys. Hunters came from all over the country to shoot pigs with Royce Rucklin, and paid three hundred bucks for the privilege. Most of them said they craved the excitement of taking a game animal that could fight back, and *would*, given half a chance. All that sounded real dangerous, brave even, over beers with the boys. The truth was that around ninety percent of Rucklin's sports shot their shoats from an elevated stand instead of foursquare on the ground, where a boar could have at 'em if it was so inclined. Their only real danger was falling out of the stand. Royce didn't mind this, of course; it saved him having to pull some hapless hunter out from under an irate pig.

I'd phoned Rockytop the day before, to arrange a hunting date, with no mention of my desire to commune with buddy Feron, since I figured to take care of that on my own.

"This's right short notice, but I guess I can find you a spot, since it's middle of the week. Weekends, forget it. Didn't know you hunted."

I'd known Rucklin awhile, having escorted shooting industry moguls and fellow writers to his place, but had never slain anything there myself.

"I'm bringing my son. He might be interested, might not. We'll see."

"What you totin', some new-fangled popper I'll read about in *Shooting and Blasting*?"

"Marlin's new bolt action .30–06."

"Marlin's into bolt-guns? Well, the oh-six will kill a hawg. Remember my rule, we flush one by you and you don't bust 'im, you owe me anyway."

I gave him my Visa number to assuage his worry, paying in full in advance.

Royce or one of his guides usually placed the gunnies on stand by 5:30 a.m., bleary-eyed but belly-full. Cullen and I arrived at 5:35; I wanted Feron to be in the woods when I got there, thus remaining happily ignorant of my presence until surprised at close range, and hopefully alone.

Rucklin was at the main house, but both his guides awaited us at the lodge. The taller one, I'd met; he reminded me of Jack Palance on Valium and his name was Jay Patay. His slightly shorter, grizzled, disheveled sidekick was introduced as Assa Pugh. Neither offered to shake. I was glad.

"This is my son, Cullen."

"Pleased to meetcha," said my son, Cullen. Emulating me, he kept his hands to himself. Good. That way he wouldn't have to wipe them on his pants.

I got out my gear; Cullen slipped into multiple layers of warm, insulated clothing, including in the ensemble his Robin Hood hat, with feather; Jay and Assa drove us into the preserve in a rusted Willys, and dropped us near a stand not far from the entrance.

"Gate's unlocked. Boy gits tired or cold, you kin walk out to the lodge and warm up."

I nodded my understanding.

"See that ladder stand, yonder?" asked Assa, pointing with a bony finger that featured a long nail with sufficient dirt underneath to nourish a tuber. The stand was perhaps ten yards away.

"By golly, I can, even in this meager illumination."

He squinted at me suspiciously.

"Y'all'll be safe up there," from Assa, still squinting.

"Safe as eggs," I concurred, shouldering the Marlin.

"Then we'll go roust some hawgs," said Jay, and left us to our own devices.

Eschewing the "safety" of the rickety stand, we settled in under a deadfall not far from a cluster of sumac that I warned Cullen about.

After five minutes of squirming to make himself comfortable, another five to admire the birds at work in the leafy forest carpeting, he said, "Daddy?"

"Yeah, babe."

"Are you going to shoot a pig?"

"Do you want me to?"

He thought about it. "Are they good to eat?"

"You bet, if they're not old and tough."

"Can you tell if they're old and tough?"

"Not always."

"Don't shoot one unless you think it'll taste good."

After an hour, four pigs came by, single file. None of them looked especially tender, so I let them go.

Not everyone did. Shortly after they wandered out of sight, other hunters rent the stillness, often repeatedly and in rapid succession.

No tasty-looking porkers came our way during the next hour. Nor old, tough ones either. In fact, none at all. Directly we hove to our feet and went to find warmth.

# Nine

A boar hog looked down at me as I poured a third cup of weak coffee while thinking, *At least it's hot.* Cullen was examining the mounted boar, a mud-colored specimen of medium size, with menacing six-inch plastic tusks protruding from its stiffly curling lips. In life, its tusks probably had been only a couple inches above the gum line, hence the plastic replacements. Ego amplification. They made the pig look mean, so its slayer could swell his suspenders with pride while he swelled his gut with beer.

It was warm and cozy inside the lodge, though furniture was sparse. A friendly fire crackled in the woodstove. Cullen sipped hot chocolate, thin and watery like my coffee.

As I looked out the front window of the lodge over the rim of my cup, rising steam veiling my eyes, I saw Feron Simmons approach, yapping and gesticulating happily with a pair of fellow hunters. Must've got his pig. I said to Cullen, "Take your cocoa out to the car, please. You can listen to the Christmas tapes."

He scrutinized me carefully. "You gonna be long?"

"Probably not."

"There gonna be a fight?"

"Probably not."

He rose, paper cup in both hands, one shoelace untied, Robin Hood hat still on his head, red feather angled rakishly. His waterproof pants swished as he walked across the room. At the door he paused, looked back at me over his shoulder. "Don't be long."

"I promise."

"And don't get hurt."

I raised my eyebrows in mock umbrage. "By Feron Simmons?"

"He has friends."

"Only two," I said, smiling. But he was concerned. "Son, Jenna could handle Feron." Jenna was his "girlfriend," five and not especially large, though athletic, and cute as a baby seal. Cuter, Cullen thought.

He grinned at that, but was still ill at ease. "Maybe I better stay, case you need help."

"Best not."

"How come?"

"Someone might say a bad word."

Smiling finally. "Like 'booger'?"

"Maybe worse."

"What's worse?"

" 'Politician.' And don't worry, Feron's lightweight stuff. I wouldn't have brought you with me if he weren't."

He gave me a thumbs-up, and went out to the car.

•  •  •

Simmons was saying, "So when he cleared the rock, I laid my sights on his front shoulder and—" when I interrupted with, "Yo, Feron. My man," stepping up close as he shut the door behind himself and his cronies. "Remember me?"

He obviously did. Around his torso, suspended in a buscadero rig, rode a Taurus .357 Magnum revolver. He went for it about a month late. I grabbed his moving hand with my left, and shucked the gun with my right.

"Hey!" he said.

"Hey!" one of his sidekicks echoed.

"Is for horses. By the way, old pal, 'front shoulder' is a tautology. There is no rear shoulder."

"What?" he said, not especially nimble of brain.

"What?" aped the sidekick, none too swift himself.

I looked at the ape. "You guys buddies?"

"What if we are?"

The man to his left said, "We just met Feron this morning." A guy with some sense.

"I'll give you fellows twenty bucks apiece to stand out front, make sure we aren't disturbed."

The sensible one replied, "Okay by me."

Feron said, "Gimme my gun!"

"Yeah, give him his gun!" agreed the ape, then made the mistake of grabbing for it. I let go of Feron's hand and hit his oversized pal an overhand left, not too much shoulder with it, but I did twist my hips a little on impact. He fell down—head going *thump* on the hardwood floor—and lay still.

"Glass jaw?" I asked the sensible one.

"Ain't much, is he?" the man answered, shaking his head.

"Drag him outside and you get his twenty to match yours."

And thus did Feron's entourage desert him.

"Finally, we're alone," I said, hefting his revolver. "Seven-shooter, huh? Nice piece."

He looked dyspeptic. "What you want?"

"Feron, Feron. No 'How ya been?' 'How's the family?' No nothing?"

"Whenever I see you, you either hit me or cover me with duct tape," he whined.

"Now whose fault is that? First time we met, you threatened not only me but my son. That was a dumb thing to do, Feron."

"Yeah, well, I found that out."

"You've lost weight. You no longer look like a pumpkin with a long stem and flat feet."

Sucking in his bay window, he said, "Thanks a lot. I been lifting weights and doing Stairmaster. Dropped about thirty pounds."

"Congratulations. Now tell me about the dough."

Instant alert. "What dough?"

"Feron, Feron, lying is not your forte. Now listen carefully. It is not my intention to spill your blood, but I will not shrink from it if necessary. We on the same wavelength here?"

"I think so. You're gonna beat the shit outa me if I don't tell you what you wanna know."

"My family's health may depend on your information."

"What you wanna know?"

"Where you got the money you've been spending on new trucks, new firearms, rod-and-gun excursions?"

"Resovic left a bundle at a safe house before he took off for the mountains with them two Diaz boys. Left that one-eyed wetback in charge."

"Ralph Gonzales?"

"Yeah, him. Ain't that a name for a fucking Mex . . . Ralph. Anyway, after the ruckus at Bobby Tew's place, I went there with Lou. We whacked Gonzales while he was asleep—smushed his head like a grape—and grabbed the bread and took off."

"Gonzales dead?"

"I dunno. Who gives a shit?"

"How much money did you get?"

"Couple hundred thou. Me and Lou split it down the middle. He left for upstate New York and I bought me my new pickup, and spread some around like you said. Heard you knocked off Emilio up at the farm."

"How'd you know it wasn't Hector?"

"Because Hector left for Mexico the day after Resovic took to the mountains. They had a big gun deal working. Hector took the two mil they got from the bank job and headed out. The rest was left at the safe house. Resovic had two or three grand in cash on him, not figuring to need more where we was going."

"I hear that you've been expecting Hector to come looking for you. He after the two hundred thousand?"

"Who the hell knows? I figured he might want to nail me for fingering Resovic. Two hundred G's is chump change to Hector. He'll be in charge now, with Resovic gone. They had a empire, man."

"How vindictive is Hector?"

"Plenty. It's why I'm paying guys to watch for him does he come after me."

"Will he be upset about my doing cousin Emilio?"

He threw back his head and laughed. "Upset? Fire'll be coming out his ears."

"That's pretty upset."

"It's the reason I been on the lookout. Figured when he came up to hit you, he'd take me out as a bonus. Sorta clean up as he goes."

"You have filled me with euphoria, Feron."

"With what?"

"Never mind."

"So, what about me?"

"What about you?"

"And Resovic's money, man?"

"That was Resovic's, not mine. I've got no beef with you."

He looked relieved.

"The Bosnians might, though."

He looked concerned.

"What Bosnians?" he said.

"The bunch the money really belongs to, kind of. They're aggressively seeking it, and 'aggressive' is the key word. They even asked me for help."

"That how you come to look me up?"

I nodded.

"If you could find me, reckon they could?"

"Reckon."

"West Virginia looks good."

I shook my head. "Too close. Know anyone in Albuquerque?"

"No. But I got me a uncle in Kennebunkport."

"Maine's not bad."

"Can I go now?"

"Sure. Say goodbye to your new friends."

I don't think he did.

• • •

After Mr. Simmons left, his two associates rejoined me. The ape had a lump under his lip. He didn't look happy.

Cullen came in to stand beside me, with no expression on his face. He eyed the gorilla with the lump distrustfully. The ape, zeroing in on some-one he figured to intimidate, glared back. If Cullen was intimidated, it didn't show. I said to him, "Why didn't you stay in the car, honey?"

"They might be tougher than Feron Simmons."

"Fuckin' A," from Apeman, still glaring.

"You just wore out your welcome," I said. "When you grabbed at Feron's gun, it cost you a twenty and a pop on the chin. Your language just shifted you permanently out of the loop. Go outside while we grownups converse."

He puffed up, opened his yap to rejoin, but the sensible one cut him off. "Fred, he knocked you on your duff once, and if you don't shut up, he's liable to do it again."

"If he can," from the primate, loath to lose face.

"He can," said my son.

"Boy's right, Fred. No question about it. And judging by the expression on the man's face, I'd say he's fixing to do it. Go on outside."

"Now wait a—"

"Fred," warned the sensible one, "if he don't, I will."

Fred went outside.

Mr. Sensible turned to me. He was redheaded, with a big nose and determined chin, and had the enlarged knuckles of a pugilist. It wouldn't be so easy to knock this one on his tail.

No need. I gave him the twenties, and he nodded thanks, then indicated Cullen. "Kid's got spunk."

I dipped my head in agreement.

As the pair turned to go, Cullen said, "Thanks for not making my daddy hit that man."

Smiling, slow at first, then broad and heartfelt, the red-haired man said, "Yep. Spunk aplenty," and left.

• • •

I patted Cullen's knee, him asleep as the noon sun streamed down on his face through the side glass. From the tape deck came a Christmas medley as we headed back to Greensboro.

My mind was filled with relief. Diaz had taken the Muslim moolah to old Me-he-co. All I'd have to do now was phone the big swarthy Muslim dude and point him and his pals south. End of Bosnian dilemma. Forever.

First I'd need to call my friend Axel Mershon, have him find out if Ralph Gonzales was alive, and around, and available. Gonzales owed me one; perhaps I could collect a debt and glean some useful information at the same time.

Things were definitely looking up.

Cullen stirred beside me, squinting one eye against the harsh sunlight.

"Hungry, sweetheart?"

"No, sir."

Sir?

"Okay. If you change your mind, tell me and we'll stop. Are you glad I didn't shoot a pig?"

After a moment's reflection: "I'm not sure. I wanted to eat one, but I didn't want to see it die."

"You should live on a farm awhile, see the cycle of life firsthand. Can't eat anything unless it dies. Goes for plants, too."

"Are you upset I didn't let you shoot one?"

"Of course not. That's why I let you decide. If it had been important to me, I'd have made the decision."

We motored on. At the outskirts of town, we were stopped by a traffic signal. Cullen watched it. Presently, a green arrow indicated that we in the left-turn lane could make our turn. Three cars made it before the arrow changed to red. We were fourth in line, so we sat some more.

"I've never seen a red arrow before," Cullen mused. "Have you?"

"Occasionally. In this state, they're uncommon."

He thought some more, watching the light, then said to himself, "Now I've seen everything. 'Cept a pelican."

# Ten

When I got back to my office, I called Axel Mershon, a buddy known to friend and foe alike as Ax. He was a former Greensboro policeman, a former NYPD policeman, a former Department of Corrections officer, a former professional boxer, a former Republican; given that he was a pleasant sort, only the latter was hard to overlook. He was currently involved in private security work, and was a devoted Catholic, a doting father of two girls, a Freemason, and mean as a Tasmanian devil when riled. What more could you ask of a man?

"Mershon Security, Carlton Calloway speaking."

"May I have the Ax, please?"

"Sure. Where do you work?"

"Great shtick, Carl. You could go on Letterman."

"Sally Jessy's more my speed."

"Axel in?"

"Hold the line."

For maybe twenty seconds, Bing Crosby crooned "White Christmas" in my left ear.

"Axel Mershon," said a gravelly voice.

"How are you, Ax?"

"Lousy. I just paid a hundred bucks for front-row seats to Hootie and the Blowfish."

"I'd pay two hundred not to have to watch them."

"Yeah, well, what do *you* know? What can I do for you?"

"I have a Bosnian problem."

Five seconds of nothing but line hum. Remembering the last time. "How serious?"

"Not sure, and I may have it solved." I told him about my nocturnal visitor up in the highlands, about Hector's not being Hector, and the rest of it.

"So how can I help?" he asked, when I'd finished.

"I need to speak with Ralph Gonzales. Try to get a line on Diaz so I'll know which way to point them. Think you can find him?"

He snorted disdainfully. "Unless he's with Jimmy Hoffa."

"Thanks. Dad and I are going to look too. Check out the local Hispanic haunts, sort of hang out, blend."

"You and Odie? Oh, yeah, the two of you will blend right in. You realize it probably won't be productive."

"I know. At least we'll feel like we're doing something. By the way, I really appreciate your efforts, pal."

"Appreciate them later, I need to go yell at somebody for goofing off. Bye."

He was gone.

• • •

A recording told me the line was no longer in service. Wonderful. Now how to reach my Muslim antagonists?

*Well,* I thought, *maybe they'll contact me.*

Unfortunately, they didn't, not right away. They did, however, speak to someone close to me.

The conversation wasn't pleasant.

# Eleven

I was at home working on an article next day, Michael Jones deftly weaving "Tapestry" in the background, when I heard Dave unlock the back door and come in downstairs, negotiate the dining area and foyer, then the staircase. His tread is singular. He stuck his equally singular head around the door-jamb and sniffed the air. "What's that smell?"

"Good morning to you, too."

"Good morning. What's that smell?"

"Hope you're feeling well."

"Hope you're feeling well, too. What *is* that I smell?"

"Snickerdoodle. New coffee flavor I'm trying. Have a cup from the carafe."

Pouring a helping, he indicated the bolt-action MR-7 rifle leaning in the corner, "That the new Marlin?"

"Yep. . . . I just brewed that, don't burn yourself."

Taking a very small sip, he nodded his approval. "Where can I get some of this?"

"Not telling."

"You don't, I'll paint your new car green."

"It is green."

"See? Can't take my threats lightly."

I went on punching keys. "I order it from Neighbors out of Oklahoma City. Now leave me alone."

"You take the Marlin to Rockytop?" asked my chum.

"Um-hmmm."

"The hog population suffer from your presence?"

"Took nary a one."

"Scared you'd muff the shot and be mauled?"

"Naw. Cullen was there to protect me." I kept prodding the keyboard.

"Little guy didn't want to see the kill?"

"He was ambivalent."

"That mean he couldn't decide?"

"Yep."

"Why don't you say that?"

"I'm a wordsmith."

"What's that big black thing on the bookshelf?"

"Taurus .357. Feel free to have a look. Maybe it'll keep you occupied—and quiet—so I can get my work done just as if you were in Sri Lanka."

He walked over and picked up the big revolver, opened its cylinder to check for ammunition—absent, of course—then snapped it shut. Hefted it in his big hand. "Thing's heavy."

"Lighter than the Washington Monument."

"Barely. Lot of holes in this cylinder."

"Seven. Rumor has it the company's discontinuing that model to make an eight-shot version."

"Taurus send it to you?"

"It was a gift."

"From whom?"

"Feron Simmons."

"Old Feron? I just *bet* it was a gift."

"Actually, he abandoned it."

"This cute litle tyke? Hard to imagine. So you're giving it a good home?"

"Someone has to."

The phone curtailed our martial discourse. Heather.

She said, "Jason's at Moses Cone Hospital. He just called. Said he needs to see you, urgently. Cullen's at school, right?"

The hair at the nape of my neck did somersaults.

"Of course. Why?"

She told me. I went to see Jason. The hospital was twenty minutes from our house.

I made it in twelve.

# Twelve

The overpowering smell of alcohol and gauze and cleaning fluid and excreta greeted me at the sliding door, the miasma of misery. I hate hospitals. Girding my loins, I took myself through the door.

It wasn't easy.

Heather, waiting in the lobby, spotted me and hurried over, leaving Web sitting in the corner on a gray plastic-and-tubular-steel chair, obviously disconsolate and dejected. I looked over at him, saying to Heather, "How's Web doing?"

"Not so good. He's worried. Jason's damage looks worse than it really is, though the doctor says he'll be going home tomorrow. You better go on up."

. . .

Jason's roommate was seated bedside when I entered. He stood, came around the bed, and extended a hand. "I'm Adam Colby." His grip was firm, damp. He was a regal man, proud of his looks, with skin the color of polished mahogany, black hair, short and tightly curled, well-trimmed mustache. He wore a Rush Limbaugh "No Boundaries" tie against a cream shirt with the sleeves rolled to his elbows. I introduced myself. Colby said to Jason, "Want me to leave?"

Jason shook his head.

I went over to the bed and said, "Heard you were a bit ruffled."

"Ha-ha," from Jason.

Colby said, "You think this is funny?"

"No, he doesn't," Jason answered in my stead. "He jokes about everything."

"Not everything, cutie," I said.

Colby'd had enough. He put a hand on my arm, prepared to deliver a lecture.

"Don't do that," Jason said.

"He can't just say—"

"He can say whatever he wants, Adam. He's here to help. One way he helps is by making light of a difficult situation. It works. I'm cheered up already. Now let go of his arm before he makes you."

Adam released me and left in a tiff.

"Sensitive," I said.

Jason nodded. "He doesn't mean anything by it. Adam's a take-charge type of guy. He doesn't realize it would take a platoon of Green Berets to take charge of you."

"Probably not even then." I touched the stitches on his cheek. "Tell me all about it."

"I was on my way to a party. Stopped by the mall for a couple gallons of Black Forest ice cream from White Mountain Creamery. On the way back out to the car, these three guys stepped out of a van. One of them, a huge sucker, held me while a second one popped me with a black thing, like in the movies."

"A cosh, or a blackjack?"

"What's the difference?"

"A cosh is usually homemade, like a pipe or a length of hose, often filled with lead. A blackjack is generally professionally made, of leather, and filled with shot. Cops carry them, to beat up drunks and college kids."

He smiled, then grimaced because it hurt. "Don't care much for cops, do you?"

I shrugged.

Very pale, very upset and trying not to show it, he looked at me and said, "The one who hit me, a thin fellow with horrible skin, said to give you a message." He paused to take a sip of water, which was difficult with his puffy lip.

I waited.

Putting the glass down, Jason continued. "Said to tell you that they could jump you just as easy, or your tata—I guess that means your son."

I shook my head. "My dad."

He nodded. "They beat me up just to send you a message."

"I'm really sorry about that, my friend." I reflected a moment. "Wonder how they knew who you were."

"I asked them that, while I lay there on the asphalt bleeding all over the skinny guy's shoes. He said they have people following you. Said you were an easy mark."

"We'll see about that," I murmured.

"Ty, you're tough. But you're not mean. These assholes are just plain nasty."

Jason had no accurate concept of Mean; he just thought he did. I, on the other hand, had stared Mean in the face, and taken its measure. He couldn't know that, of course, and I spent many of my waking hours trying to forget.

"If you're right, then these lads need to go back to their own baili-wick," I said.

"Europe?"

"That's not the place I had in mind."

# Thirteen
Next morning, I waited until after nine o'clock for Axel to call with word about Ralph Gonza-les. No news. Since I needed to go to the firing range to chronograph a batch of handloads for an upcoming article on the .38–40, today was as good a day as any. Cloudless, low forties, no wind to speak of. So into the Subaru went my gear, and out to the range I trundled. After spreading the gear on two benches, setting up the Oehler chronograph, and arraying my ammo supply in methodical order, I decided to give Feron's .357 Taurus a quick spin before getting to the morning's serious work. I stapled up a target at twenty-five yards, walked back to the firing line, sat down at one of the benches, loaded the cylinder to capacity, rested my extended arms on some folded towels, then sent three rounds downrange. The revolver's single-action trigger pull was light, but there was a discernible hitch at let-off. After firing three rounds, I went down to the target frame to check the result.

It was obvious that Feron's sight picture was different from mine, or that he'd sighted in with a different bullet weight, or not at all. The point of impact was three inches high and an inch left of point of aim. Out came the screwdriver. The elevation screw turned easily, its click detents positive; the windage screw was another matter. Evidence that someone else had found it so was a buggered-up screw slot. I managed to make my adjustments without further marring of the screw head.

After shifting the sights, I fired another three-shot string, walked down to check the result and mark the holes. Despite my blasting, a murder of crows populated the pasture adjacent to the range, cawing raucously to their sentinel high in a denuded elm, his ebony plumage gleaming in the presolstice lambency. No one else was at the range to annoy them, and I guess they didn't consider me a threat.

I was looking for a tin can or large chunk of rock on the fifty-yard bank for my seventh shot when a voice behind me said, "We must speak with you."

I turned, mildly startled, though I shouldn't have been since I was wearing both earplugs and earmuff-type protectors, and thus wouldn't have heard an elephant tap-dancing on a tin roof, let alone two Bosnians in sneakers sneaking out of the trees. The guy on the left was my bulky Muslim confrere; with him was a slender fellow with an automatic and an attitude. His dark hair appeared to have been cut with a lawn mower; his skin, pale and blotched, surrounded mean rodent eyes.

Jason's attacker? He wanted badly to attack me, too; the desire was in his eyes.

He waved the gun around like a wand, indecisively. I thumbed back the hammer on my Taurus and pointed it at his nostrils, decisively.

"Put the gun down," I ordered.

"Mr. Vance, we have come to talk. Karl has no plans to shoot you."

Unconvinced, I repeated my demand, "Put the gun down, NOW!"

Lawn Mower Head moved his eyes and his feet and his gun, but the muzzle was still pointed roughly in my direction.

"If he doesn't drop the fucking gun right now, I'm going to drain his sinuses."

My foliated pal said something in Bosnian or Croatian or pig Latin and the antsy one walked over to the bench nearest him and put the pistol (a Hungarian Frommer—the ugly Stop model, of all things) on it. There he hovered.

"Tell him to step away from the table," I said, lowering the still-cocked Taurus to arm's length by my leg, its muzzle pointed at the ground.

"Or you will do what, Mr. Vance? Shoot him with your empty revolver?"

"Tell him!"

"You think because I do not speak English so good I cannot count to six?" he said angrily.

Aha. He'd been counting the shots, waiting for my gun to run dry before the confrontation. No point in correcting him, so I said, "I may have located your money."

"Good. Now how will you get it?"

"I won't. You will."

He smiled pleasantly. "I do not think Mr. Diaz will hand it over. Do you?"

That stopped me. "You knew Diaz had the money?"

"Of course. We are not fools."

"Then why did you come to me?"

"For us, getting in and out of Mexico is very hard. Further, Hector Diaz owns many policemen, judges, politicians. It would be difficult, perhaps impossible, for anyone to take anything from him so long as he is on his own surf."

"Turf."

"Turf, that is right." He showed me the gold tooth. "Which is why we come to you."

I had an incredible sinking sensation. This was not going according to plan. "Why?"

"It is said he nurtures a hatred. Against you, your entire family. If anyone can bring him here, it is you."

"How will luring him up here for a go at me get you your two million bucks?"

"Is your problem. Perhaps you might pretend an arms deal, or narcotics. For lots of money. Perhaps we might even make a profit, eh?" He laughed.

I thought about it. Might work, at that. But I said, "And if I refuse to help?"

The splotched one gave me a leer. "I hope you do not," he said, voice raspy and irritating, like a cat's tongue on dry skin. "I look forward to it if you do not."

"Must we threaten you constantly?" interjected the large one. "Did not our beating of your friend teach you a lesson? We can get to any of you, at any time."

"Like the pretty lady with the honeycomb hair. Or the boy," added Lawn Mower Head, sidling closer to where his bitty .32 lay beckoning on the table. His feet fairly danced, fingers drumming against his filthy sweatpants. *Let's get it on here, bro,* his body language said.

A sharp word from the bearded giant stilled the drumming, but his feet kept shuffling, grinding gravel. He faunched for a piece of me.

I said to the man in charge, "Give me a number where I can reach you. The one you gave me is out of service."

The hirsute one seemed genuinely surprised at that, but withdrew from a side pocket a scrap of paper, from another a crayon.

Crayon?

He wrote on the scrap a seven-digit number, then handed it to me. "Should we hear from anyone other than you—" he began.

"You won't. And it won't be long. By the way . . ." I looked him in the eye. "Jason was unnecessary. I owe you for that."

Splotchy Face just grinned and fidgeted.

"We shall see," said the big man, and turned to leave. His crony took a step toward the pistol, hand reaching.

"Leave it," I snapped.

The big Muslim snapped something too, but the splotchy one was torn between obedience and his weapon, puny and fragile though it was. The gun won. He continued his boardinghouse grab until my seventh shot blew the Frommer out from under his reaching hand, off the bench and onto the ground, its slide and frame askew, the strident boom of the Taurus ringing painfully in our ears.

Their facial expressions almost made up for Jason. Not quite, but almost.

# Fourteen

On the way home from the range, my cranium was filled to overflowing with worry and concern. The cell phone interrupted my absorption.

"Talk fast, it's my nickel," was my greeting.

I was irritable, you understand.

"A bit crabby, are we?" chided Dave Michaels.

"You would be, too, if you just had to destroy a perfectly good gun, even if it *was* owned by a perfectly obnoxious cretin. What do you want?"

The repartee is our way of showing how much we care.

"Jason called. Fanner's coming over to his place this afternoon, to see if he wants to file charges against his beater-uppers."

"And?"

"He called to see if you want him to."

"You betcha. I'm planning to do the same."

"You get beat up too?"

I recounted the happening at the range.

"You pegging the one with the nice complexion for assault?"

"Yes indeedy. He may have intended to shoot me."

"With a Frommer? Gun prob'ly wouldn't have worked. If it had, it wouldn't have done much damage."

"Yeah, well, he hurt my feelings."

"His trying to shoot you just as if you didn't have a big red *S* on your chest?"

"Damn right."

"Some people got no respect."

I thought a moment. "What time's Fanner meeting with Jason?"

He told me when.

"At Jason's apartment, right?"

He told me yes.

"Will you call Jason and tell him I'll be there?"

He told me to go to hell and hung up.

Taking that as a refusal, I called Jason myself.

• • •

Patterson's apartment was, as always, as neat as a hospital operating room, though not so austere. Paintings and pottery decorated the walls and halls, upstairs and down, in bright colors and done by local artists. Jason wasn't into elitism. I stood gazing at a watercolor near the kitchen, as Jason walked over and handed me a cappuccino. He smiled, as best he could given the condition of his lips, and said, "Take a load off."

I did, in the living room, in my favored leather armchair. Jason's big silver Persian immediately jumped into my lap, rubbed her handsome face against my abs a few times, purring loudly, then rotated and settled. I scratched her ears. The purring intensified.

"Doesn't this idiot feline know I hate cats?"

Jason settled across from me—somewhat catlike himself—on the couch, putting his teacup on the walnut end table, beside a color photo of Web. "I suppose not."

A hint of cannabis teased my nose.

I sniffed and said, "The police are coming and you smoked a joint?"

Frown of disapproval. "Adam. I told him to go outside. Instead he went upstairs, to the bathroom. At least he turned on the fan."

We spoke of disparate things as we waited there for Fanner: books we'd read recently; our choices in HMOs; Jesse Helms. Jason grew red in the face only twice.

• • •

On my second cup, the doorbell sounded. Adam, newly arrived from upstairs and looking uncharacteristically mellow, answered the buzz, if you'll pardon the expression. Lieutenant John T. Fanner strode in, dapper as ever, parked his chapeau on the coffee table, hiked his trousers, and sat.

"What is that in your lap, Mr. Vance?" he questioned.

"Christmas dinner. Jason's been fattening her up."

He nearly showed his incisors, so wide was his grin, then turned to Jason Patterson. "I understand you wish to file a complaint."

Jason nodded. "Tea, Lieutenant? Or some of Ty's cappuccino? I make it just for him, but I'm sure he'll share."

"Speak for yourself," I objected, then smiled to show I was kidding.

"Tea would be fine," Fanner said.

While Patterson went to get the tea, I related to Fanner my problems at the shooting range.

"And your intent is to file charges against a gentleman you shot at?"

"Only at his gun, and he reached first."

"And you do not know for certain that he intended to shoot at you, correct?"

I nodded.

"Well, then." He held up his hands.

"Lieutenant?"

"Yes?"

"Last spring you did very, very little to help me and my family. I kept expecting you to, so I let things get out of control. I nearly lost both Cullen and my dad, not to mention my mother-in-law, and a close friend was killed. All for nothing."

He looked at me, waiting.

"I won't let things get out of hand this time."

"A threat, Mr. Vance?"

"Take it any way you like."

He uncrossed his legs—argyle socks sag-free at his exposed ankles—and recrossed them. "I have already issued an APB on the Bosnian assailants, based on the descriptions provided by you and Mr. Patterson . . ."

Jason had returned with the tea, and held it out for Fanner to take. He did so, taking a sip—so good he took another—then propped the cup and saucer on his ample knee and continued.

". . . but the results have been nil. I suspect that our suspects are holed up at a safe house, and come out only for necessities."

"Like threats and mayhem?" I said.

"Exactly. They will have gofers for the acquisition of food and beverage—this tea is excellent, by the way—and running to the laundry."

"So once again the situation is in my hands. Is that what you're telling me?"

He shrugged. "We will do all we can. In the meantime, you might wish to call in professional help, as you did before."

"That's what you suggest?"

"Not officially." He removed the tea from his knee, enjoyed a quick mouthful, leaned forward, confided, "But it is what I would do. If I were you, of course."

"Great."

"You have resources, after all, that the rest of us do not. Not to mention," he went on, "your well-developed, ah, personal skills. All work to your considerable advantage."

"So I can take care of my own family, in my own way."

"As we all must, ultimately. We seek perpetrators, Vance. We are not bodyguards. But I will help you all I can."

"Now don't I feel safer, just knowing that."

"Your sarcasm is misplaced."

"So is your inactivity," I said, standing and placing kitty in Fanner's lap. She jumped down and left the room. Smart cat. I thanked Jason for the coffee, shook hands with Adam, and followed her lead.

• • •

When I reached home, I called Colonel Rufus Earl McElroy at Fort Bragg, and told him what I needed, and when.

I let him worry about the how.

# Fifteen

The rain pounded the roof as I pounded the speed bag; hail kicked off the windowpanes as I kicked the heavy bag, the sky as dark as my mood. Pop had driven Cullen and Web to see the Christmas display at Tanglewood, over near Clemmons, and allowed Ethyl to accompany them without a fuss. Lately his behavior had been very odd, and this was yet another example. As I went through my squat routine, I looked out the window of my home gym, hoping that the weather wouldn't hinder their outing.

My first set was with the bar only, twenty reps; then 95 pounds for fifteen; 135 for fifteen; 185 for five; 225 for five; 275 for five; 350 for five;

405 for five; finally, 455 for five. Back down to 350 for ten, 315 for eight; 250 for fifteen. Then time out to throw up.

I was doing crunches—three sets of one hundred per, two minutes between sets—when Dave arrived. Late. "Sorry," he said, slipping on his gloves. "Thurman couldn't close this afternoon."

"No problem," I grunted.

"I said I was sorry," he went on, rotating his neck to loosen the kinks, then doing jumping jacks to up his heart rate and grease the shoulder joints.

"And I said no problem." I went to the mat, moving into a t'ai chi kata. He jumped and jacked and I flowed and fumed, the two us side by side in the loft, each with his own thoughts. To ease my brown study, Dave joined me on the mat. Step forward, deflect downward. Parry and punch. Withdraw and push. Turn body, lotus leg sweep. We perspired and pursued. Dave is a Master. He says I'm better than him. Maybe. Maybe not.

Finally, we sat.

"What's the matter with you?" he asked.

I ignored the opening.

"Tyler?"

More ignoring.

"If you don't answer, I'm gonna trot out my repertoire from *Oklahoma*."

"Please. You'll scare the mice."

He looked around the loft uneasily. "You have mice?"

"If you sing, not for long."

The ice was broken. I spilled the beans. He lent an ear. Do I know my clichés, or what?

When I finished, he said, "So all you have to sweat is a bunch of Bosnians, that pussycat Hector Diaz, and your father getting his ass in a sling. Phooey. Did you know they're thinking of pulling *Lucy* off Nickelodeon?"

Dave has a way of putting things in perspective.

Helping each other up, we trudged downstairs to shower and lap up homemade potato soup, not necessarily in that order.

Outside the windows, darkness had chased the rain away. A nearly full moon peeped hesitantly through the remaining cloud cover. I winked at it, in a better frame of mind, despite "Oh, what a beautiful morning . . ." assaulting my ears from the guest bathroom.

The assault continued. ". . . what a beautiful day. I've got . . ." followed me into the master bath, until I closed the door and missed the rest.

•  •  •

Dad brought Cullen in very late and sound asleep, and handed him to me. I carried him upstairs to his bed, throwing back the covers while holding him on my shoulder, his gentle respiration in my ear, then eased him down onto his back. Off came the shoes, socks, jeans; then I covered him, kissed his cheek, whispering "I love you" into his ear, as I'd done every night we'd been together, all his life. He made a child's sound and rolled over, reaching for his blanket. I watched him sleep for a minute, then joined Dad in the kitchen.

"He like the lights?" I asked.

"You bet. Me too, and I've seen 'em a dozen times. Every year's different, though."

"How about Web? And Ethyl."

"She didn't say nothin', but Web seemed to enjoy himself, in his way."

He hesitated. I said, "Did you want anything?"

"A little palaver."

"Sure. Sit down."

We sat at the kitchen table. I waited. Finally, he began. "I want in on it, Tyler."

"In on what, Pop?" I knew damn well what.

"The whole thing. The Bosnians, Diaz, the two million. I want to be part of it, help out. I ain't useless, you know."

"Nobody said you're useless. But I've got Dave, and the Ax, and McElroy. They'll protect me." I grinned to lessen the blow.

"I know that," he snapped. "It ain't just you, it's . . ."

He folded his rough old hands and looked at them awhile. The nails were cut short, his fingers blunt and honest and honed from years of honorable labor.

"It's what, Pop?"

"It's this. I'm seventy-three years old. I got arthritis, gastric reflux, diabetes, my prostate ain't what it used to be, and my pecker is hardly good to pee with. I ain't goin' to live forever, and I don't want to!" He finished with such vehemence it set me back.

"But—"

"But nothing. And I'll tell you something, son. I don't plan to sit around in some nursing home someday, wastin' away, losin' my ability to think or even control my own actions. Nosir, not me." He looked away, embarrassed.

Aha. Am I obtuse, or what?

I said, "What worries you is the wasting-away part. That little fiasco last spring showed you there are other ways to go, quicker ways, more exciting ways."

"Dang right," he agreed, thumping a big fist on the table for emphasis.

"What about Cullen?"

"What about him?"

"You don't think he'd miss you?"

" 'Course he would, but it wouldn't kill him. You done okay when God took your mama."

"Like hell! I cried myself to sleep every night for a month, and even now . . . Besides, I was older than Cullen."

"Only a few years."

I fretted over this situation for a while, him sitting there looking at me like he did when I was a teenager and had done something stupid. Which was often. Now I knew how he'd felt. When someone you love more than yourself seems to be heading down a black hole, you want to jerk them around and show a better way, at least by your lights.

On the other hand, it *was* his life.

This was hard.

"Okay," I said.

"Okay, what?"

"You're in. I told you I wanted you to help me find Ralph Gonzales. So we'll go find him. But remember, the object here is to remove a threat to Cullen, not soothe your ego."

He brightened. "We, huh? Me and you."

"You think I'd let you go it alone, like at Bobby Tew's?"

His eyes dropped.

Oops. Did one bolster another's self-confidence by deriding them?

"Forget I said that," I apologized, and he brightened again.

"How we gonna do it?" he asked.

We got down to specifics as he rubbed his big old rough hands in anticipation.


# Sixteen

Meanwhile, other people had plans for us. According to phone company records, the following calls were made in early December 1995:

A call from the jail in High Point, North Carolina, placed collect to "Curly Joe" in Dallas.

A call from a Dallas pawnshop to Mexico City, its recipient later identified as one Hector Diaz.

A call from Mexico City to Lorraine's Beauty Nook in Portland, Oregon.

A call from a pay phone in Portland to an auto body shop in Memphis.

A call from Memphis to a pay phone at the University of North Carolina Chapel Hill.

In nearby Durham, a man later described as in his middle thirties, slight of build, hair either light brown or medium gray, who walked with a slight limp in either his left leg or his right and wore a Chicago Bulls cap and blue work clothes, checked out of a motel and headed west in a black Nissan Pathfinder with Florida plates, Dade County. He had registered under the name Herman Clandestine; his real name, so far as is known, was Victor Beauville. His luggage was minimal.

The Pathfinder refueled just east of the Route 421/I-40 intersection on the south side of Greensboro.

# Seventeen

"Legato! Legato! Connect those notes!" Strains of "Good King Wenceslas," courtesy of Cullen at the keyboard, five months into this new discipline, trying hard to do well, Ethyl at the helm also trying hard. To keep her blood pressure in check. Dad just shook his head and kept on beating vanilla into a bowl of creamed butter and sugar, with flour, baking powder, chocolate chunks, and pecan halves on the counter awaiting their turns. He was busy preparing chocolate-chunk cookies and restraining himself from charging into the other room to Cullen's defense.

"Dang that woman, she yells at everyone!"

"Cullen knows that as well as you. He tunes her out."

"Like hell. You go in there and watch his face. He's trying so hard to please he'll have hemorrhoids 'fore he's eight."

On that scatological note, I went into the sitting room to witness firsthand the effect of Gran'ma's exhortations.

Cullen was doing "Jingle Bells" now, occasionally plunking a sour note.

"Did that sound right to you?" Ethyl asked, when he had finished, remonstration oozing from every pore.

"Gra'maw, sometimes this finger stutters a little."

I bit my upper lip, striving mightily to remain countenancially neutral.

Didn't work. Ethyl, noticing, tossed me a look capable of inducing paroxysms in a lesser man.

I gave her a beatific smile in return.

Cullen returned to "Jingle Bells," fingers dancing in an attempt to harness the recalcitrant digit, his little shoulders swaying to the melody. Sounded better to me. I motioned to Ethyl. She came over, making it look as if she were doing me a favor.

Whispering, so as not to disturb the young maestro, I spoke into her ear. "I appreciate the free piano lessons, but chances are he won't play Carnegie Hall next year, so ease up a little, please."

"How do you know?"

"Know what?"

"He won't play Carnegie Hall."

"Ethyl. He's just five. Cut him some slack."

"Maybe you should teach him then."

"I could hire Debra Kirk. I hear she's great with kids, and so adept at the keyboard she makes Bruce Hornsby sound like he's playing in mittens."

"Hummph," she said, more or less.

"We agreed?"

Firm, reluctant nod of the slender, pointed face. I kissed it, inhaling the faint essence of lilac and camomile, surprised that she let me.

"Thanks," I said. As I turned to leave, she asked, "Who's Bruce Hornsby?"

•  •  •

The lush smell of Fraser fir, lights twinkling merrily, tinsel moving in the gentle eddy of forced heat, on my way upstairs seeking Dave. I found him sitting at Cullen's work desk, on Cullen's little blue chair, knees about at ear level, singing and painting wooden Christmas ornaments for the kids down at the shelter to fill the nine-foot tree he'd purchased and transported there yesterday. I watched and listened from the doorway.

"Willie, take your little drum . . ."

Dip of the pointed brush into the pigment.

"Tu-re-lu-re lu . . ."

Stroke, stroke, big hands quick and accurate and loving.

"Let us sing on Christ-mas day."

Dab at the paint again.

Coming up behind him, I said, "Were you just singing 'Pat-a-Pan'?"

"What's it to you?"

"Nothing, nothing. But if you were, I'll have to tell the Ax, then he'll mention it to the guys at the gym and . . ."

"I don't care who you tell. Get out of here. Can't a guy have some solitude? Thought you wouldn't find me in Cullen's room."

The phone sounded.

"Want coffee?" I queried, turning to go answer it.

"Rather have some warm cider."

"And a sandwich, press your shirts?"

"Not too warm, though."

I left the room.

• • •

It was Axel.

"Am I dumb, or what?" he said.

"Or what. But tell me how specifically."

"Shoulda checked the jails first, not as an afterthought."

"Okay. And?" I said, by way of encouragement.

"Talked to the chief of police over in High Point, just nosing around, you know. He claimed he had no Ralph Gonzales in lockup, but didn't I know a guy named Tyler Vance. I admitted it, and he said they had some Mexican who's been asking after this Vance guy, and I said who's the Chicano, and he said they were holding him under a Juan Doe, ha-fucking-ha, and I said describe him. He did, and viola."

"That's 'voilà.' So, the Mexican you're referring to is Gonzales?"

"In the Popeyed flesh."

"Can you set up a meet, quickly?"

"Does a possum have a pointy prick?"

"I'll take that as a yes," I said, and ruminated a moment.

"Why do you think Gonzales wants to see me?" I queried.

"How should I know? Maybe it's your pleasing personality and rugged good looks: When you want this conference?"

"As soon as."

"I'll relay that information to the chief."

I told him thanks, we disengaged, and I yelled "HOO-HA!" at the ceiling.

• • •

Heather arrived with Web in tow—but not as clingy as usual—just as Dad was taking the cookies from the oven. Noting that, I arched my brows at her; she smiled and shrugged while Web walked over to examine the cookies at close range. Pop eyed him peripherally. "Want one?" he asked.

Webbish nod.

Heather said, "Can you say 'please,' Web?"

"Please, Web." Ah, little humor there, touch of insouciance, rebellion. Very non-Webbish, lately. Good sign.

Dad used a spatula to lift a cookie, deposit it on a plate, then covered it with a Christmas napkin. "Glass of milk?"

"Sure," replied Web, mouth en route to a first nibble.

"That's hot, now," warned Dad. "They just came out."

Web nibbled carefully. "Mmmm," was his assessment.

Dad poured him some milk in a tall Tupperware glass. "Think you could gag down three or four more of those?"

"Yephh," responded Web between chews.

"Help yourself."

I said to Pop, "Dave would like a warm cider."

"He knows where the kitchen is."

"He's painting ornaments for the shelter kids."

He thought about it. "Reckon that entitles him to room service," he opined, digging the cider out of a cabinet.

Heather and I snuck upstairs.

# Eighteen
The next day, when I went to pick Cullen up from school, a black Pathfinder was blocking the path of an after-school care van. The van driver—a chunky lass with coccyx-length tresses and brown work boots—was stalking around the Nissan, looking for someone to yell at; the driver was nowhere in sight. I smiled to myself, glad I wasn't the target of her ire. She fixed me with a jaundiced eye as I drove past, as a warm-up.

I retrieved my progeny, spoke to several teachers and children I knew, and returned to the truck. When we left the parking lot, the Pathfinder was gone. *And with an earful, I bet,* I thought to myself, as we pulled out into traffic.

I was about to ask Cullen how his day had gone when the cellular rang. Picking up the phone, I said, "Kris Kringle."

Jason chuckled in my ear. "I can hear the sleigh bells. You left a message for me to call."

"Cullen and I're en route to Latham Park, to kick his soccer ball around. After, we're supping with Dave and the Ax at J and S Cafeteria. Will you join us?"

Cullen leaned over and said "Pleeassse" into the phone.

Jason said, "Tell him thanks, and I wish I could, but Adam's parents are coming for dinner at five. Is it important?"

"Dunno. Might be."

"Could I drop by your house around nine?"

"We'll be there," I said, and bid him adieu.

. . .

As the four of us waited in line—my senses enticed by the admixture of aromas, tempted by the array of desserts, dazzled by the abundance of salads—Axel diverted my attention by filling my ear with information, none of it about food, dammit. Dave and Cullen kibitzed.

"This Gonzales character, known affectionately in some quarters as Milk Eye, is pretty much an unknown quantity. When he was busted for trespass, he had no ID on him. He did have a dime bag, however, so was jailed on possession. Inside, there was a fight. He put two scumball inmates in the infirmary, one in traction. High Point ran his prints and got a who-the-hell-is-this? from the Fibbies. The guy's back is still wet from crossing the Rio Grande, but no green card, so he's looking at hard time, then deportation."

"I wonder," I wondered, "why he asked for me."

"You two are simpatico," said Ax. "You whipped his . . ." He glanced at Cullen. ". . . hinder, then let him hoof it, leaving his pals to cool their heels downtown. Now you're joined at the hip."

"Can you walk if you're joined at the hip?" from Cullen, to let us know he was paying attention.

"With difficulty," I answered, with a wink to acknowledge that he was doing well, keeping quiet and listening and not interrupting the grownups.

Cullen, first of us to reach the trays, doled them out, placing napkin-wrapped flatware on each. The trays were blue, to match my eyes. When his turn came, Cullen with no vacillation requested a chicken leg, broccoli, and sweet potato casserole, soft roll on the side.

I, on the other hand, can vacillate with the best of them. Torn between baked spaghetti and country-style steak, I chose beef stew.

"Can I have sweet tea?" asked my heir.

"No. There's sugar aplenty in those sweet potatoes. Milk or water."

He got water. The lady at line's end punched all four of us into her machine. Cullen waited patiently for the ticket. She handed it to him, asking, "Need help with that, honey?"

"No, thank you," he replied, and carefully carried his tray to a table.

After we'd arranged ourselves and our provender, Cullen took the four trays across the room and placed them on a stack of others. Then we all dug in.

"What you intend to get working with Gonzales?" queried the Ax.

"Not sure, but he owes me from the fight at the bait shop last spring. He'd have been locked up with the rest of them if I hadn't let him slide. Maybe I can appeal to his better nature."

Dave snorted.

"I've nowhere else to go here. I figure Gonzales could still be in touch with Diaz, and can help me think up a way to draw the big galoot off base. Get me a crack at him."

"Or him at you," said David.

An elderly couple took the table next to us, unloaded their food, then put their empty trays on a clean table beside them. Cullen, mouth full of broccoli, put down his fork, got out of his chair, went to the trays and gathered them up, took them across the room to the tray receptacle, and placed them there.

Ax asked, "What's he doing?"

A forkful of tender corn-fed beef suspended in front of my mouth, I answered, "He's affronted when someone puts their trays on a clean table, forcing the next customer to sit elsewhere or move the trays themselves."

"The fella busing tables'll get them."

"Poor guy's got enough to do. Besides, why should he? The tray receptacle's there for empty trays. When someone puts one on a clean table, it inconveniences everyone else, and for no reason other than laziness and lack of consideration."

"Wonder where Cullen picked up that philosophy," said Axel.

I popped the bit of meat in my mouth, shrugged, and said, "Beats me."

Cullen rejoined us, forked up some casserole.

Continuing, I said, "If I can convince Diaz, through Gonzales, that it could be lucrative for him to come to the States—say for a narcotics score, or gun buy—then maybe he'll just zip right on up here."

"He might be planning to do that already, but to wax you, not spend money," Dave theorized.

"Well, that would give me a chance at him, but wouldn't get me any money. Then what would I do about the Muslims? I'm not even sure how many of them there are. I *am* sure they're dead serious about getting their money, and that they figure I'm the guy to do it. No, I've got to come up with a way to lure Diaz out of Mexico with his pockets full of green."

"More than just his pockets," said Axel, voice muffled from a mouthful of potato salad.

Three teenagers lit in a booth nearby, downloaded, stacking their empty trays on an adjacent table. Cullen got them, gave the teens his version of a hard look, and put the trays where they went. Came back, sat down, shook his head disgustedly, and bit into his roll.

Dave, not a heavy eater, took a sip of tepid coffee and asked, "How soon do you think you can get Diaz rolling? The Muslims aren't going to sit on their hands forever. They already went after Jason, and only half seriously. Who's next? And how soon?"

"That, old pal, is what really has me worried. At least Hector is a known quantity," I said, and with a wedge of egg-custard pie beckoning, took my cup over to the coffee urn, filled it with regular (the decaf there is fit only for emergency consumption), went back, and reseated myself.

Dave said, "Next time, just jump on up, go get your coffee, never mind that I'm trying to get some information here."

"Sorry."

"No problem. So what're you going to do about the immediate situation with the Muslims?"

"Circle the wagons while hoping they'll give me a little time. After I talk with Ralph, I'll give the bearded ringleader a call and tell him I've a plan in the works."

"What if Gonzales won't play along?"

"Then I'll lie to the Muslims, to buy time. And go to plan B."

Cullen looked stricken. "You're going to lie?"

Patting his knee for reassurance: "It's an emergency, son. I don't owe these guys the truth. They started the hostilities, not me. And remember, they hurt Jason. Badly."

"This plan B you mentioned," interjected Dave. "Wanna clue me in?"

"You and I might have to check the weather out in Juarez."

"Not our territory."

Nodding, I said, "That's why I'm putting so much faith in my Hispanic friend over in High Point."

"I hope it's not misplaced," from the Ax.

I just shrugged. "Best I got, until I see what Gonzales has to say."

A tall cowboy came in. Shiny boots, turquoise belt buckle, huge black Stetson, tight boot-cut jeans with what appeared to be a balled-up sock for strategic anatomical enhancement. He slid into a booth, hat still in place, and set out his food. Behind him came his sister, I presume, comparably dressed but with cotton-cord trousers instead of jeans. Painted on; no panty line.

Tex, predictably, placed their trays on a table not far from his elbow.

Cullen said, "I like her corduralls," and got up to get the trays.

"Corduralls?" said Ax.

"Corduroys," I said, watching Cullen, who retrieved the trays, gave the ostentatious would-be cowboy a look of disapproval, and turned to convey the trays to their proper destination.

Tex climbed to his high-heeled feet and said gruffly, "Where you goin' with them trays, boy?"

Cullen, ignoring him, just kept on walking.

"Did you hear me, you little—"

I started to stand, but Dave was nearer. "No, no, no, no, no," he said, suddenly eye to eye with Tex. "You don't want to say anything else. Sit down and enjoy your meal."

Eyes blazing, the cowpoke from Hoboken said, "And what if I don't?"

I didn't hear what Dave responded—he was facing away—but his voice was as well modulated as if he were forecasting the weather.

My bet is that he wasn't.

From her place in the booth, the woman's eyes grew very large. She said, "Herb, I'd sit down if I'uz you"

Cullen walked over to stand beside Dave. "I was just trying to help, mister, since you couldn't seem to carry those big old heavy trays way across the room yourself."

All eyes in the room were on Tex, and there was no real way for him to save face. He showed what he was made of.

"You're right, boy. Thanks for the help."

"Don't mention it."

And then we had dessert.

As I forked up a load of pie, I noticed a slender gent watching us intently from a corner booth. Early middle age, in need of a shave, sandy brown hair under a red and black Bulls cap. I looked back at him with equal interest. Quite unhurriedly, he took up his paper and began to read.

I was disquieted, and had no idea why.

•  •  •

Our quartet stayed intact as we meandered out to the parking lot. As I was preparing to insert the key into my truck door, I stopped. Three vehicles away was a black Pathfinder. I went over to it, looked inside, Dave saying, "What's up?" from behind me. Gray upholstery, manual shift, plastic wood-grain on the dash, CD player, the interior clean as a dental tray.

A shiver traversed my spine and my nape hair did "Blowin' in the Wind."

"What?" Dave insisted.

I shook it off, got in my Toyota, and left.

In retrospect, I should have hung around to see who got in the Nissan.

• • •

At home, Cullen read me a bedtime story, *The Littlest Angel*. Each year since he was one I've tried to read it to him, but can never get all the way through it. His mama couldn't either, God bless her. This year he volunteered to read it to me. And he did, with just a little help on a word here and there. It choked me up as badly to hear it as it did to read it, but Cullen was patient, pausing at the emotional parts to let me catch my breath, then forging on.

Afterward, I mopped up, tucked Cullen in, listened to his prayers. Then he asked, "Will you sing me Christmas carols until I fall asleep?"

Not just being polite, you understand; he really likes my singing. So I sang. He drifted off during "I Saw Three Ships." Five minutes later, I put the teapot on and waited for Jason with a copy of *Rapport* magazine in front of my nose.

# Nineteen

I went to the door, peeped through the peep-hole, opened to a very pale person. Across the street, carolers caroled. "You're still a bit wan," I said to Jason.

"I've never heard that word used in conversation," he said. "Are you sure of your pronunciation?"

"Sir," I said, looking up my nose at him, since he's taller. "I am a professional writer. Words are my life."

"Let's look it up," he insisted.

We repaired to the dictionary.

"See?" said I.

"I'll be damned."

"You might be if I don't come up with something to keep your Muslim friends from filling up your dance card again."

"Please. Not even in jest."

I grinned. "Lighten up."

He smiled. Wanly.

I filled a flagon with tea, a robust blend that he likes, handed it to him, and said, "Come upstairs for a moment, if you will."

In the office, I took a trio of small handguns from the safe and placed them on my desk. Jason looked at them. "You going to shoot me and save the Muslims the effort?"

"That would solve your problem, wouldn't it? But no, I guess not. I want you to choose one."

He was astonished.

"For what?"

"What do you think?"

"I don't like guns."

"You like being bludgeoned?"

He was uncomfortable.

"Why show me three? Just take one, load it, and give it to me," he protested.

"I'll elucidate. The one on the left is a revolver."

He was insulted.

"I *know* that."

"Holds only five rounds, and is thicker through the middle than the autoloaders. But some folks are more comfortable with a revolver than a pistol. Easier to ascertain whether it's loaded, no safety to fool with, no slide release, no having to jack a round up into the chamber."

He was interested.

"Aren't revolvers more reliable?"

"Not necessarily. The one in the middle is a Colt Pocketlite .380 automatic. Its power level is comparable to the revolver, which is a .38 Special, but the auto's easier to shoot well, especially under stress. The downside is that it has a safety to manipulate, unless you carry it hammer down on a loaded chamber. And then you'd have to thumb back the hammer for the first shot. That's not very fast unless you're thaumaturgic."

He was curious.

"What about that ugly little guy on the right?"

"I won't tell the PR lady at Smith and Wesson you said it was ugly. That's a Sigma, also a .380. Its advantages are that there are no external controls—no slide release, no safety lever, no hammer. You simply point and shoot, like the revolver, except it holds seven rounds instead of five. Why don't you try the trigger on each gun—they're unloaded, of course—and see what feels best to you?"

He did, concentrating on the task. For two minutes he picked them up and put them down, hammers rising and falling repeatedly, checking them out. He settled on the Sigma.

"Since there is no slide lock, it's best to put one round in the magazine, like this." I showed him. "Then insert the mag in the butt until it clicks into place. Pull the slide all the way back and let it slam forward; don't ease it shut. Then remove the magazine, making sure the muzzle end of the gun is always pointing in a safe direction, and fill up the magazine."

I let him do so. He couldn't get the seventh round to go into the magazine. "Thought you said this gun held seven bullets, like the Colt."

"Cartridges, not bullets. The bullet is what comes out of the barrel. And it does hold seven."

"Well, I can't get the seventh one to go into the clip."

"I said the *gun* holds seven, not the magazine."

He was puzzled for a moment; then light dawned. "There's one in the barrel."

I nodded. "There's hope for you."

"Light on the feet does not mean light in the head."

"Ha-ha, to quote a famous gay guy I know. And Jason?"

"Yeah?"

"Carry that on you all the time."

He was uncomfortable again.

"Isn't that illegal?"

"And better than being dead. Besides, the concealed-carry law just went into effect. In an emergency, which this is, an applicant doesn't have to wait the normal sixty to ninety days. If this situation drags on, maybe we'll consider that option. Meanwhile, you're Mister Meanor."

"Mister . . . Oh. It's not a felony?"

"Not at this point. There's talk in Raleigh that with the new law in effect, it may become one.

"And Jason," I said again.

He was stuffing the Smith in a pocket. "Hmmm?"

"This is no game. Last time they just beat you up. Next time they may decide to gut you like a fish. Or hurt someone who's with you."

That got his attention.

"Use your best judgment, of course, but be prepared for the worst."

He swallowed hard. "Okay."

"I meet with Gonzales on the morrow, first thing. Hopefully, this will be over soon and you can bring that back."

He didn't look convinced.

Neither did I.

# Twenty

In a cubicle the size of a steamer trunk, Gonzales and I conferred, knee to knee, sitting at a table big enough for an ashtray and our elbows, and nothing else. He stuck a butt to his lips and whipped out his Bic. I said, "You wanted to see me, I understand."

"*Sí.*"

"You light up and you'll see me going out the door."

He didn't light up. Instead, for twenty minutes he told me about Hector Diaz, how he had returned to Mexico just before the big battle in the mountains in which Valentin Resovic had been killed, and Emilio Diaz, Hector's cousin. Emilio was a ringer, snuck into the States through New Orleans to take Hector's place, thus freeing Hector to make a two-million-dollar gun buy. Resovic had known that he and Hector were under close surveillance by multiple national and interna-tional agencies, and that as a consequence, his movements were too tightly monitored for the arms deal to go through. As long as he and

Diaz were still in the United States, and in plain view part of the time, the gun buy was in abeyance. Hence look-alike cousin Emilio's presence; he was a red herring, allowing Hector to slip off and consummate the deal. Resovic even called Emilio Hector, so any mole in his organization wouldn't know the truth. Only Ralph Gonzales, now seated across from me and third man in the group's hierarchy, was supposed to know that Hector was no longer Hector.

Did Ralph still maintain contact with the real Hector?

Sure. They occasionally talked on the phone. There were loose ends here in Los Estados Unidos that he, Gonzales, had been tying up. I was supposed to be one of them.

So Hector was mad about my capping his cousin?

"You betcha," Ralph assured me. "Plenty mad for sure."

"So what do you want with me? Chances are good you won't off me right here in the High Point jail, even if you could. Maybe if this were Davidson County . . ."

That got a laugh. *"Es verdad."* He laughed again, then told me why he'd wanted to see me. He was looking at some real hard time on this dope charge, bullshit though it was. They were talking intent to distribute, not simple possession, plus resisting arrest, assault on police officers . . .

"How many officers were there?"

"Only *tres.* But they were *muy malos,* tried to use their clubs."

An error in judgment. The cops should simply have pointed many guns at Ralph until he was cuffed. Threatening him with batons would only make him mad. Gonzales mad was a handful, and I had scars to prove it.

Now, they did too.

Anyway, Milk Eye was looking at serious time here, and in a *gringo* prison. That was not to his liking.

But what could I do?

Help get him out.

Why?

"Because I have *información.* Very importan' *información.*"

"And if I help you get out of here, you'll tell me things I ought to know."

"*Sí.*"

"How do I go about getting you out?"

*Quién sabe?* That was my problem. Maybe I could call the governor, get him to pull some strings over here in Gritsville. Ha-ha. The guy had a real sense of humor.

Even if I could pull some strings, why should I?

He hesitated. He needed a hook to reel me in, knew he had one, but didn't want to give away too much.

"Hector has a contract out."

"Just on me?" I asked, mouth suddenly dry.

He shook his head. "And on your *papá,* and *muchacho.*"

Heart encased in a lump of ice, I asked just what I could do about it?

Big Latin grin. "I can bring Hector here. *Con mucho dinero.*"

Was he a mind reader? I asked how.

Ralph told me to set up a dope buy, a big one, and he would pass the word to Diaz. Then Diaz would come, no question, with much money for the dope and perhaps a gun to do the job on me himself, if the contract had not already been fulfilled.

Just like that?

"*Sí.*" He snapped thick fingers, winked his good eye at me. "He trus' me."

"And you'll arrange the buy, exactly how I tell you? Set Hector up just to get out of jail?"

Nod. "An' money. For espenses."

The nitty-gritty. "How much?"

He showed me lots of teeth. "You decide. I trus' you."

"And I suppose you want a ride to the border, or a ticket on a plane."

More teeth, very white. I wondered if they were all his.

"Okay," I said.

"*Es verdad?*" he assured himself.

"You can trus' me," smiling back at him.

He laughed at my Ralph Gonzales impression, unoffended, and clapped me on the shoulder. "We are brothers, no?"

"Perhaps in spirit. I'll call you."

"Soon, *amigo.* This scum they put me with . . ." He spat on the floor. "Pretty soon mebbe I kill one. Then even you cannot get me out."

He was probably right. I hurried to make his bail. Fortunately, I knew a magistrate. Nonetheless, I had to cash in a formidable CD.

Maybe I'd ask for a finder's fee, or at least expenses.

Ha.

And in the end, I was right.

• • •

At The Old Hole in the Wall for lunch, I told the Ax about my meet with Ralph Gonzales.

"So, Diaz has issued a contract on your whole family. Wonderful," said Mr. Mershon.

"My sentiments exactly. I don't know what I'm going to do about Cullen and school."

"He's not in danger at school. Too many witnesses. To and from, though, is a problem."

"I usually take him, though sometimes Ethyl or my dad picks him up."

"I can do that, for a while anyway. At least when you can't."

"Much obliged. Dave too, if you're tied up. And I really appreciate your dropping everything to help with this."

"Hey, a man protects his family above all else."

"More coffee?" from Deloris as she swept by.

"Thanks," I said, and she refilled the Holloware.

"Now, about the details of this bogus dope buy. Here're my thoughts." We talked through the lunch hour, ironing things out. Deloris kept our cups filled, and with nary a fuss nor an impatient glance. We could've sat there until we fused with the booth and she'd never have complained, God bless her, because that's the way she is. The most underrated person in life is a good waitress; the most overrated is a Mexican drug lord, gun trafficker, killer of old men.

My plan was to tip the former and defuse the latter.

I took care of the first as I left the restaurant, and with the second part well on its way, I allowed myself to feel good.

Prematurely.

• • •

Dad and Cullen were watching a game show by the light of the Christmas tree when I got home late that afternoon. My son rushed over and gave me a hug and a kiss, then hurried back to the TV. Odie waved a hand.

"What, no kiss?" to Pop.

"You need a shave," he said, and kept on watching.

"Daddy, who do you want to win?" Cullen asked.

"I don't know, sweetheart. You pick."

"I like intestant number two."

"Me too, then," I agreed, riffling through the mail. Two royalty checks: one for thirty-five dollars, one for nine-thousand, eight-hundred, twelve. And four cents. An assignment from a British gun magazine, due in sixty days. A letter from Rick Jamison inviting me to . . .

Odie was saying, "You just like her because she's pretty."

"Nuh-uh," Cullen insisted. "It's 'cause she knew dimetrodon was a lizard, not a dinosaur."

"Nope, it's because you think she's pretty."

"Is not," from Cullen, rising to his knees on the couch.

"Is too."

Cullen launched his wiry body, which Dad diverted, my son ending up on the carpet giggling hysterically. And loudly.

"Boys? I'm trying to read the mail."

They paid me no attention, squealing and laughing until I marched over and piled on, three generations of Vances rolling and laughing and roughhousing under the tree's watchful gaze. Cullen's mom, too, perhaps, from heaven.

I never did find out which intestant won the game.

• • •

Heather joined us for supper. After Cullen went upstairs to dance with sugarplums, and Dad had borrowed *The Santa Clause* and gone home, she and I engaged in a time-honored yuletide pursuit: smooching in front of the Christmas tree.

No groping.

Yet, anyway. Santa might catch us if he came a few days early.

The tree was redolent and sparkling, angel at the crest looking down; the fireplace crackled merrily; festive candles flickered here and there. Between smooches, hot buttered rum for her, Gevalia's Royal Vinter Kaffe for me. Nobody up but Heather, and me, and us.

"Would it be seemly for me to paw and whinny?" she whispered, liquid lips nearly touching my cochlea.

"Certainly not. But you can prance coquettishly and swish your tail."

"If I did that, you'd reduce the room to shambles," she giggled.

"I might anyway."

"Talk, talk, talk," she breathed, shifting strategically. Then the slow grin, full of threat and promise.

Would bite marks show?

We quit talking as Pan beguiled us with his flute.

• • •

Later, at the kitchen counter, with me wearing yellow gym shorts and Heather in one of my plaid flannel shirts with the sleeves rolled up to her elbows and looking not at all like Lamar Alexander, we sat with our thighs touching and munched day-old butterscotch brownies, washing them down with cold milk. Heather spilled nary a crumb, not easy when you're eating brownies.

I got crumbs all over. No milk mustache, though. Think I'm a slob?

Heather was saying, "So Diaz has a contract out?"

"Um-hmm," losing some crumbs with my response, at least on the counter, not in my lap.

"What does that entail, exactly? I mean, I've seen plenty of movies, but . . ."

"It means he has engaged somebody to eliminate me, and probably my family as well."

"Aren't you afraid?"

"Of course I am. But there are things I can do, and I'm doing them. Besides, McElroy is coming up from Bragg, Fanner has his eyes open, and Dave and Dad and the Ax are helping."

"And you and this Gonzales gentleman are in cahoots on a scam intended to entice Hector from his cave."

"Indeed we are."

"What about the Muslims?"

"I called them this afternoon, after the Ax and I made our plans. They said they'll wait, for a while. A short while."

"Can I help with any of this?"

"Sure. Stay close by. Provide me with obedience and honor and adulation, as always. You know, keep me limp and stress-free."

Her smile irradiated the room. She put her hand in a lap. "Don't know about limp, but stress-free I can handle."

I jumped.

Then, in deep register, like Garbo, she said, " 'Handle' is the operative word here."

When we got around to finishing the brownies, they were two days old.


# Twenty-one

It was Monday. I'd just dropped Cullen at school and was headed home when in my mirror appeared a Nissan Pathfinder. A *black* Nissan Pathfinder.

I couldn't tell who was behind the wheel, just a vague shape wearing a red and black ball cap. Tired of his games, I pulled over to the curb, fetching a Kahr 9mm from the glove compartment, and stepped clear of my truck, gun held against my leg discreetly to avoid terrorizing passersby. Instead of slowing, the Pathfinder accelerated, whizzing by me in a whoosh. I jumped into the Toyota and gave chase.

Out Fleming Road he went, with me in hot pursuit. His truck had 168 horses and weighed 3,700 pounds; I was in control of 190, in a vehicle half a ton lighter. Unless he was Richard Petty, he couldn't outrun me.

He wasn't Richard Petty. My front bumper glued to his rear, we hove left onto Inman in front of the Food Lion, swept past A Cleaner World, then the Cornerstone Baptist Church, and took the hard left-hand curve at High View Road on two wheels. After we both did a little airborne whoop-de-doo courtesy of a break in the tarmac at the Bryan Boulevard construction site, he ran the stop sign at Old Oak Ridge Road, jumped the left-side verge, and four-wheeled it into a field across from the fire station. I waited at the sign for a Nova to pass, then went over the grassy verge after him. The two of us performed what must have been quite an odd vehicular dance for a while, spinning and dodging, mud flying, as I tried to ram him. Inevitably, my Toyota, doing its best but with only two driving wheels, became mired in a soggy depression. I had to sit helplessly and watch the Nissan roar out of sight down Old Oak Ridge, toward Airport Boulevard.

I said *Shit* seventeen times and walked to the fire station, hat in hand, metaphorically speaking. Three pleasant but suspicious firemen helped me out of the mud.

Tooling around the airport area for an hour, up one road and down the next, no Pathfinders did I see, except a dirty red one driven by a tall blonde, long hair unkempt and uncombed. On his rear bumper was the sticker:

HEART ATTACK
God's Revenge on the Eaters of His Animal Friends

I went home in a funk. And ate some tenderloin.

• • •

Dad called from Cullen's school just after noon, using the cell phone he toted in a fanny pack. "Had lunch with Cullen. Been in and out of the building all day. No sign of a black Nissan."

"Good. I called the principal and told her the situation. She was afraid I might take Cullen out of school, which she seems to think is a poor idea. She also pretty much disdains the danger aspect, echoing what Axel said, that there are simply too many adults at school for anyone to risk making a grab for Cullen."

"I ain't so sure, son."

"Me either. That's why you're there. I'm still considering pulling him out. Ethyl says she'll school him here, at home. So long as you or Dave are with them, he should be okay. I'm going to nab the guy in the Nissan, one way or the other, and soon."

"You plan to send Cullen away if you don't? Like last time?"

"Hope I won't have to. McElroy's due tomorrow. We'll wait and see what he has to offer."

"Okay, but let's don't wait too long. Hector's not only mean, he's smart. Not smart as Resovic, but wily," he concluded.

"I know, Pop."

"Be careful," he said, and hung up.

I needed to zip to Fed-Ex to ship off a manuscript, so hopped back in my truck and cranked her up. As I drove away, I found out later, portly Mr. Rummage was peeping through the curtained front window of his house down at the corner, watching a black Nissan Pathfinder parked on a hill in a sheltered copse, well within eyeshot of our houses. He'd seen the vehicle twice before. Its occupant, he reported to the police, was using binoculars to watch something at my end of the street. Mr. Rummage said he couldn't see the person well enough to give a description.

. . .

That evening I was scheduled to address a wonderful group of ladies at Jamestown United Methodist Church. Theirs was a book club that had been in continuous existence for more than sixty-three years. They were appreciative, attentive, delightful. And afterward, they let me eat cake. I asked if I could come again. Soon.

On the way home, I watched my mirrors. No Nissan Pathfinder. Didn't matter. I'd spot him sooner or later.

Turned out to be sooner.

# Twenty-two

Will Peeples had a carrot up his nose when Cullen and I sat down with our trays. "That's disgusting," opined Laura Taggard, her view seconded by at least three other girls at the lunchroom table. Out of deference to their sentiments, Will removed the carrot and ate it. "That's gross," Laura further opined, accompanied by multiple exclamations of "Eeau-uiou" from the ladies. Will, undaunted, simply chewed.

Cullen bit into his sandwich—grilled cheese—and munched quietly. Me too. The table talk—at least among the boys—centered around the morning's soccer game, played at recess just before lunch. I'd watched; it was a doozy. Lots of kicks, no scores, much bickering. Like a session of Congress. I absorbed the recount stoically, so as to remain impartial.

Directly we polished off our eats, dumped the residue, and quit the scene, Cullen to class, me outside for a look-around. I'd been at the school all day, doing bodyguard duty. Pretty boring stuff. I would have volunteered to assist with a reading program or tutoring session, but that wasn't what I was there for.

Circling the parking lot once, I started back into the building. Stopped. Checked the lower parking lot, well away from the school. I couldn't see well for the trees, so I moved a few steps to my right. There! Black Pathfinder. I headed toward it at a run. The driver spotted me, pulled out of his slot, and spun away in a rush. I changed direction, aiming for my truck. In twenty seconds, I was off after the Nissan.

Scooping the cellular from the glove compartment, I punched out 911. And got nothing. *Shit!* Dead battery. I tossed the useless instrument on the floorboard, mentally kicking myself. I'd noticed the battery was low that morning, but since it takes a while to recharge and we were late already, I'd decided to wait. Wrong move.

The Nissan was barely in sight up ahead, weaving in and out of traffic. I did the same. Only faster. He zipped left onto Swing Road, probably headed for the interstate. I hustled after him, gaining a little every second. At the intersection of I-40 and College Road, instead of hitting the on ramp, he sprinted across the College Road bridge. Me too. We zoomed past a curb market, the vet's, the cable company, then left onto Wendover and back toward I-40. The Nissan ran two red lights. Me too. At the third he squeezed through, but a Pepsi truck loomed in my path and I had to jump the curb and plow through a parking lot, luckily missing almost everything in my path. Note that I said *almost* everything. A concrete planter I did not miss. Grabbing reverse, I backed away from the planter—now missing a sizable chunk of itself—and took off after the Pathfinder. We crossed the I-40 bridge doing seventy, encumbered more by traffic than prudence. He whipped left onto Dolley Madison with me inhaling his exhaust. Since he showed no signs of stopping, and since there were no cars coming at us, and since this was a two-lane road with a nice ditch on either side, and since few houses were near the road, and since Market Street and its heavy traffic were coming up, now seemed as good a time as any . . .

I punched throttle and passed him on the wrong side of the road, then cut him off, turning directly into his path. He plowed into my passenger-side door at maybe fifty miles an hour. I fought the wheel as we went into the ditch, locked together by g-forces too strong to overcome. He wound up in someone's yard, right side up, but my truck tilted drunkenly . . . tilted . . . tilted . . . and fell heavily onto its side. Quick as a raccoon, I climbed out the passenger window and went after the driver of the Nissan, who was trying to restart his engine.

When I reached his truck, I snagged his jacket, spun him out and onto the ground, then pounced on his prostrate body intent on serious bodily harm. He covered his face and yelled, "She paid me! She paid me!"

Fist cocked, I held back. "Who paid you?"

"I don't know who she was!"

Fear settled in the pit of my stomach like a hundred-pound sinker. I said, "Tell me all of it! Quick!"

Very shakily, he said, "Some broad. She came into the store this morning, where I sell cars, and wanted to test-drive a Pathfinder. Had the exact one picked out. Black SE."

I could scarcely breathe.

"After we drove around awhile, she made me a proposition."

"Hurry it up!"

He held his hands palms out, as if to ward me off. "Okay, okay. She offered me five hundred bucks to drive the Pathfinder to that school and sit in the parking lot. Said she and her husband were in a custody dispute over their son. Said she drove a black Pathfinder, and if he saw one, he'd think it was her and come over. Said if I could decoy him away from the school, she'd pay me . . . Hey!"

But I was sprinting to his Nissan. Eight seconds later, I burned rubber getting to a pay phone.

. . .

The phone at the school buzzed busy. . . .

The police would require too much explaining; there was no time. . . .

Dave and Dad were farther away than I was. . . .

Jason!

He answered the second ring. "Patterson residence."

"Jason! Get to Cullen's school! It's an emergency! Someone decoyed me away! He's in serious danger!"

"I'll go now."

"Take your gun!"

"Oh, God. . . . Okay, I will!"

"Hurry!"

I jumped in the Nissan and headed for the school, scared out of my wits.

# Twenty-three

Though the actual chronology of events can never be known, various police agencies, compiling data from disparate sources, posited the following:

Looking down from the woods surrounding the J. R. Lanham Elementary School, Harmony Cahill, seated behind the wheel of a black Nissan Pathfinder with Florida plates, watched Tyler Vance hotfoot it after the dupe from the Nissan place, who was now shoveling pavement behind himself at a frantic pace at the wheel of a black Pathfinder identical to hers. "There goes my red herring," she muttered, and picked up the phone.

At the other end, Victor Beauville, an unconscionable man of moderate size and bland disposition, answered the buzz. He too sat at the wheel of a black Nissan Pathfinder registered in Dade County, Florida. "Talk," he said.

"Number One is hightailing it after my rabbit," she said.

"I suppose the geek from the car store provided you with no difficulties?"

"Only monetary. And Hector will cover that loss, no problem."

"You're going after Number Two now?"

"As we speak," she answered, shifting into gear.

"Number Three will be terminated within fifteen minutes."

They broke connection simultaneously, the man popping a mint into his mouth and putting on his Bulls cap. Switching on the engine, he took a final magnified look at Number Three's house, eased out the clutch and began to roll, gravel crunching under the tires.

*Looks like rain,* he thought, as he dropped a Walther .32 into a side pocket of his jacket, silencer in place. He was interested in seeing what damage those sixty-grain Silvertips would do, since the gun magazines seemed to regard them highly.

*We'll see.* He began to whistle as he drove, happy to be alive and doing what he liked best, killing people. *It's always good when a man can combine vocation and avocation,* he reflected, and popped a stick of Juicy Fruit in his mouth.

•   •   •

As Harmony Cahill was parking her Nissan Pathfinder near the front door of J. R. Lanham Elementary, Colonel Rufus E. McElroy was pulling off I-40 at the airport exit, en route to the home of Odie Vance. The two had arranged to have lunch there, a short time later to be joined by Tyler and Dave Michaels for a strategy session.

It was not to be.

•   •   •

Harmony Cahill—not her real name, of course; no one does wetwork under their real name—screwed the silencer in place, then tucked the

Walther semiauto into her waistband, a very tight fit. "Gotta lose a few pounds of ugly fat," she said to herself, as she stepped out of the Nissan. "I'll cut off my head." She cackled at her own wit while striding to the front doors, heels clicking on the sidewalk, calves large as Arnold Schwarzenegger's working to propel her stout frame.

She entered the double doors, bypassed the office, and went straight to Mrs. Creed's room. She entered without knocking. The teacher looked up, mildly startled, then stepped forward to greet the newcomer, smiling pleasantly. "May I help you?"

Harmony Cahill looked around irritably. "The children aren't here. Where are they?"

Taken aback by the surly attitude, Roberta Creed said, "May I ask who—"

"I SAID WHERE THE FUCK ARE THEY?"

The teacher, shocked to her marrow, never having heard that word within the confines of this room and very seldom at such close range, not to mention having loathed it since childhood, simply goggled at the burly, foulmouthed intruder.

Harmony Cahill reached out a strong-fingered hand, grasped Ms. Roberta L. Creed's slender neck, and squeezed. "Listen to me. I have to ask you again, I'm gonna rip out your fucking trachea!"

That *word* again. There was no way Roberta Lynne Creed—minister's daughter, den mother, Sunday school teacher—was going to yield information to a filthy-mouthed hussy such as this, not while there was breath in her body.

Soon there wasn't much. Harmony kept squeezing until Roberta Lynne Creed slumped to the floor, head impacting the linoleum with a dull thud.

"Fuck! Shit! Piss!" Harmony ground through her teeth. "Now what?" She whirled into the hallway.

•  •  •

Odie Vance was halfway down the driveway to his mailbox when a black Nissan Pathfinder pulled up. He knew about the Pathfinder Ty had chased, so was instantly suspicious. Being too far from the house and too close to the Nissan to make a run for it, he used his wits. Looking past the Nissan and its driver, he raised a hand and yelled, "Hi, Mr. Wilkins. Come on over. We'll have lunch."

Mr. Wilkins, Odie's neighbor for more than a decade, was not out in his yard, nor yet even in the house. In fact, he was visiting a nephew in Pawtucket, but Victor Beauville didn't know that. So he hesitated, uncertain what to do, as Odie walked toward him. Drawing abreast of the Nissan's open window, Odie smiled and said, "Howdy." Victor just sat.

Not long.

When he was close enough, Odie pivoted on the balls of his feet and hit Victor Beauville on the hinge of his jaw, putting a lot of his weight behind it. It was not only the best punch Odie had thrown in forty years, it was the hardest Victor Beauville had ever been hit. His head snapped to one side; stars burst in his head; his body went limp. Odie, noticing the latter, wasted no time in turning on his heels and scattering for the house—and his World War II carbine, stored with a full magazine where Cullen would never find it. His sneaker-shod feet slapped the sidewalk as he ran for his life, chest aflame, adrenaline surging through his overwrought system.

He made it to the porch before Victor Beauville came to his senses . . .

Through the door before Beauville reached for his gun . . .

To his trusty carbine before Beauville could climb out of the Nissan.

Had chambered a cartridge before Beauville staggered shakily up onto the front porch.

Prone at the end of the hallway, rifle trained on the front door, Odie waited, heart pumping erratically, head swimming, chest sawing for air.

Until he passed out.

•  •  •

Tyler was within a mile of the school, traveling eighty miles an hour, when the highway patrolman spotted him and U-turned in front of a Honda driven by an elderly tourist from Des Moines. The Honda tagged the patrolman in the right-rear quarter panel, causing its ancient driver to impact the steering wheel with great force. The highway patrolman, caught up in the passion of the chase, ignored the accident and roared off after the speeding Nissan, the very model of indeflectable determination. The fact that the Honda driver's pacemaker was malfunctioning as a direct result of the accident would not have deterred him, even had he known about it.

Patrolman Everette Everhart was in hot pursuit.

. . .

Putting on her pretty face, so to speak, Harmony Cahill sashayed into the front office. An officious, attractive woman with skin the color of nutmeg was seated behind a desk, phone at her ear. She held up a finger to indicate, *One minute, please.* Harmony thought about shooting the fucking finger off, but whoever was on the other end would hear the silly bitch holler, so she bit her lip and went out into the hall.

A man was coming toward her, about her height and weight but with a crimson hue. Strong drink or natural? Maybe high blood pressure. He smiled at her, displaying shiny teeth. "How can I help you?"

Displaying her own choppers, shiny enough, she said, "I'm Cullen Vance's aunt. My brother asked me to pick him up and bring him home."

The red one hitched up a sleeve to glance at his Timex. "School doesn't let out for more than an hour."

"Our daddy's sick."

"Mr. Odie? Sorry to hear that," he commiserated.

She proffered a genteel smile, or what she hoped was one.

"Cullen's at music. Come on, we'll go to my office and phone Ty or Odie for verification. Won't take a minute. I can't let you pick him up otherwise. You understand."

"Of course," replied Harmony, as they began to walk down the hall.

"I didn't know Tyler had a sister," said the man.

"I'm from out of town."

"My name's Gerald Huff. Assistant principal," he averred. "You sure don't look much like Tyler." He winked at her. "If you'll pardon my saying so."

"Different mothers," Harmony said, truthfully enough.

Huff looked puzzled. "I wasn't aware that Mr. Odie had divorced."

"My mom died."

"Oh. Sorry to hear that," solicitously.

They were approaching an office door. Above the door was a sign that said "Assistant Principal." On the door was a placard that read: "Mr. Gerald Huff."

"This your office?" Harmony asked sweetly, as they drew near.

"Sure is," Huff replied. "After you."

She smiled as he stepped aside for her to enter. Once inside, he closed the door, then said "Hey!" because she had stuck the muzzle of a small black pistol against his upper lip.

Without so much as a hint of a smile, she said, "Tell me where Cullen's music class is. Exactly." He did, exactly. Then she whacked him across the head, very hard, and again as he fell back against his desk and slumped to the floor.

She stepped over his still form, opened the door to peer carefully up and down the hall, pressed the lock button, then closed the door behind her and headed for the music classroom, where at that moment Cullen Vance was singing "Hark, the Herald Angels Sing" along with twenty-five classmates.

• • •

Standing on Odie's porch, Victor Beauville thought, *If I walk through that door, I deserve to get shot,* and rubbed his aching jaw. His head still hadn't cleared, so he shook it, regretting the move instantly. *Man, that old guy can hit,* he thought, then started around the house to search for another way in.

If he'd known that Odie Vance was inside the house having a heart attack at that moment, he might have left . . .

And fewer people would have been shot that day.

• • •

Tyler Vance saw the blue lights coming up behind him before he heard the siren. *Great!* he thought. *I'll have official help after all.*

But he didn't know Trooper Everette Everhart.

Ty slid the black Pathfinder into the parking lot and stopped behind *another* black Pathfinder, exited, and waited impatiently for the patrol car to arrive. It soon did. As he ran over to explain the situation, the trooper shoved open his door and jumped out of the vehicle, drawing his sidearm. Tyler stopped and raised his hands overhead.

"Put up your hands!" Patrolman Everhart screamed, thumbing back the hammer on his Beretta.

"They *are* up," Ty answered.

"Don't get smart. Just keep 'em where I can see 'em!"

"Officer, we don't have *time!* If you'll—"

"Shut up! Get down on the pavement!"

"My son's in danger in that school!"

"I SAID GET DOWN ON THE PAVEMENT! NOW!"

The stridency of the patrolman's voice led Tyler to do what he was told, all the while worried sick about what might be happening inside the school.

Trooper Everhart approached warily, cocked pistol held in both hands, arms quivering from excitement, and said, "Put your hands behind your back!"

There was no way Tyler was going to let himself be handcuffed until Cullen was safe, so instead of placing his hands behind his back, he laced them behind his head. When the officer knelt on his back, put the Beretta against his temple, and gritted, "I said behind your back, mister, not your head," Tyler deflected the gun barrel away from him, rotated his body clockwise, and grabbed the officer by the shirtfront. Patrolman Everette Everhart discharged his weapon into the pavement when Tyler grabbed him, then climbed to his feet. Vance let the officer pull him upright, getting a grip on the man's gun hand as he did so. Patrolman Everhart fired the weapon again, this time into the windshield of his patrol car, and was about to shoot a third time when the gun was wrenched from his grasp. The next thing he saw was a hammer-hand aimed at his nose.

It was the last thing he saw for five minutes.

After putting the officer down for the count, Tyler took the Beretta and ran into the school building.

•  •  •

Harmony Cahill did not hear Highway Patrolman Everhart's pistol discharge. Instead, she heard twenty-seven voices raised in song, a few of them on key. She had slipped into the cloakroom unnoticed, and stood there a few seconds trying to pick out Cullen Vance. There! First row, fifth child, little mouth an O as he sang. She advanced on the teacher—facing her choral group at the front of the room—and beckoned with a finger. The teacher stopped conducting and came over, a questioning frown on her face. "Yes?" she said.

Turning her back to the kids, Harmony showed the music teacher the Walther, now back in her waistband, and said, "I came to get Cullen Vance. If you raise any kind of commotion, I'll shoot everyone in the room. After I leave, you stay in here with the children. If anyone tries to stop me, whoever is near me dies. Understood?"

The teacher nodded.

"Good. Now get that Vance kid over here."

The teacher turned to the children.

•  •  •

That Vance kid was suspicious the moment the strange woman entered the room. She didn't look nice, and he'd had dealings with people before who didn't look nice. He glanced toward the back door, gauging the distance, just in case. The not-nice-looking woman—who reminded him of a chunky, unkempt Cruella de Vil—was whispering to Mrs. Ward. Mrs. Ward didn't look happy. Cullen checked the back door again.

Uh-oh. Mrs. Ward was motioning for him to come over. He did so, very slowly and reluctantly. When the not-nice-looking woman impatiently reached out to grab his shirt, he saw the gun at her waist.

His reaction was instantaneous.

•  •  •

Colonel Rufus McElroy made the turn onto Odie's street and slowly accelerated. The Vance house sat back by itself, but there might be young children playing in the neighborhood. Spotting the black Nissan Pathfinder in the driveway, McElroy wondered who was joining them for lunch. He knew Ty had a new truck, but if his memory served, it was a Toyota. Hell, maybe not.

Since there was insufficient room to park behind the Nissan, McElroy pulled into the curb, well past the mailbox, and stilled the engine. There was no one in sight, on the street or elsewhere.

Things seemed quiet as he got out of the Army sedan.

Too quiet. No birds singing, no squirrels chasing. Probably not even a mole burrowing.

Why this bad feeling?

Trying to shake it off, he strode to the front door and rang the bell.

•  •  •

The first thing Tyler Vance heard when he burst through the school's double doors was someone screaming. He ran to Cullen's room, where he found a teacher kneeling beside Roberta Creed, screaming something through her upraised hands, repeatedly, unintelligibly.

"WHERE'S CULLEN?" he hollered.

She continued to scream.

He shook her, not gently. "Where are the kids?"

No coherent response.

From behind him: "What are you doing? Where's . . . Oh, God, what—"

The school secretary had come in and spotted Roberta Creed on the floor.

Tyler grabbed her shoulders. "Where are the children from this class?"

"In music. What happened? Did you hear those shots?"

"Listen to me! Where's the music class?"

"Across from the lunchroom. Who did . . ."

But he was out the door.

•  •  •

When Harmony Cahill took hold of Cullen's shirt, she got a surprise. It wasn't pleasant. The boy instantly grabbed her wrist in both hands, his grip surprisingly strong, then stepped in close to her right hip and spun clockwise, placing his left shoulder directly under her right elbow. Bending forward at the hips, he jerked down on her wrist with all his strength and weight and fear.

He did the move exactly right, and lightning quick, and he was very strong for a five-year-old. Harmony's elbow hyperextended, pain shooting up the arm and into her neck. She let go of the boy's shirt just as the little shit kicked her on the shin with his heel, which hurt almost as bad as the elbow. Then in a flash he was across the room and out the door.

Harmony Cahill grabbed the anguished music teacher by the left breast and jerked her off balance. "Remember what I said!"

Then she too was out the door.

The teacher fainted.

•   •   •

James M. Farley was in his last year at Guilford County, having been a custodian for forty years, the best in the system. Had letters of recommendation to prove it. Which he didn't need. He'd always prided himself on his work. He was wringing out a mop outside the AG classroom when he saw Cullen Vance squirt out of the music class and aim for the playground.

That was surely odd.

Odder still was the woman who came hoofing it after the boy. She had a *gun* in her hand. Stopping to look both ways when she stepped clear of the building, she must have spotted the boy because she broke into a run, heading the same way he had.

*Those must have been shots I heard, not backfires like I thought,* Farley thought to himself. *What's going on here?*

He followed the lady with the gun.

•   •   •

Victor Beauville heard the doorbell ring just as he stepped inside the back door. *Now who the hell is that?* he thought, and moved into the kitchen. Odie Vance, unconscious on the floor not twenty feet away, was out of sight around a corner, in the hallway.

Beauville walked catlike toward the hall as the buzzer sounded again. He stopped. Listened. Then moved again, into the hall.

• • •

"Start, start, start," Jason Patterson said over and over. But his Corvette wouldn't. He pounded its steering wheel in frustration, then ran next door to borrow his neighbor's Mazda, if she'd let him. Five minutes later, he was on his way to the school, doing seventy, about as much as he could wring out of the aged GLC.

• • •

One of the kids from Cullen's class met Tyler at the door of the music room, tears on her face. "Something's the matter with Mrs. Ward," she cried. When Tyler entered the room, Mrs. Ward was sitting up, pale and disoriented. On seeing Ty, she seemed to snap out of it.

"Mr. Vance! There's a lady with a gun after Cullen! They went out that way," she said, pointing to the door. He was through it and gone before she could lower her arm.

• • •

Cullen hid in his favorite spot, between an air-conditioning unit and a Dempsey Dumpster. He couldn't see his backtrail, so didn't know that the not-nice woman had seen him scamper into his hidey-hole and was closing fast. His breath was coming in gasps, and the smell of fear was on him. But he was thinking. About what to do next.

• • •

Patrolman Everette Everhart awakened slowly, head spinning, nose hurting like hell, and climbed laboriously to his feet. Blood was all over his face; some trickled down, onto his shirt now that he was upright. He looked for his gun.

Gone.

*Shit!* That lunatic must have it.

From the trunk of his patrol car, its windshield starred from his own bullet—*How the hell am I going to explain that away? Hey, I'll say the lunatic did it*—he removed a Remington 870 pump and shucked a round up its chamber.

He considered calling for backup. *Hell no, I won't. Gonna nail that bastard myself,* he thought. And headed for the school building.

• • •

When no one answered the doorbell, McElroy was worried, so he went around back to see if Odie's car was there. It was. *If Odie is here, and the driver of the black Nissan Pathfinder is here, why doesn't someone come to the door?*

He brushed back the tail of his suit coat and drew an abbreviated issue .45, the one only general officers were supposed to carry. Snicking off its safety, he went up the back stairs like Sundown.

• • •

Harmony Cahill was practically on top of Cullen when James Farley yelled at her, "Hey, lady, whatcha doing?"

If she'd had normal nerve endings, she'd have jumped. But she didn't have normal nerve endings.

So she spun and fired, her black automatic making a spiteful spitting sound, its little hollow-point bullet striking a drainage pipe near Farley's head and zinging off into space. He ducked around the building, his mama not having raised any foolish children.

Nor cowards either. He took a pipe wrench from his pocket and peeped around the corner. The lady had disappeared.

• • •

Jason Patterson jumped the light at the corner of Friendly and College Road, to the irritation and consternation of several motorists. The pistol in his pocket made an unfamiliar, uncomfortable lump as he floored the pedal, tires protesting vigorously, and resumed the quest.

• • •

When Cullen heard Mr. Farley yell at the not-nice woman, the custodial worker sounded very near. Which meant the woman was probably very near as well. Oh dear. Having looked around quickly, and seeing no other choice, he squeezed his small body into the extremely limited space between the Dumpster and the building.

Not far, though . . .

Because he got stuck.

He wanted to cry but was afraid the not-nice woman would hear. So he just struggled for breath in the constricted space, and fought down the panic.

• • •

When Tyler came through the door from the music class, Harmony Cahill had just stepped into the open space recently vacated by Cullen, and so didn't see her. He did see James Farley peering around the corner of one of the mobile classrooms. "James," he hollered, "have you seen Cullen?"

"Yeah," Farley answered, "and some lady with a gun."

At that moment the lady with the gun appeared and began to shoot it, first at Farley, then at Tyler. Ty hit the dirt and fired back with Trooper Everhart's Beretta, his bullets whanging into the Dumpster behind which his son was hiding, although he didn't know it.

"I think your boy's back there!" Farley yelled. Hearing that, Tyler jumped to his feet and charged the woman, not daring to shoot since he didn't know exactly where Cullen was. She fired two shots, then took off running, kicking out of her shoes and grabbing a fresh magazine as she went.

"Stop!" Tyler yelled, dropping to one knee and drawing a bead on the rapidly retreating woman before him.

"Daddy?" came a muffled sound from the direction of the Dumpster.

"Cullen!"

"Over here. I . . . can't . . . breathe . . ."

Ty rushed to the Dumpster, realized his son's plight, grabbed a corner of the huge trash bin and heaved.

Nothing.

"Daddy . . ." Weaker now.

Ty shoved with all his heart, his will, his being.

The Dumpster didn't budge.

*Help me, Lord!* he prayed, and pushed, and shoved.

Suddenly James Farley was there, pushing alongside, the two of them, feet digging in, Farley spinning around, shoving his big work boots against the air-conditioning unit, his broad back to the Dumpster, Cullen crying, "Daddy . . ."

Over and over . . . as the men grew weaker, more fatigued, more desperate . . .

And then it moved.

An inch . . .

No more . . .

Enough.

Cullen staggered out and fell into his daddy's arms, wheezing, gulping air . . .

Safe.

"Please don't leave me," Cullen said in a whisper.

Tyler hugged him hard.

•  •  •

Harmony Cahill was running around the side of the building just as Trooper Everette Everhart entered it with his shotgun at the ready, scaring everyone in sight. Seconds later, Jason Patterson wheeled into the parking lot, slewed to a stop behind the patrol car, and jumped out in time to see an unpleasant-looking woman careen around the corner of the building with a gun in her hand. Jason—neither slow-witted nor indecisive, and possessed of quick reflexes—grabbed for his own pistol, unfortunately fumbling the draw from his pocket. The little autoloader clattered to the pavement, skittering under the GLC. Jason took a quick glance at the woman, noted her gun lifting toward him, then followed his handgun under the car.

•  •  •

Victor Beauville was squatting beside Odie Vance, feeling for a pulse, when he heard the back door squeak on its hinges. He straightened up and flattened his slender body against the wall of the hallway, gun in hand.

And waited.

•   •   •

Dave Michaels was running a little early, no big deal; he and Odie would play dominoes until Ty and McElroy arrived. When he pulled up to Odie's house and spotted a black Nissan like the one Ty'd told him about, he jumped out of his car and ran to the front door, uncertain of what to expect.

He was reaching for the knob when he heard a shot from inside.

•   •   •

Trooper Everette Everhart was five feet inside the front door of the school, trying to listen to twenty people at once, when someone yelled, "There she is!" and pointed out a window. Where he'd just come from. *Shit!* He moved to the door, opened it with a foot, and peered out.

A man was down—not the lunatic though, too bad—on his belly half under a Mazda parked behind his patrol car. *What's happening here?* thought the highway patrolman, and stepped outside. As he did so, a woman hove into view, aiming a peashooter with a silencer toward the man lying on the tarmac.

"DROP THE WEAPON!" Everhart yelled at the woman.

She didn't, instead moving faster than any human he'd ever seen, spinning toward him, her gun coming to bear as his finger tightened on the trigger . . . too late. He felt a blow just above his navel, not especially painful, just a thumping numbness of the skin, but his mind knew what it was and panicked, causing him to jerk the trigger of his Remington and miss the damned woman, giving her time to fire again, her second bullet striking the door behind him as he pumped the action and shot at her again, saw the pellets impact, her body lurch slightly, until she caught herself and fired at him a third time and the lights went out.

•   •   •

McElroy had just stepped into the hallway when he caught a bullet in the chest, causing him to fall back against the doorjamb and fire his own gun inadvertently, his slug digging a chunk from the banister down the hall. Kicking himself backward to dodge a second bullet, he was vaguely aware of the front door bursting open as he fell.

• • •

Tyler heard shots coming from the front of the building, and remembered.

"Jason!" he said.

"What, Daddy?"

"Son, I need to go. Jason was on his way here to help you. Do you understand?"

Cullen nodded unhappily. Ty handed Everhart's Beretta to James Farley. "Ever use one of these?"

"I know the basics," Farley said.

"Don't let anything happen to him."

"I'll take care of him. You take care of you."

Tyler raced to the building.

• • •

Jason Patterson was still under the Mazda GLC, trying to be as inconspicuous as possible lest the monster woman remember him and lower the boom. He could see her feet, blood running down one of her ankles. *She must be giving up,* he thought. *She's getting into the truck.*

Indeed she was, and getting blood all over the upholstery. Four of Everhart's shotgun pellets had found flesh. Harmony Cahill had felt better.

She'd felt worse, too, she reflected as she climbed into one of the black Nissan Pathfinders, started it, slipped into first, and pulled away from the curb.

Just as Tyler burst through the school's twin doors.

• • •

When Dave came through Odie's front door, he noticed three things:

Odie facedown on the hall floor.

Blood on the wall near the kitchen doorway.

A man pointing a gun at him.

So he dove into the stairwell—to his right—as a bullet smacked into the doorframe behind him. Scrambled up the stairs as fast as he could make it, hearing feet pounding the floor below him, topping the stairs and diving onto the floor as two more *sputs!* from below indicated bullets flying in his direction.

Knowing Odie kept an old Smith & Wesson in a sock drawer, he headed for it, hoping it was loaded. He slammed the bedroom door behind him and shoved the chest of drawers against it, then rooted through the socks for the gun.

There! He checked the cylinder—full.

All right!

. . .

*This is getting pretty complicated,* Victor Beauville thought, as he climbed the staircase. *Who else is going to show up?*

He pussyfooted along the upstairs landing to the door so recently slammed, and tried the knob. It turned, but wouldn't open. Something was blocking it.

A foot?

He fired the remainder of his magazine through the door.

Nothing fell on the other side.

He put in a full mag, tried the knob again, then leaned his weight against the door.

No dice.

He was about to leave when someone behind him said, "If you move, I'll kill you."

Beauville moved anyway, pivoting at the hip and filling the air with hollow-points. McElroy went down the stairs headfirst, which hurt his chest something awful. Another magazine in place, Beauville eased across the landing and peered over the banister . . .

And caught a bullet in the cheek, its spinning pathway cutting a groove below his right eye, blood splattering the wallpaper behind him as he recoiled, recovered, leaned back forward over the railing and tossed off three rounds of his own, more careful now that his ammo supply was dwindling.

Then no sound.

•  •  •

Tyler tried his best to catch the black Nissan Pathfinder and its bloody driver. Said driver, noting this, applied the hand brake, punched the gas, and did a bootlegger's one-eighty in the parking lot. Poking the Walther out the window, Harmony fired southpaw until it ran dry, then stomped the gas pedal and aimed the vehicle at her pursuer. Ty dove between two parked cars and she missed. Him anyway. She sideswiped a Buick two cars down. Again a change of direction, with Tyler jumping up from behind the sheltering cars as she roared past . . . and away . . .

From the lot, the property, from sight.

He stared until there was nothing left to see, then went to find Jason.

•  •  •

While all the shooting had been taking place on the upstairs landing, Dave had quietly shifted the chest of drawers away from the door. Opening it a crack, he saw the man who'd shot at him standing at the railing, peering down into the stairwell.

Dave stepped into the hall and said, "Hi."

Though the man was very, very fast, Dave had not only seen faster, he *was* faster. The man's gun was still coming up when Dave shot him five times with Odie's old revolver. The gun didn't have much power, but whatever it had was enough; the guy went over the railing and down the stairs. Dave looked to make certain, only one cartridge left in his gun. McElroy knelt beside the dead man, his .45 auto held against the guy's ear.

"You all right?" wheezed McElroy.

"Yeah. You?" from Dave.

"No," said McElroy, and fell across the body.

# Twenty-four

At the school, the situation was this:

Roberta Lynne Creed, age thirty-four, was slowly recovering from her near-death asphyxiation.

Highway Patrol Officer Everette Clyde Everhart, age thirty-three, was dead from multiple gunshot wounds.

Assistant Principal Gerald Theodore Huff was en route to Wesley-Long Hospital, having suffered a serious concussion.

Rachel Ann Ward was inside being treated for syncope.

And Sergeant Carl McDuffy, Greensboro Police Department, was interrogating yours truly. "Tell me again how you shot Trooper Everhart," he said, and popped a piece of Juicy Fruit into his mouth.

"Tell me how your likeness came to be beside the word 'pinhead' in *Webster's*."

He grinned at me unpleasantly, his carrottopped face bespattered with freckles, his nose out of joint. "Same old smartass Vance."

"Same old brain-dead McDuffy."

"Can we go through this again now that we've pissed on each other's geraniums like a couple rottweilers?"

"Sure," I said.

"You were where when Everhart bought it?"

"Out back with Cullen and Jim Farley. The woman had chased Cullen out that way. Jim probably saved his life."

"Then you intervened, right?"

"She shot at me. I shot back."

"With Everhart's handgun."

"Yes."

"And you missed."

"Far as I know."

"Thought you hotshot gun writers never miss."

"You going to start up again?"

"Naw. Go on with your story. I'm on the edge of my seat."

"When the woman opened up, she was beside the Dumpster. I fired at her, but Jim warned me that Cullen was somewhere near. So I stopped shooting and charged her."

"Why in the hell did you do that?"

"Figured if I got close, I'd have a better chance of hitting her. Plus, I thought it might cause her to break and run."

"Getting close can work both ways, Vance."

I shrugged. "Cullen was too near her. I had to do something constructive."

"Getting shot ain't constructive."

"Anyway, she took off. I was considering taking a shot when Cullen called. He'd slipped behind the Dumpster to hide and gotten stuck. Jim and I got him out."

"How'd you do that?"

"Moved it."

"The Dumpster? The hell you say!"

I shrugged again. "Cullen squeezed out and we all sat there until I heard shots, and remembered that I'd called Jason to come for Cullen."

"Jason? Why didn't you call us?"

"He lives nearby. Besides, there might not have been a squad car in this vicinity, plus I'd have had to spend five minutes explaining. There just wasn't time."

"Meanwhile you hustled your ass over here, thereby sucking a highway patrolman into the situation. Were you driving a little fast?"

"You bet, and glad to see the trooper."

"He glad to see you?"

I hesitated. This was the tricky part. "Not really."

"So he pulled down on you?"

"Yes."

"Ordered you onto the ground?"

I nodded.

"Tried to cuff you?"

Another nod.

"And you used some of that martial arts crap to disarm him."

"No choice."

"You could have explained the situation to him."

"I tried. He wouldn't listen."

"So you whacked him."

"If I hadn't, Cullen might be dead. I barely made it to him as it was."

"So I got you for speeding, maybe careless and reckless, resisting arrest, assault on a police officer, obstruction of justice, carrying a firearm on school property, theft of a firearm, reckless endangerment, and attempted murder."

"Don't forget running in the hall."

McDuffy shook his head. "You're a trip, Vance," he said, then went over to his car and used the radio.

• • •

Jason and I were sitting cross-legged on the grass near the flagpole. Around us hummed considerable official activity. Jason said, "They've pretty much sorted things out, but they'll be interviewing witnesses forever."

"You sure you're okay?" I asked.

"Fine as can be expected in my weakened condition," he answered. I noticed the swelling from his beating had about disappeared, though the cuts and bruises were still very much in evidence.

"Let me tell you," he went on, "I was making some pretty fancy moves for someone recently hospitalized." He looked over toward the front of the school, to where Everhart had died. "Shame about that officer. He undoubtedly saved my life."

We watched the activity awhile, then I said, "Wonder how Huff is making it."

"Haven't heard. There was a lot of blood."

I nodded. "Head wounds bleed a lot."

We saw Fanner approaching and climbed to our feet. He opened with, "The highway patrol commander is adamant about wanting your scalp."

"Gonna let him have it?"

"I suppose not. You appear to have thwarted the person responsible for all the carnage."

"Too bad I couldn't have kept her here to meet you."

"I understand she was hard hit."

"Jason thinks so. I got only a brief look when she was trying to run me down. Can I get my son and go home now?"

Before he could answer, the school secretary came running with a cordless phone in her hand, face a mask of consternation. "Mr. Vance, it's your father. He's . . ." She stopped.

I didn't want to take the phone.

Did anyway. And was immediately sorry.

# Twenty-five

Dave met me at the door. I raised my brows; he shook his head. "Be prepared. He doesn't look very good," he said. I looked past him, where my father lay trying to live, Ethyl sitting silently by the bed.

"McElroy was there too."

"At Dad's?"

Nodding, Dave said, "He's down the hall with a hole in his chest. Doctors say he'll be fine. Right now he's sure as hell not."

I took a deep breath.

"The colonel saved your papa."

Another deep breath.

"Odie's going to be all right."

Another.

"You have to believe that. 'Cause if you don't, it won't do him much good. You know?"

I nodded. He squeezed my shoulder and let me by, whispering, "He's heavily sedated," as I passed.

Pop was ashen. An IV line ran from his arm, and there was an electric heart monitor pinned to the sheet. Attached to the bed was a catheter bag, its tube snaking up and out of sight.

I tried to swallow. Couldn't.

I touched his hand lightly, taking the gray fingers into mine.

"Dad?"

No response.

"He won't hear you for a while," Ethyl said quietly.

I dropped into a vacant chair, and held his hand. For two hours he never stirred.

•  •  •

Heather was on a bench in the waiting room, Cullen curled up beside her, head on her lap. Jason sat at her side, Web's head on his shoulder, sound asleep. The two of them looked very tired.

"How's Odie?" she asked.

"No change."

"I'm so sorry."

"Me too."

"You plan to stay all night?"

"As long as it takes."

"Where do you want Cullen to sleep?"

"At Dave's. He'll take him. You too, if you want."

"And Web?"

"Of course. Jason as well."

"Adam is worried sick," Jason said. "I'd better stay at home, unless you need me."

I shook my head. "That's okay. So long as Dave is there, they'll be fine."

"How's McElroy, have you heard?" he asked.

"Dave told me he was okay. I haven't seen him yet. I'd better go see if they'll let me take a peek."

Dave came over and handed me a cup of coffee, and one to Heather, and one to Jason. "Tyler?" he said.

"Yeah?"

"Eat something."

"Not hungry."

"Tyler?" he said.

"What?"

"Eat something."

"I said I wasn't—" I began, irritatedly.

"Tyler?"

I put a hand on his big arm. "Sorry."

"Don't care about sorry. Eat, you hear me?"

"Okay."

"I want your word."

I didn't say anything.

"Tyler?"

"Okay!"

Heather, shaking her head in amazement, said to Dave, "Incredible. Nobody in the wide world can get him to do something he doesn't want to do, except you."

"Not so," Dave said.

"Who else?"

"Him," Dave said.

Pointing at Cullen.


# Twenty-six

Colonel Rufus Earl McElroy was awake, and in pain. A clear plastic tube had been inserted into his chest just under and in front of his left armpit, its opposite end going to a gallon-sized glass jug filled with water. Each time he breathed, bubbles rose to the water's surface.

"How are you, sir?" I queried.

Weak smile. "Must be dying. You haven't called me sir in twenty years."

"Old habit."

He breathed and bubbled awhile, me standing there wondering what to say. The doctor'd told me that McElroy had taken a bullet in the thorax from nearly point-blank range. The slug had smashed a rib, followed it for a few inches, then tunneled under the outer edge of the left pectoral, bulldozing its way inward to exit the muscle just in front of the sternum. His heart had been missed by maybe two inches. No one seemed to know exactly what had transpired after the hit, but concerted movement must have been involved because the busted rib had lacerated a lung, causing considerable internal bleeding and trauma, then loss of consciousness. The prognosis was good; McElroy would likely be up and dancing in three or four days, released in five.

"How's Odie?" he said, wincing as he spoke.

"Still hasn't come around."

He grunted in response.

"I understand you saved his life."

He grunted again. "Dave tell you that?"

I nodded.

"Figures. It was him saved both our asses."

The perplexity must have showed on my face, because he continued to expound.

"When I got there . . ."

Air bubbles in the jar as he spoke.

". . . Odie didn't answer the bell."

More bubbles.

"Went around back . . ."

Bubbles, face a mask of severe discomfort.

"His car there, and a black truck . . ."

He paused from the pain.

"Tell me later."

Slight shake of his head. "So I went in through the kitchen . . . and got ambushed."

He rested again, quite a spell. Then went on. "When I got hit, I kicked backward, heard a commotion . . . Dave busting in. Guy tried to pop him, too."

Rest.

"I went upstairs. Still had my gun . . . tried . . ."

More rest while I waited.

"Dave nailed the guy. Dunno how. Can't remember after that," he finished.

He suddenly gripped my hand very hard.

"Want something for the pain?" I asked.

He nodded, teeth set.

I went to find a nurse. Twenty minutes later, he was out like a light.

• • •

I slept a couple hours, awakening to a crick in my neck. Went to check on Dad. No change. Ethyl still sat beside his bed, wide awake.

"I'll sit up with him awhile, so you can get some sleep," I offered.

She shook me away. I sat in the other chair and tried to sleep. Forget it.

So I sought coffee, finding some in a machine.

I'd tasted better.

I'd felt better, too. My head hurt and the crick hadn't gone away and my mouth tasted like Elmer's glue. On the other hand, I'd felt a lot worse, and not so long ago.

Having promised to eat something, I plundered the snack dispenser. Chips, cheese crackers with peanut butter, Honey Bun, washed down with orange juice. Haute cuisine.

At daybreak, Ethyl came to find me.

Dad was awake.

# Twenty-seven "Hey, Pop."

His eyes were open and staring at nothing. I looked at Ethyl. Her expression, normally keen-edged like flint, was soft.

"How you doing?" to my dad.

Nothing.

Leaning closer, I said, "Do you need anything?"

No sign of coherence.

I looked at Ethyl again. She kept looking down at Dad.

I tried once more. "Can you hear me, Pop?"

He gazed into what only he could see.

A doctor appeared at my elbow. She said, "Are you the son?"

The son. "Yeah. I'm the son."

"Can I speak with you? Outside?"

"Sure." We moved to the hallway. Ethyl stayed bedside.

The doctor said, "It's possible he may not come out of it," the words like a blow to my wind. "It's also possible that he suffered a stroke along with the heart attack. In fact, it's probable. The damage done to his heart was minimal, based on the X rays. We've scheduled a CAT scan for this morning. We'll know more afterward."

"Okay," was all I said.

"Were you here all night?"

I nodded.

"Go home and get some rest. There's nothing you can do here. If there's any change, good or bad, we'll call, you needn't worry."

I went back into the room where my father lay staring. To Ethyl, I said, "I'm going to his house. To take a nap."

Her acknowledgment was a curt nod, never taking her eyes off Dad.

"You going home soon?"

Head shake.

"Okay," I said, and left.

•  •  •

I stopped at home to recharge the mobile phone and call Dave. "Everyone's still sound asnooze," he told me.

"How about you?"

"I'm not."

"Did you sleep any last night?"

"Some."

"How much?"

"Some."

"Sitting up?"

"Sure. Thurman's coming over in an hour. I'll grab a few winks. You eat like you promised?"

"After a fashion."

"Out of a machine, right?"

"It's food."

"In theory. Now that you're home, drink a couple Instant Breakfasts. I know you don't feel like eating."

"Good idea," I agreed.

"So you'll do it?"

"And you'll get some sleep?"

"Sure. That's why I called Thurman. Can't slay dragons half asleep. Or on an empty stomach."

"I'll fix 'em now."

I did, mixing them in a blender with two frozen bananas. Then I went to Pop's.

•   •   •

Someone had fixed the front door, at least sufficiently so that a teenager with a credit card couldn't pop the lock. I used my key to enter the back way, defying the police tape. Dad had been baking, something for him and McElroy to enjoy. The smell lingered. There was dried blood— McElroy's I presumed—on the wall in the hallway, beside the kitchen entranceway. Not much, brownish now. The chalk outline of a body was at the foot of the stairs.

What had happened here?

I called Fanner. He wasn't in. They took my number.

I lay on my dad's big double bed, eyes damp. Watched the ceiling fan, like I'd done so often as a boy. Sometime during the morning, sleep claimed me.

•   •   •

The old clock said 1:17 when the phone rang. Heather.

We talked desultorily for five minutes: Sure, Cullen and Web were fine. Of course they weren't outside; they were watching *Homeward Bound*. Yes, Dave was asleep, and Thurman was sitting by the window with a long black gun on his lap, chewing tobacco and spitting into a mason jar, which was disgusting. She'd called the hospital and been told that Dad was in and out, still unresponsive; that Ethyl was in but equally unresponsive.

"She should go home for a rest, Ty."

"I agree. Go tell her to leave."

Heather said, "You bet I will," and put Cullen on.

"Hi, Daddy."

"Hey, sweetheart. The movie good?"

"Web likes it. After five times, it's kinda old to me."

"Um-hmm. You eat lunch yet?"

"Yes. Bunsrick stew."

"Brunswick."

"Yep. Heather fixed it. With scratch."

"*From* scratch."

"Right." Lengthy pause. "Is Paw-paw okay?"

Uh-oh. "I don't know, babe. It's too early to tell."

"What happened to him?"

"He had a heart attack, and maybe a stroke."

"What's a stroke?"

"It's when something stops the flow of blood to the brain."

"Like when you faint?"

"Yes. Except it's more serious."

Long pause. "Can I go see him?"

"We'll see."

"Are you coming over here?"

"Do you need for me to?"

"Yes."

"Then I will."

"Right away?"

"Right away."

He sounded relieved. "Okay. I love you. Bye. SMACK!"

I kissed him back and left the house in which both of my parents had suffered strokes. One of them had left me. I hoped not both.

• • •

Dave and Heather and I sat on Dave's patio, tea and coffee and beer among us. Christmas lights were strung along the periphery; they winked at us methodically. Holly and mistletoe and evergreen sprigs, and carolers down the way, their voices uplifted and uplifting.

Dave had his long legs propped on the railing. Mine wouldn't quite reach. I took a sip of black tea, not really tasting it, and watched the lights.

Heather said, "Cullen seems to be okay. Considering all that happened, at the school and with his grandfather, that's amazing."

I nodded. "He's resilient. I was worried to death when Tess was killed. But he got through it."

"He had you," Dave said, holding his coffee in both hands to blow on it.

"And Pop, and Ethyl."

"You made the difference. Your dad is great with him, and Ethyl, in her own way. But it was you who brought him through. You're always there for him. You always listen to him, and I mean really listen. You don't talk down to him, treat him like he's too young to understand things."

Heather smiled. "Today, he was trying to explain to me how kites work. He'd been reading *My Weekly Reader.* He patiently went through the process, but got his facts a little crossed up. Nonetheless, he plowed on. At the end, he paused, looked me in the eye, and said, 'I don't know exactly what I'm saying, but I know what I'm talking about.'" She smiled again.

Me too.

Until Thurman brought me the phone and Ethyl said, "You need to come. Now."

.   .   .

A cardiologist met me outside Dad's room, introducing himself as Dr. Marvin Fielder.

"We've done all we know how to do for your father," he began. "He's just not responding. Every test we've conducted indicates that there is no physiological reason for his malaise. No permanent brain damage showed on the CAT. A catheterization indicated only moderate blockage of two coronary arteries, remarkable for a septuagenarian diabetic. In my opinion, he doesn't require even a balloon angioplasty, and certainly not a bypass."

"Then what's the problem?"

"Unofficial diagnosis?"

I nodded.

"The will to live doesn't appear to be there. He seems to want to give up, go on to whatever's next. He's a widower, right?"

"Yes."

"How long?"

"Nearly thirty years."

He thought about that; obviously he'd expected it to have been more recent.

"Grandchildren?"

"I have a five-year-old son with whom he spends a great deal of time. My sister lives in New Jersey and has four children, all grown," I said.

"Perhaps he doesn't feel needed anymore. Like he can let go and it won't turn anyone's life topsy-turvy."

He quickly held up a hand. "Don't misinterpret that. I know he'll be missed, and I'm sure he knows it, too. But his loss may not be life-disruptive to anyone, or so he may think."

I remembered what Dad had told me just a few days before. Perhaps the doctor was right.

He put a hand on my shoulder. "You want your father well? Give him a reason to be well."

·  ·  ·

With Ethyl looking on, I leaned over my dad, whose eyes were now closed, and talked low and close and sincere.

"Pop, I remember what you told me the other day, and I respect your viewpoint. Maybe if my life was too miserable to bear, and my son was grown, I'd lean the same way. The only thing is, the doctor tells me your health isn't all that bad. You don't even have a decent heart condition, for Pete's sake. And if you really had a stroke, there are no identifiable aftereffects. I realize your arthritis is a pain, that the reflux is no fun, and that taking three or four diabeta a day is a major nuisance. So, do what you think is best.

"One thing, though. You probably don't know it, but the guy who tried to kill you shot McElroy. The colonel's down the hall, and they say he'll make it, but he's out of commission for now, and there's to be no official military help forthcoming, like we had last spring.

"Another thing, the guy who came after you wasn't working alone. His female partner made a play for Cullen. At the school, if you believe that. Obviously, nowhere is safe. I managed to get there in time to save Cullen, but not to snare the woman. She got away and the authorities have no idea where she is.

"With you out of the picture, that pretty much leaves Cullen's safety up to me and Dave, though Jason and Thurman are willing to help. Of course, willing and able aren't quite the same, but you do what you can, right? So if Dave and I can stay awake, and Dave's business doesn't pull him away, we can probably keep Cullen safe. That's if we keep him home from school, of course, which means that Ethyl will have a lot of input in his life, since she'll have to home-school him. Picture his personality in a couple years.

"Oh well, nothing else to do. His safety comes first. Too bad we don't have more help. Anyway, I love you, and so does Cullen. Whatever you decide is okay by me, and he'll get over it. In time."

I kissed him on the forehead, saying, "If you're still alive, I'll see you tonight," and left, not daring to look at Ethyl.

•   •   •

I was helping Cullen choose clothes that evening, for his impending visit to see Paw-paw, when Dr. Fielder phoned.

"What the hell did you say to him?"

"He awake?"

Laughing, he said, "Awake? He ate three bowls of orange Jell-O and pinched a nurse."

"Female, I hope."

He was still laughing when we hung up.

# Twenty-eight

While awaiting a visit from Lieutenant Fanner next morning, I occupied myself with an hour's worth of cardiovascular exercises and a short kata punctuated by twenty minutes of the local paper, its journalists in a tiz about the uproar at the school, as were their broadcast brethren. Fanner finally arrived, sparing me further elevation of my boiling point. He had two Egg McMuffins and a pair of tiny baked-apple pies in tow.

"What, no grits?" I said, rummaging through the bag.

"Rather a bowl of sheep-dip," he rejoined.

"Matter of opinion," I said, pouring us coffee, its pungent aroma even more beckoning than the McMuffins, though I know that's hard to swallow.

"Anyone who would consume grits would curry a warthog with his teeth."

"And be glad to do it," I concurred. He smiled and sat and bit into his rectangular apple pie.

"Dessert first?"

"Does breakfast involve dessert?"

"Now there's an interesting item for discussion."

"Better perhaps that we discuss Hillary Eloise Harmon."

"That Cullen's girlfriend at the school?"

He nodded, chewing, too polite to speak around the apple bits. As always, he was neat and thoroughly dressed, although his head was uncovered; a navy fedora lay on the hall table beside his tweed topcoat.

"Like the tie," I said. "Italian?"

He nodded between chews.

We abandoned the small talk and tackled the tuck. Later, over refills of Colombian, Fanner elaborated on Ms. Harmon, aka Harmony Cahill.

"Very little is known about her. Her talents were once employed by the CIA, but it seems she took to her work too readily. Collateral damage was often very extensive, even for the agency."

"That's why she didn't think twice about going after Cullen at school."

"Precisely. And although we do have that name for her, there is no absolute corroboration of its validity."

"Not even by the CIA?"

Shook his big head. "On the two occasions that she has been arrested, she provided different identification."

"Prints?"

"Can be altered."

"So how do you know what you know about her?"

"We ran her MO, and physical description, through federal channels. Her methodology is quite recognizable, and she is very lethal."

"No shit. What else?"

"Cullen was very, very lucky."

I nodded at that, watching a determined squirrel on the ground outside my dining room window. A nut was in trouble. "Tell me more."

"The lady has been described as between five feet four inches tall and five seven, and between a hundred and twenty pounds and one-seventy-five."

I snorted at that. "Now there's a weight range. I'll tell you this, the woman I chased around the school weighed no hundred and twenty pounds."

"The point is that she alters her appearance easily, even so far as gaining and losing a considerable portion of body weight."

I considered that, the discipline it would entail. Thinking about it did not make me happy.

"Can you shed any further light on Madame Harmon?" Fanner asked.

"She's fearless, and very quick. But careful. She turned to shoot at me with no hesitation whatever, but when she realized she was cornered with only a silenced pocket gun for an ally, she was equally unhesitant to quit the scene. Showing up at the school as she did, and in broad daylight, I'd peg her as bold, smart, and ruthless. Someone who'll kill a child will do anything."

"One caveat," Fanner pointed out.

"That is?"

"We do not know that she was planning to kill Cullen. She hurt no one but adults."

"Somehow I doubt she intended to take my son to see *A Christmas Carol.*"

"I agree. Still, kidnapping and murder do not necessarily go arm in arm. She is credited with twenty-one killings, and none was a child."

"Oh, I feel better already. Despite the fact that her partner was taken off, do you share my feeling that she's still lurking, despite her wounds?"

"Indeed I do. You can count on it. She has a reputation for tenacity, not to mention resiliency. And she always wears a vest."

"Great. Maybe I can hire her as a nanny."

· · ·

For the next few minutes, Lieutenant Fanner filled me in on what had transpired at my dad's, so far as was known.

"So both McElroy and Dave merely stumbled into the situation," I interrupted at one point.

"That appears to be the case. Our supposition is that somehow your father knew someone was after him, or at least trying to gain entrance to his home. Hence the rifle there with him on the floor. The deceased had a very pronounced swelling at the jawline, as from a hard blow. Can your father hit hard?"

"You bet."

He smiled grimly. "The voice of experience?"

"You bet." I grinned back. "Seriously, one of Dad's brothers was Golden Gloves, and Pop used to spar with him. Uncle Darryl once told me that Dad could have gone pro. If he popped this guy on the jaw like he meant it, you bet it'd swell, not to mention putting his lights out."

Fanner thought about that. "That might explain how your father managed to get to his gun. Also why he had a heart attack. Fear, agitation, abrupt stressful activity. When he is better, perhaps we shall find out.

"McElroy told us," he continued, "that he was suspicious when no one answered the doorbell. He circled the house, noticed your father's car parked in back, and slipped in unannounced. And was shot for his trouble. Enter David Michaels. He too was to dine with your father, and must have arrived just after the colonel did. He went to the front door, heard a shot, and immediately kicked open the door. That probably saved McElroy. The hit man was distracted."

"Just by Dave bursting through a doorway? What a limited attention span." Trying to keep the tone light.

"So David, dodging bullets, took to the stairwell. He claims to remember that your father kept a revolver in a bedroom drawer. He sought the gun. With his attacker close at heel, he entered the bedroom, secured the doorway by means of a chest of drawers, and acquired the revolver.

"In the meantime, McElroy regained his feet and negotiated the staircase, searching for his assailant. The two exchanged fire briefly, then the colonel sought sanctuary on the ground floor. Such fevered movement, we suspect, caused the damage to his lung.

"While his antagonist was thus engaged, David removed the obstacle from the doorway and shot the man to death."

"Not in the back."

"No. No indeed. All five wounds were from the front, over the heart, in a cluster the size of a lemon."

"A lemon? He must not have been used to the gun."

"David is that good, is he?"

"You never saw anyone as good, Lieutenant."

"Present company included?"

"Well . . ." I said modestly.

Fanner continued to enlighten. "The deceased is Victor Beauville, or so his driving license reads. From Florida."

I waited for more, not forthcoming.

"What else?"

He shook his head.

"Nothing else?"

"His height, weight, predilection for erotic tattoos in unusual locations."

I smiled at that, in spite of myself.

"Something amuses you?"

"Thinking of a friend. She hails out of Florida too. So," I continued, "didn't you run the prints on this hard case who almost nailed my daddy?"

"Mr. Vance, please, do not question my abilities. His fingertips had been adjusted. Chemically."

"Dental records?"

"We are checking, but there were no filled cavities or bridgework."

"Must have brushed and flossed regularly. Since birth," I said, grimacing. "Reminds me of last spring and that guy at the bank. I thought when a body turned up, you guys knew within an hour whether he was anal-retentive or had an aunt in Cleveland."

He spread big hands. "What can I say? We are doing our best."

"As usual, that's not very damn good. More coffee?"

"No, thank you. I will spend half the morning in the head as it is. Well, do not let me trouble you further. My regards to your father. And Colonel McElroy." He made as if to leave, then paused.

"When your personal, er, sources identify the remains, you will tell me, correct?"

"Oh, by all means," I said, fetching his fedora. He put it where it belonged, gave me a look that would jump-start a cotton thresher, and departed.

# Twenty-nine

Over the varied protestations of the hospital staff, Dave and Heather and Jason and I crowded into McElroy's room late in the afternoon. Jason brought a poinsettia, placing it on the window ledge. It cheered the room considerably, though doing little to mask the harsh hospital effluvium.

Dave was saying, "These were professional hit persons, Tyler my lad, not folks pissed at you for cutting them off at a traffic light. And damn good ones, too. The lady at the school sounds like hell on greased wheels, and the one at Odie's was fast as a mamba. I didn't shade him by more than half a tenth."

"What does that mean?" Jason asked.

"Half a tenth. As in tenth of a second."

Jason's jaw dropped. "You're saying you beat the guy by five hundredths of a second!"

"That's just for perspective," I answered. "What Dave's saying is that the fellow was really quick. However, since Dave shoots IPSC competition regularly, his estimate of half a tenth is probably accurate, so long as he wasn't in the grip of tachypsychia. If so, the actual difference may have been, say, eight hundredths of a second."

Jason looked stricken by the minuscule numbers.

"That's a long time when you're talking first shot, Jason. Remember, that's not for the whole string. Probably took him nearly a second to get off all five."

Dave snorted derisively. "In your dreams."

I looked at him. "C'mon, you aren't used to Dad's gun."

"Yeah, well, my finger still works," he rejoined.

"The DA pull on that Smith will go at least fourteen pounds. Besides," I continued, "those original grips are too petite for those hams you call hands."

"Oh, boys?" said the colonel.

We looked at him.

"I have a hole in my chest. Can we cut to the chase?"

Jason asked, "What's tachypsychia?"

Heather shook her head, saying, "Men," in that way women reserve for themselves.

"What do you mean *men,* in that tone of voice?" Dave said. "All we're doing is having a simple disagreement about skill levels and perception. When you and Tyler are discussing the tie-in between ear infections and lengthy pacifier dependency, I never shake my head condescendingly and mutter, 'Parents,' under my breath. Not to mention . . ."

For the next hour we discussed and designed and discarded and divagated.

But we came up with a plan.

Pacifiers had nothing to do with it.

•   •   •

Cullen was in Dad's room, the two of them playing poker. With Pop out of danger, Ethyl had gone home to collapse. I patted Pop's arm, kissed Cullen on the hair, and told them of our solutions. To wit:

If Ethyl was agreeable, she would move into my house for the duration to home-school Cullen. Maybe Web too.

McElroy and Dad would recuperate at my place, with two of Axel's men on guard around the clock, one inside the house, one out. Additional security would be provided by McElroy's top soldier, a tender Special Forces E-6 who was using some leave time to reinforce our little team, claiming a desire for some real-world experience, not just constant training.

Ethyl, accompanied by at least two of these men, would take Cullen and Web to the Y daily, for whooping and hollering and skipping and jumping and swimming, all intended to preempt cabin fever. Once or twice a week, they'd maybe go to a play or movie. House arrest this close to Christmas would be a trial, but couldn't be helped.

Dave and I, in concert with Ralph Gonzales, would try to lure the three-hundred-pound slug up from Mexico City. And smush him.

Dad liked everything except being stuck in the same house with Ethyl long-term.

"It'll be all right, Paw-paw," Cullen reassured him. "She'll feed you lots of soup."

"Yeah. That's what I'm worried about."

# Thirty

Dave and I had finished our run—only ten miles today, due to time restraints—and were racing one another in bent-knee sit-ups on incline boards, five sets of one hundred per, one minute rest between sets. I was on my fourth set, fifty-seventh rep, when Ethyl stuck her disapproving head in the room and said, "Phone," in that special tone of hers.

It was Ralph Gonzales, calling to tell me that he'd spoken to Hector

Diaz about our bogus dope deal. Hector, Gonzales said, had been all up in the air, having heard that his contracted double hit had gone awry, and that the Vance male trio was not only well but bullet hole–free. After ranting for five minutes about how one couldn't trust important work to hirelings, how he'd probably have to journey north to do the job himself, how crappy the current political and environmental climate was in Mexico, he'd gotten around to asking Gonzales the purpose for his call. Dope, Gonzales told him. Lots of dope. Seemed he—Gonzales—had while enjailed met a guy who knew a guy who knew another guy who had recently lost a major distributor to a DEA bust in Charlotte. This guy was sitting on roughly three million in uncut heroin, and was so sorely vexed and perplexed and in need of cash that he had agreed to cough up Gonzales's bail if he'd help remedy the situation, either personally or through a reliable contact. Hector Diaz was as reliable as they came, Gonzales had assured the friend of his new friend's friend.

Set it up, Hector Diaz had ordered Gonzales, saying that he'd fly up to handle the deal—and the extremely irritating Tyler Vance—himself. Thus:

The trap was set.

Diaz would be on the move immediately.

Ralph Gonzales wanted out of jail, equally immediately, to make "arrangements."

· · ·

Ralph phoned again an hour later, and told me everything was a go. "Okay," I said. Then: "What do you figure as your cut of the three mil?"

Gonzales answered, "Twinny percen'."

I said, *"Estás muy loco!"*

Gonzales warned, "I can tell him not to come."

I said, "Twenty percent is not entirely unreasonable."

Gonzales agreed, *"Sí.* Is very fair."

I said, "We need to meet."

Gonzales invited, "Come see me. Pretty damn soon." Then he hung up.

· · ·

I called McElroy, still in the hospital, and told him of my conversation with Gonzales. He said he'd get back to me after calling some of his friends in the spook community. If McElroy assisted in snagging Diaz, it would be a nice feather in his beret. Besides, he had a personal score to settle, having lost a couple of men to Hector or some of his compatriots last spring.

"You plan to use real smack as bait for Diaz, or a substitute?" asked the colonel.

"Where the hell would I get three million in heroin?"

"No problem. My friends in the Drug Enforcement—"

"Forget it. With my luck, three bicycle-riding kids with UZIs would knock me over. No thanks."

We said goodbye and I made a pot of Snickerdoodle, then whipped up some mix for a Belgian waffle. Or two. Would three be gluttonous? Probably. I could make an extra, freeze it for Cullen for later. Of course, frozen isn't as good as fresh, and it would be a shame to throw out that much batter. Besides, I could mix him up a fresh batch. If I ate three, then ran an extra four miles, plus did two hundred—

The phone again; McElroy. "Your Mex pal was right. Diaz is on the move. Pan Am to Chicago."

"Where to from there?"

"Punker City. How the hell do I know, Vance? We'll pick him up in Chitown, attach ourselves to his rump like a wart. Big guy like that shouldn't be hard to tail."

"I'll wait for word."

"Oh, you'll be the first to get it. I'll call the Bureau later."

"Can I go fix my breakfast now?"

"You making one of your pepperoni omelettes?"

"Belgian waffles."

"No shit? What do you put in the mix?"

"Combine three cups of whole wheat flour with one and a half teaspoons of baking soda, two-thirds teaspoon of salt, then separate three eggs, beating the whites until—"

"Wait! Let me get a pencil. . . ."

I ended up eating two waffles.

Ethyl came in and ate the other one while I was talking to McElroy.

# Thirty-one

It was just after sunrise and I was parked outside Sports Unlimited on Burnt Poplar Road. At the moment, me and the Subaru were alone in the paved lot, except for the leavings of a careless shopper. A plastic bag flitted past, borne by the wind.

After ten minutes that felt like forty, I was suddenly no longer alone, but surrounded by Muslims. Well, three anyway, including my huge, bearded friend. Karl, the splotchy one, was nowhere present, far as I could tell. He was probably across I-40 looking at me through a rifle scope.

Who gave a flip.

I got out of the car, met the bearded one, passed him some information, gave him instructions, watched his hard face lighten up, received a curt hairy nod of agreement, got back in my car and left, covin enacted.

. . .

"About your bond," I said to Milk Eye, aka Ralph Gonzales, aka Captain Kangaroo so far as I knew.

"*Sí?*"

In a little park on Big Tree Way, we sat side by side on a swing set. The chains were cold, plastic seats hard. The sun, nearing its zenith, shone weakly down.

"It comes out of your twenty percent, off the top."

"*No problemo.*"

"Has Diaz hit the States?" I ventured, probing for veracity.

"*Sí,* yesterday. He is expected here in a couple days." He began to swing in the chill air, thick hair wafting in the breeze created by his movement.

"You have the plan straight?"

"I call you to set up the buy. He will not know who the seller is."

"And Ralph?" I was swinging now too, stomach flipping at each peak.

"*Sí?*"

"Arrange not to be there when it goes down."

"I mus' work on that."

"Fur is going to fly."

"Don' I know."

As we swung there together, my stomach protesting (did I really enjoy this as a kid?), I considered warning against a double cross, but decided against it. Something told me I could trust Gonzales to keep his word.

Which he did and he didn't.

•  •  •

The ad read:

> UKc Registered American-eskimo pups.
> Six-weeks old, no shots. $250. Two Males.
> Christmas is coming. Hurry.

Cullen and I hurried. Out Old Randleman Road, watching for the turn as I'd been instructed by the voice on the phone, finding it, steering left into a small subdivision, left again at an intersection, one of Axel's operatives following close behind us, probably with a bazooka under his seat.

"There!" said Cullen excitedly.

The Vance household had been poochless for several months, due to very unfortunate circumstances. Since we're dog people, I'd promised Cullen that for Christmas we would remedy the situation.

Until recently, we'd had a pair of West Highland whites, a terrific breed, full of themselves and wonderful companions for my boy. Me too. But one of them had been killed last spring, in my stead. Her demise had so dispirited Nubbin, her mate, that he'd developed an inoperable tumor within two months of her death.

Tearfully, Cullen had asked after we'd buried Nub in the yard under a sugar maple: "Has he gone to heaven to be with Mama?"

"I don't know, son. Maybe."

Not satisfied with that answer, Cullen had run to his room and slammed the door. His sobs could be heard all the way downstairs.

"Why didn't you just tell him yes?" Ethyl reproached.

"Because I don't know whether dogs go to heaven."

"Know, schmoe. You should have told him what he needed to hear."

"I never lie to him, Ethyl."

A pursing of lips indicated: a) she'd exhausted the subject; b) I was being characteristically obdurate.

Cullen had come down in fifteen minutes, walked over to where I sat in my old platform rocker watching a group of pundits butting heads with a clutch of politicians, and climbed onto my lap. With his unhappy little head on my shoulder, he'd said, "I don't want another dog. Ever."

"Okay."

He'd begun to cry again. I switched off the homiletics and held him, rocking gently, until he fell asleep, cheek damp against mine.

Recalling that moment vividly now, three months later, I stepped out of my truck, took Cullen's hand, and went to look at a fluffy ball of spunk.

•　•　•

Motoring home, Cullen holding the puppy very carefully in his lap. "Think I'll call him Lucky," he said.

Since my Uncle Lawrence had a dog by that name, which Cullen had spent hours playing with, I assumed he was purloining the monicker.

"Why don't you make up a list of names, not just pick the first one that comes into your head. Then you can give it some thought and settle on one."

"Nope."

"Why name him Lucky?"

" 'Cause I'm lucky to have him," he answered. The pup, obviously agreeing, licked him on the nose.

"Lucky" it was.

•　•　•

Web and Cullen and Lucky were playing in the den, under Ethyl's watchul eye. I was at the sink slicing tangerines for snack time—the occasional piece finding its way into my mouth—when the phone sounded.

"Hewwo," I answered juicefully.

"I can tell Odie's doing better all the time," said Dave's voice.

"Yeah? How?"

"Your appetite's back."

"How do you know I'm not chewing tobacco?"

"Haven't heard you spit."

"Maybe I swallow."

"If you'd ever chewed tobacco, you wouldn't be able to jest about that. You meet with the Muslims?"

"Indeed. And bailed out our Hispanic pal."

"Any word from the colonel's contacts?"

"Not yet. We're waiting. Diaz has had plenty of time to get here, unless he's coming by burro."

"Or dogsled."

"Not that much snow in Mexico."

"Ever hear of pontoons?"

"Goodbye."

•  •  •

"Cullen wants a pair of Rollerblades for Christmas," Dad said over a cup of Irish Creme decaf, the two of us watching the boys—still playing with the puffball, which at the moment was running around on stubby legs, an old sock in its mouth.

"When I die, you can buy him some."

"What's your problem with Rollerblades?"

"Because I've watched Cullen skate, and I use that term loosely. He spends more time on his knees or his seat than he does vertical. Besides, I like him having a full complement of unbroken bones."

"He might wanta play hockey someday."

"Yeah, and he might want to race at Le Mans. You want me to buy him a Lotus?"

"Suppose I'd had that attitude when you was comin' up?"

"As I remember, you did."

"And so you did what?"

Since I would gain naught answering that question, I took a sip of java and let it slide.

"You gettin' hard of hearin'?" he pressed.

Sigh. "I did stuff when you weren't around."

"But he's too dumb to do that."

"Of course not, but when I tell him not to do something, I expect . . ."

He looked at me over his bifocals.

Another sigh. No matter how old you get, you can't win an argument with your parents.

"So. Can I get him some?"

I sighed yet again. Pop smiled to himself and drained his cup.

• • •

I had just stepped from the shower, hair plastered wetly to my skull and reeking of soap and shampoo and hygiene, when McElroy phoned from the hospital, presumably to say it was time to turn him into an outpatient. Wrong.

"Just got a call. They lost him."

"I take it you mean Diaz," I said.

"Yeah."

"The person who, you told me only yesterday, was of sufficient size and facade that following him would be a snap."

"They'll spot him when he hits Greensboro, don't worry."

"Oh, I won't. He merely wants three million bucks' worth of junk and my life. Why would I worry?"

"They'll find him, Tyler. Besides, you're covered at the house, aren't you? And I'll be out of here tomorrow."

After I punched off the instrument, Heather said, "What?"

"Loose rat."

"Diaz?"

I nodded.

"What are you going to do?"

"Put out some cheese."

# Thirty-two

I was dressed to the nines in a charcoal glen plaid, center vent, my scarlet cravat picking up the subtle hint of red in the suit's weave. Shirt robin's-egg blue, cordovan Weejuns with matching belt, my Kahr 9mm in an inside-the-pants rig. We were at my house, preparing to leave for a Christmas party at the home of a local literary celeb, when Heather said, "Are you sure we should do this? That madwoman is still around, and Hector is supposedly on his way. Won't we—and the boys—be safer here?"

"Unquestionably. We'd be safer still downtown in jail, and McDuffy'd be happy to arrange it. Maybe McElroy could make a few calls, arrange for a sleep-over at Fort Knox. Cullen would love that, get to camp inside one of the—"

"Tyler?"

"Yes, ma'am?"

"Shut up."

"The point is that I refuse to put my life on hold. Two of Axel's men are on the job right here at the house, not to mention one of Uncle Sam's finest. Dad's upstairs and Ethyl is down here. Fanner has two roving patrols in the area, and the sheriff assured me that one of his cars would tool by regularly. It's only for a couple of hours. We'll be fine. The kids will be fine."

We went upstairs to say goodbye to our boys, who were in Cullen's room listening to music and playing Chinese checkerds. Web was winning. I turned the music down, drawing "Daaadd" from my offspring.

"I have some instructions, and I'm not going to talk over that," I said.

Sigh of exasperation, a little civil disobedience for Web's benefit, to show who was really the boss around here.

"Eat fruit if you two get hungry. No Cheeze Doodles."

Nod of concurrence.

"If you watch a video, no Surround Sound. Ethyl's got a headache, though I know that's hard to imagine. She's in the living room reading. And no videos from the closet, just the ones on your rack."

"*Okay*, Dad," moving a marble, a red one. Double jump. Web responded with a quadruple, landing inside Cullen's triangular base.

"Son. Don't talk to me with that tone."

"Sorry," he said, meaning it.

"I wouldn't be putting you through this if you hadn't opened that bag of Doodles yesterday, or if I hadn't caught you slipping *The Wild Bunch* into the VCR last week."

"But it's a cowboy movie. I thought—"

"I told you before, no movies from the grown-up selection in my closet."

"All right." He took another double jump.

Web scratched his leg and examined the board, brow creased in concentration.

"Is there anything else?" Cullen asked, looking up from where he sat cross-legged on the carpet. What he meant was, *You can go now, Dad.*

I leaned over and gave him a kiss. "Just this."

Heather had already bussed Web, so we took our leave. As we descended the stairs, one of the boys turned the volume back up and George Frideric Handel—courtesy of the Mormon Tabernacle Choir—filled the second story.

•  •  •

"Why don't you simply keep inappropriate movies out of Cullen's reach?" Heather asked, from behind the wheel of her Porsche, while I was slipping a Glock 19 and two extra mags into her glove compartment. A Benelli shotgun was on the floor at my feet, stuffed with Number 3 buck.

"It's impossible to keep everything out of his reach, my dear, unless I resort to lock and key. And then how would he learn what's appropriate and what's not?"

"But what if he'd watched the movie?"

"*The Wild Bunch*? I doubt it would have scarred him for life. I don't keep poison where he can find it, but I do keep some medicines within reach that he shouldn't take, like Tylenol. He's been told never to touch them, or even his own children's aspirin, without me or one of his grandparents present. He isn't three. He needs to learn what he can do and what he can't, not just be protected by someone who watches over him constantly. Who's going to do that when he's thirty?"

"He'll be grown, Ty."

"Right. And how will he have learned what's acceptable and what's not? Not to mention what is safe? It's called accountability."

After a moment, she said, "I'm not sure I agree with that."

"You don't have to. You're free to rear Web any way you see fit."

With a scathing look, she said, "But my views have no validity so far as Cullen is concerned, right?"

"I didn't say that. I will say that I give how I teach and discipline my son a great deal of thought, and never take anything for granted. The foregoing is an example of a decision on my part about what is best for Cullen in the long run. It's based on logic, not happenstance or something I read in a book on parenting."

"I think we need not pursue this discussion," she said.

"Fine by me. I didn't initiate it."

We rode the rest of the way in silence.

•  •  •

Thirty or so guests were present when we arrived. The room was brightly lit and seasonally decorated. Heather immersed herself in conversation with the host immediately, avoiding me. Still miffed I reckoned.

I spotted Jason Patterson and Adam Colby over by an enormous punch bowl. Drinking punch. Surprise, surprise. Jason, offering a filled crystal cup at my approach, said, voice low, "I'm happy not to have to wear that gun anymore. It dug into my ribs."

"Where'd you carry it?"

"Inside my waistband, just aft of my right hipbone."

I grinned. "Aft?"

"It means behind," Adam said smugly,

"He knows that," Jason said.

"More correctly 'to the rear of,' but 'behind' is close enough."

Adam, his back up, waded in. "Him wearing the thing at all is absurd."

"Not as absurd as being beaten up twice when the second time might be prevented."

"I can take care of Jason, and without a gun."

"I don't need taking care of," Jason protested.

"Not to mention the fact that you aren't always around," I said to Adam.

"Relax, guys," Jason interrupted again. "This is going nowhere. Both of you were after the same thing, covering my ass. We're all on the same team."

He had a point, so I quit arguing and went over to greet a friend and his date.

•  •  •

At the time I was drinking punch and arguing with Adam Colby, Cullen was crawling under his bed, flashlight in hand, to retrieve a stashed copy of *Caddyshack*, which he'd previously snuck out of the collection in my closet.

While he was doing so, Jonathan Barrie, McElroy's top man, was having his throat slit in my backyard.

# Thirty-three
When the arm slipped around his chest and the knife entered his throat, Sergeant Jonathan Barrie was thinking of his girlfriend Cheryl—a waitress at Dora's Dinner and Dance in Fayetteville—not his job of providing security for those inside the Vance household. Nearing the end, when blood had turned his shirtfront into a warm soggy mass and his heels were drumming uncontrollably against the hard ground, his thoughts turned to home. Then those too were gone, like a flame extinguished by the wind. The killer laid Jonathan's head down gently, to avoid sound, and moved into the backyard.

•  •  •

Tim Wentword, one of Mershon Security's most able employees, leaned against an elm. Strictly against orders, not to mention common sense, Tim was smoking a butt. All this rigamarole about some hotshot killer on the loose didn't worry Tim none; he'd seen action at the tail end of Nam. *All this over one person. Shit, let the creep come,* he was thinking, when a hand clamped over his mouth and jerked him back, cutting off his air, and the knife pierced straight to a kidney, twisting—right-left, up-down—razor-sharp, slicing his insides into chum, blood spurting from the wound all over the killer's right hand, the two of them going to ground, Wentword on top, the knife coming free with a sodden meaty *swiiick,* then plunging in again, under the ribs in front, angled upward, finding the heart, twisting excruciatingly, until the pain and blood loss took its toll and Tim was gone.

The killer lay a moment, entwined with the quivering body, savoring. One mustn't let moments like this go to waste; they were too deliciously rare.

Ah well, dawdling was no good. To the phone wire, *snip,* then the electricity meter at the side of the house. Through a gap in the curtains, the old lady was visible, reading in the living room at the front of the house, violet glasses in place. The second security guard was at the kitchen sink, directly in front of the window—the putz—washing his hands.

No other sound. No TV, kids playing. Upstairs? Asleep? Maybe. Upstairs, anyway. First, the guard.

• • •

Coy Waringhouse had not quite finished washing his hands, which he always did very thoroughly, including each nail, where germs can tend to collect. He kept those fingernails trimmed, straight across, natch. Shaking the residual water from his hands before reaching for a towel, he dried as carefully as he'd washed. No chapping in his future.

The bullet came through the window, and struck his left eyebrow instead of the eye as intended, having been slightly deflected by the glass. The effect was the same: the spent bullet wound up against the inside rear of Coy's cranial cavity; his body wound up twitching on the floor.

The coroner later commmented that Coy's hands were unusually clean.

. . .

Ethyl heard the sound of breaking glass, followed quickly by a heavy thump. She deduced correctly the origins of each sound, dropped her book and her glasses, grabbed up the cordless phone. No dial tone. She tossed the useless instrument onto the chair, moved quickly to the hall and glanced toward the dining area off the kitchen. Nothing. She was at the foot of the stairs, one hand on the banister, about to ascend, when the lights went off.

. . .

Odie Vance, asleep upstairs in Tyler's king-sized bed, had for all his life been a very light sleeper. Old age had merely exacerbated the tendency. He was also afflicted with tinnitus—courtesy of World War II—thus always slept with a fan on. The white noise from the whirring blades to some extent masked the constant ringing in his ears.

Suddenly the whirring stopped, waking Odie as effectively as an alarm clock. He looked at the digital across the room; no numbers were visible. *Power's out*, he thought, sitting up and swinging his legs around to place his bare feet on the floor. He rubbed his eyes to clear them, feeling a twinge of discomfort deep in his chest. Through the curtains, a luminance. *Streetlight's on*, he thought groggily.

The significance of that brought a sharper discomfort to his chest. Then he was up and moving.

. . .

The youngest Vance was rooting around under his bed, still seeking the elusive *Caddyshack*, when Web said, "Cullen."

"Yeah?" returned Cullen, training his flashlight on a far corner.

"I heard a thump."

"What kinda thump?"

"A big thump."

Aha! There it was. Cullen's little hand closed on the tape and he wriggled out from under the bed clutching it triumphantly.

"I'm scared," Web said.

Cullen directed the light at the tape. "Don't be. Look, I got the movie."

The lights in the boys' room were off, lest one of the adults open the door and discover them with a verboten item. *Wait a minute*, thought Cullen, noting the absence of light coming under the door from the hall. He switched off the flash.

It was dark.

*Really* dark.

He moved to the window, peeped out at the house across the street. They had lights. Moved to the radio, punched *on*. Nothing.

Uh-oh.

Where was Paw-paw? Or Gran'ma? He thought about going into the hall and calling to someone. An inner voice voted against it.

Seldom slow at coming to a decision, Cullen whispered, "Under the bed, quick."

•  •  •

The killer used a pick on the back door, taking maybe thirty seconds to gain entry. After two days' surveillance of the house from an adjacent unoccupied one ("FOR SALE—By Owner"), the number and gender of those in the Vance household was a given. It was known (by means of wiretap) that: Tyler and his ladyfriend were gone to a soiree; the rough-looking number named Dave had been called to work by his employee, some asshole named Thurman, if you can believe that. As things stood, only the two security types, one soldier-boy wuss, the old man and the old woman, the Patterson kid, and the mark had remained.

No problem. And so far, that's what it had been—no problem at all. The old broad presented no difficulty, but the geezer, now . . . somehow he'd thwarted Victor, and Beauville was no pilgrim. No indeedy. *But what can one lone seasoned citizen come up with? Let's go see.*

•  •  •

Ethyl heard scratching at the back door, like someone picking a lock. What to do? If she went upstairs, she'd simply draw whoever was there right behind her. Where was Mr. Mershon's outside man? And that

young soldier, Barry something-or-other? Assuming the worst—that
she was the sole surviving defender on the ground floor—Ethyl rea-
soned that made her the sole protection for the boys upstairs.

Her and Odie.

*Good Lord,* she thought. *Can he survive another heart attack?*

She looked around frantically, then went to work.

.  .  .

Odie dug his ancient Smith & Wesson .32 out of the sock drawer where
he'd hidden it. Although Ty didn't allow loaded guns accessible to Cullen, circumstances were such that he'd allowed Odie to bring along his
trusty old mouse-gun. It felt good in his hand now, comforting. He
checked the cylinder: full. Too bad he hadn't thought to bring some
extra ammo. Must be slipping.

*Well, hell, I did have a heart attack, and probably a stroke, too. Can't
be expected to remember everything like when I was only seventy.*

He eased open the bedroom door, peered quickly down the hall,
then headed for the boys' room.

.  .  .

Cullen heard creaking in the hall. He hefted the long four-cell flashlight,
its checkered metal surface comforting in his hand. *Anyone big will
have to get down on their hands and knees to look under here. When they
do that, I'm gonna bust 'em a good one,* he thought.

Web said, "Why did the lights go out?" Sniffling.

"Maybe thunder," Cullen said, worried about his friend.

"Didn't hear any." Sniff.

"Me either, but it can be way far away."

"How does thunder knock off the lights?" Sniffles abating.

"'Lectricity does it, not the thunder. Like in your socks."

"Huh?"

"Daddy told me thunder and lightning is like when your socks
crackle when they come outa the dryer. Kind of."

"My socks aren't that loud."

"Shhh!" Cullen put a hand on Web's arm.

"Cullen?" came a low voice.

Paw-paw's low voice. So flooded with relief he couldn't quell the tears, Cullen shout-whispered, "Here!" and wiggled out from under the bed just as a crash and a heartfelt "FUCK!" reverberated up the stairs.

· · ·

When the killer put a foot on the bottom step and shifted balance, something on the stairs slipped underfoot. A stack of magazines! *"FUCK!"* Down on one knee and the old lady was suddenly there, going for the head with a lamp the size of Rhode Island! *Whap*, right on target. Stars for a second, then the killer bounced up to ward off another blow with an elbow, *"OUCH!"*—pain shooting up the arm and into the neck, drawing a heartfelt yell once again.

Then the old battle-ax and her fucking lamp were gone.

· · ·

"Ethyl!" Odie bawled, and ran to the top of the stairwell. A shadowy melee was in progress on the landing below. Two figures, one getting beaten with a huge object.

Not daring to shoot—since he did not know who was who—he stuffed the gun in a side pocket and charged down the stairs, having no idea that Cullen was right behind him.

· · ·

Ethyl jumped back around the corner into the living room and there awaited the intruder, lamp raised for combat. Said intruder, having had enough of the lamp and the old bitch wielding it, stood swaying at the foot of the stairs, ears singing from the head shot.

Not for long.

Suddenly a body sailed down from above, sending the killer to the floor. Again. Odie lashed out with a fist, impacting his opponent's cheek under the left eye, followed immediately by a hard right to the chin.

*Enough!* thought the object of said pummeling.

Well trained, much experienced, fearful of life and capture and more suffering at the hands of this swarm of ancients, the killer gave Odie the heel of one hand to the bridge of his nose, shoving the old man back and providing an opportunity to strike again, harder, ridge-hand to the jaw. It was Odie's turn to see stars as he fell heavily. Lying there, winded, he reached for his .32. Gone!

Suddenly Ethyl was back, swinging the dreaded lamp, impacting the killer's right shoulder to draw another pained expletive and a looping left arm that took Ethyl by surprise and knocked her several paces down the hall.

"LEAVE HER ALONE!" Cullen shouted, and landed on the killer's back, muscular little legs attaching like staples, supple fingers clawing for the face, seeking eyes, missing, finding nostrils instead, a rigidly crooked forefinger going deep inside, jerking sideways, the killer's head going along, no choice.

Then Cullen too was dismounted, flying through the air to land atop his grandmother in a heap, the killer advancing, drawing a second gun—having somehow misplaced the first in the scuffle—until Odie swung a tripping leg and everyone was down, Odie on top briefly, until once again he was dislodged, then Ethyl rose, pushing Cullen aside, out of reach, and punched ineffectually at the killer's face, garnering anger, not damage. Up came the gun, long and black, silencer in place, rising toward Ethyl's fighting heart, finger jerking the trigger, the angry *sphut!* of discharge punctuating the struggle, Odie's hand barely arriving in time to redirect the killer's arm sufficiently for the bullet to miss, *sphut!* the second one going into the ceiling, and then Cullen grabbed the gun arm, sinking small but sharp incisors deep into wrist flesh, drawing, "FUCK!" and *sphut!*—this third bullet taking out a vase on the table by the door—and an open-handed cuff to the face that sent the boy sprawling.

The killer retreated, moving to the kitchen end of the hallway to pause, rest, all the while holding the flagging group under the gun. Slow smile of impending pleasure, the kill in sight, blood trickling from one nostril, the pistol pointed at Ethyl's torso. Cullen saw, and would have none of it. He flung himself in front of his grandmother, screaming, "Don't you hurt my gran'ma!"

"You're next, kid. I'm popping Gramma first because she knocked the shit outa me with that fucking lamp," the killer laughed.

Then stopped laughing . . .

Because something sharply pointed was pressing just behind an ear. Into that ear a voice, soft and melodious, spoke.

"No, Lugo. The kid's not next. You are."

The killer stiffened, tried to lean away from the pointed object.

"I told you in Lisbon," continued the voice, "never, never deal yourself into a contract that I've already undertaken. You told me you understood. Obviously you didn't."

"Hey, wait! Hector told me you and Vic fucked it up. Said you were both dead."

"Dying ain't my thing, Lugo. Other people dying, that's my thing."

"Come on, baby. We had some good times, me and you."

"Not good enough."

"Please!"

"Stop whining, for God's sake. You sound like a mark."

And then she poked the ice pick through the skin, the muscle, the bone and tissue and gray matter, wiggling it rapidly in a circular motion, scrambling the killer's brains. Lugo slumped to the floor.

Harmony Cahill stood and surveyed the group before her.

Nobody else moved.

"Hey, kid," she said.

"Leave him alone," Ethyl said, placing her body in front of Cullen's.

"I'm talking to *him*, lady, not you. Hey, kid," Harmony said again.

Cullen stepped forward to stand defiantly, not looking away though he was terrified.

She smiled down at him. Grim, hard, deadly, but humor there, in the eyes, lurking, like death. "That trick you pulled on me, at the school?"

Cullen nodded, too scared to speak, his little chest heaving from exertion.

"Nice move," said Harmony Cahill, aka Hillary Eloise Harmon.

Cullen blinked, confused now, but not quite so frightened.

"Please don't kill the boy," Ethyl said.

Harmony Cahill was taken aback. "I don't kill kids, Grandma."

"Then what . . ."

"I'm supposed to grab him. For bait. It's his papa Hector wants wasted. And that old fart." She pointed at Odie.

"By the way, Gramps. How'd you take Vic out?"

Odie didn't answer; his chest was on fire.

With no answer forthcoming, Harmony said, "No matter. Hey, kid?"

"Yes, ma'am."

Chuckling, Harmony Cahill said to Ethyl, "Hear that? Calls me ma'am."

Looking back at Cullen, she said, "You're some kid," then appeared for a moment to be lost in thought. "You know something? You deserve a reprieve." Her eye wandered. . . .

Ethyl placed herself between Odie and Harmony Cahill. "Take me. He's recovering from a heart attack. This could kill him."

Harmony shook her head. "Sorry, Granny, but you aren't blood. But you're right. I don't need a sick man on my hands."

From the floor, Odie said, "You're after my son, right?"

Harmony nodded. "You betcha. He's worth a hundred grand, and I got big-time VISA payments. Wouldn't want me to fall behind, wouldja?"

Odie pressed his case. "You want Tyler face-to-face, get your chance at him, right?"

Big Harmonious smile. "You bet your ass."

"Then you don't need nobody. After tonight, my son'll be lookin' downright forward to meetin' you, I guarantee. Just give him a call."

Ten seconds passed. Maybe twelve. Then Harmony Cahill said, "Damnedest family I ever saw. I'll keep in touch."

Down the hall and out the door, tousling Cullen's cowlick as she went.

# Thirty-four

I steered around a Saab, its driver doing all of thirty, maybe thirty-one miles an hour; it was a forty-five zone. The driver flipped us the rod as we drew abreast. Heather smiled sweetly at him, then mouthed, *Asshole*. He blew his horn and switched on the brights, gunning his engine to keep pace.

Of course. *Now* he was in a hurry.

"What do you know?" she said. "A sob driving a Saab."

"Is that observation politically correct?"

"Of course. It certainly isn't stereotypical. Not all Saab drivers are SOBs."

"As far as you know."

The cellular interrupted our philosophical intercourse. Dave said, "You heading home?"

The hairs at the back of my neck began to weave and wave like wheat in the Nebraska sun. "As we speak," I answered.

"Drive faster."

"Tell me," I said.

He did.

I drove faster.

• • •

Police cars, sheriff's cars, one Army vehicle, and some unmarked Fords. The Feds.

Dad met me at the door. "Cullen's fine. He's up in his room with Web and an Army captain. Ethyl's okay, in the downstairs bathroom gettin' a butterfly put on a cut. That's one salty gal. Put up one helluva battle."

I reached out, turned his face gently with a hand: both eyes beginning to blacken; angry welt on his portside jaw; scrape on his forehead, high, near the hairline.

"You should see the other guy," he said, grinning.

"Yeah?"

"He's in there." He pointed toward the kitchen with a thumb. "Covered with a blanket."

"Tell me exactly what happened."

He did so, all the way up to the moment of the man's demise. "While he was jerkin' and twitchin' there on the floor like a puppet with a broken string, Ethyl had the presence of mind to grab Cullen and put his face to her bosom, so he didn't see none of that part, thank God.

"Then the woman palavered with us some, allowin' how she'd originally intended to steal Cullen, but she liked the cut of his jib. She thought about taking me instead. Ethyl told her my heart was on the fritz, and that it'd be better if she took *her* in my place."

He stopped to shake his head, "Who'd have thought? Anyway, she ended up deciding not to take any of us."

"Why, you reckon?"

"She claimed she was really after you, and just needed one of us for bait. . . ." He paused to touch his jaw tenderly, like it hurt.

"So?"

"Don't rush me, son. I don't feel all that spry."

"Sorry, Pop."

"Forget it. Anyhow, she agreed that she didn't need no bait, that after tonight all she'd have to do was call and you'd come a-runnin'."

"You're right about that."

"You reckon she'll call?"

"Who knows? Are you sure Cullen's okay?"

"Said so, didn't I? He's havin' a high old time bein' debriefed by a real Army officer. Web seems to be enjoyin' it too, in his way."

Given that, I went to see Gran'ma first.

• • •

I kissed Ethyl on the butterfly.

"Does it hurt?" I asked.

She gave me a troubled head shake.

"You okay?" said I.

Troubled nod.

"You don't look okay. Come clean, Ethyl. What's the matter?"

A tear formed, then left her eye, trickling down into the furrow around her mouth. Another. "I broke your mother's lamp."

"What?"

Another tear joined the first two. "The one she got from *her* mother, and gave to you and Tess when you were married."

"That big table lamp in the living room?"

Nod.

"How'd you break it, dear?"

Characteristic purse of the thin, prim lips. "I hit that evil man with it. Several times."

"Hard?"

"You're damned right!"

I grinned, because I'd never heard her cuss. "Dad tells me you saved the ranch."

Shrug of disclaimer.

"Including Cullen," I said.

No further response.

"I surely loved that old lamp, it coming down through the family and all," I fretted. "So did Mama."

Another tear, her wounded eyes on my face.

I stepped closer. "But I love Cullen a whole lot more, Ethyl. Mama would too, had she known him."

She looked directly into my eyes.

"Mama wouldn't care about the lamp. Me neither. I care about you," I said, pulling her stiff form to me, kissing the scented forehead.

"You done real good, lady. You and Dad."

"Cullen too," she reminded. "He fought like a tiger."

"It's in his genes. Gets it from his gran'ma." I kissed her again.

And by golly . . .

She kissed me back!

• • •

"Daddy!" yelled my son, and jumped into my arms.

I kissed him a hundred times, then said, "What's this?" fingering his bruised little cheek.

"A battle scar!"

The Army captain, sitting on Cullen's bed, smiled. Heather was over in the corner, holding Web in her lap, stroking his hair.

"That ol' bad guy popped me one," Cullen continued. "But I bit him good, and stretched his nose some!"

"His nose?"

"It was all I could reach."

"One must make do," I said. The captain smiled again. I put Cullen down and held out a hand. She stood and shook it firmly.

"You from Fort Bragg?" I queried.

"Yes."

"McElroy's unit?"

"*Colonel* McElroy, yes."

"Sergeant Barrie . . . ?" I let it trail off for the boys' benefit.

She shook her head gravely, short brown hair framing a streamlined mocha face.

"I'm sorry," I tendered.

She nodded her agreement.

I turned to Web. "So, Webster. I hear you took good care of Cullen."

Cullen took his cue. "You bet. He never let me get scared. And he stayed up here all by himself with my flashlight, ready to bop anyone who came up the stairs!"

Web, pleased with the praise, half smiled in his shy way, then rested his head against his mama's chest.

Good.

Everyone was okay.

Except me.

I was pissed!

•   •   •

David met me in the upstairs hall. "You all through in there?"

"Yes."

"You sure?"

"I'm sure," I said. "Why?"

"McDuffy's downstairs wetting his pants. I told him you needed time with your family. He seemed to disagree."

"You must have been convincing, since he's not up here in my face."

Dave smiled his special smile, the one that if directed at me, would send me packing. To Paraguay.

"I was, at that," he said.

"If you'll come down with me, I'll try hard not to be ascared."

"Come on, sweetheart," he said, taking my hand. "I won't let him yell at you."

We went to beard McDuffy in my den.

# Thirty-five

Sergeant Carl McDuffy was talking to another Homicide dick—this one from the sheriff's department—when Dave and I joined them. McDuffy was wearing a plaid madras tie and oxblood Weejuns, like he was right out of the sixties, though he couldn't have been more than thirty years old.

The sheriff's man was less of a fashion plate and more of a cop. He looked tired but competent. We shook hands and introduced ourselves; sorry, I can't remember his name.

McDuffy opened with, "You all finished with kissing the baby?"

I turned on my heel and marched out of the room.

"Get the hell back in here!" he shouted, starting after me. Dave blocked his way.

"What the hell do you think you're doing?" McDuffy yelled up at Dave.

"Preventing a rise in your health insurance rates," Dave answered mildly.

"He can't just—"

"Yes. He can." Dave looked over at the sheriff's officer. "Is Tyler under arrest for anything?"

"Nope," said the deputy.

"Since he wasn't here when it all came down, he's not a material witness, is that correct?"

"Correct."

"Any chance of an obstruction charge?"

The sheriff's guy was enjoying this. "Don't see how."

Addressing McDuffy again, Dave said, "See, carrottop? Ty can do anything he wants."

I came back into the room in time to catch McDuffy's complexion reach the color of his hair.

"Oh, one more thing," from Dave. "His son was almost killed tonight. You make another comment like that first one and *I'll* put you in the hospital, badge or no badge."

McDuffy, livid, turned to the sheriff's man. "Threatening an officer! Did you hear that?"

The deputy shook his head. "Can't say I did, McDuff. Well, I need to go speak with the medical examiner. 'Less y'all think you need a referee."

"We'll be fine, thanks," I said.

Then we were alone in the room—me and Dave and Carl McDuffy, GPD Homicide.

"What do you want to ask me, Sergeant?"

"Where you been tonight?"

"To a party."

He got out pad and pen. "Where was this party?"

"I wasn't here, McDuffy. That's all you need to know. Charge me with something and I'll provide names. Otherwise, I'm not involving anybody in this unnecessarily. Folks don't like surprise visits from the police, hard as it may be for you to imagine."

The cellular rang. McDuffy started to reach for it until Dave said, "Do you live here?" stopping the sergeant's hand in midair. I answered the phone.

It was Fanner. "So disaster once again strikes the Vance household."

"Those guarding it, anyway. My family's all right."

"Glad to hear it. I have personnel on the way. We will cover your family like skin on a grape until you make suitable preparations. Will you spirit them away as you did last time?"

"I haven't thought it through."

"For several days, then, we shall keep them from harm's way. After that. . . ."

"I know. Don't worry, Lieutenant, I'll come up with something. Soon."

"Of that I have no doubt. May I have McDuffy, please?"

"You sure as hell can, if you'll take him home with you."

"Very amusing."

"Who's trying to be amusing?" I handed the receiver to McDuffy.

The sergeant listened a lot and said little, but turned redder and redder as the conversation lengthened. Directly, he put down the instrument.

"Leaving now, are you?" asked David.

McDuffy did, and without saying goodbye.

Dave and I exchanged high fives and went to make coffee.

# Thirty-six

Harmony Cahill had to place seven calls to reach her ultimate party. When she did, the conversation, conducted in Spanish, translated thus:

"*Hola?*"

"Hector, you sorry son of a bitch."

"It is you?"

"Fuckin' A, you bag of monkey puke."

Hector Diaz, laughing, said, "*Cómo estás?*"

" '*Cómo estás*' my oversized ass. Whaddya mean retracting my contract and giving it to *Lugo*, of all fucking people?"

"You and Victor made a mess. Besides, I heard you were dead, *chiquita*."

"Up yours. When I get dead, I'll call and tell you. This is the second time you've double-crossed me, you tub of llama guts. Never, never do it again. *Comprende?*"

Diaz was getting angry. No one, but *no one* dared talk to him in such a manner. "Careful, or I might place a contract on you and your filthy *gringa* mouth."

There followed twenty seconds of silence, except for a modicum of line hum. Then Harmony Cahill said, ever so slowly, "Hector, that does it. Color me quits, and I advise you to stay the fuck out of my way. And if you do decide to put a hit out on me, make sure to place the money in trust, because you won't be there to cough it up at the end."

Slamming down the phone for dramatic effect, she walked to her car, cackling all the while. "Fuck it. Who needs a hundred grand."

She was still cackling when she drove away, eating a soft chicken taco.

• • •

It was nearly five in the morning, still dark as the inside of an ostrich, when I walked out my front door, headed for Harris-Teeter and breakfast makings. Dave had made a pizza run a few minutes earlier, on behalf of all the policemen still cluttering up my house, including teams from Forensics and Homicide. Everyone in the house was resting or asleep except me and him and the army of cops. His red Taurus SHO was parked in the drive behind the Subaru. My dented Toyota was in the garage.

Shit.

Back inside to ask him to move his car. Instead, from his place on the den couch, he tossed me the keys. "Take mine. And fill it up while you're at it."

As I quit the room he was singing, "Runnin' on empty . . ."

• • •

Climbing into the Ford, the leather interior treating my nose to its exquisite aroma, I inserted and turned the key, bringing the engine to life. When I heard the word "Hi" spoken softly into my left ear, simultaneous with the painful prick of a pointed instrument near my carotid, I gained a whole new perspective on the term "involuntary evacuation."

I didn't move—at all—until a hand slipped past my left shoulder and hovered below and in front of my chin. Slowly, very slowly, I reached up and grasped the hand. It shook mine and the voice said, "Pleased to meet you. Finally."

"Ms. Cahill?"

"In the flesh—ample, I might add. Don't you know that you should always, always check your rear seat for stowaways, muggers, loose change?" Soft chuckle against my ear, near the uncomfortable piercing sensation. Then a sigh, equally soft. "Now that we meet, what should I do with you?"

"My understanding," I said, spine writhing and crawling with maggots, "is that your intent is to snuff me."

Again the soft laugh, her breath—not unpleasant—wafting warmly around my face. "That's what Hector offered me a hundred G's to do. Of course, that was before his defalcation?"

"His what?"

"Defalcation. Failure to meet an obligation or promise. Don't you ever do crossword puzzles?"

"I confuse 'down' with 'across.' "

More soft laughter. "Dammit, Vance, I like you. I like your whole fucking family. Normally, that would make things hard for me. I never killed anyone I liked. Except one time. Ah, well . . ."

" 'Ah, well,' what?" My skin at point of entry was beginning to leak a little, the warm trickle threading wetly toward my collar. Maybe we'd simply sit here and talk, with the engine running, until I bled to death. Or ran out of gas, whichever came first.

" 'Ah, well,' meaning it's a moot point," she said.

"Moot as in arguable, or academic?"

"Hey, you're not entirely ignorant." She laughed. "The latter."

"And why is it academic?"

She removed the pain in my neck. "Because Hector and I have split the blanket."

"Does that mean the contract has been voided, or merely assigned elsewhere?"

"You talk well for a bumpkin."

"And you, for a contract killer."

"Don't hurt my feelings, I have a Glock pointed at your ribs. One of the new minis, a .40. Seen one?"

"The nine-millimeter, not the .40."

Abruptly, unbelievably, she handed the weapon over the seatback, butt first. "Have a look."

I did, saying, "Nice gesture of trust."

"Naw. I got two. Other one's trained on your navel, from behind. Having any prostate trouble?" Again the soft laughter.

Returning the Glock, I said, "What now?"

"Nothing. Just wanted to meet you before I leave this burg."

I thought a moment. "You said Diaz was paying you a hundred thousand for my harried hide?"

"Yeah. Vic was getting half that for your papa. Poor Vic," she mused—sincerely, judging by her tone.

"But Diaz welshed on the deal."

"Reneged, not welshed."

Semantics lessons from a wet-work specialist? Where's Rod Serling when you need him?

"Want the dough?" I asked.

"Sure. I got an appointment at the beauty parlor." She paused to cackle at herself. "What you got in mind?"

I told her.

She seemed to like it.

"Seems fitting," she said, after a spell. "Diaz double-crossed me twice, which is three times too many. If what you say is correct, that he's on the way here to good old Greensboro, then I'll deal myself in. For one-hundred thou. Oh, Vance?"

"What?"

"Never, never try to double-cross me."

"I wouldn't think of it, Ms. . . . . Should I call you Harmony?"

"Call me anything you want, long as it's not Eloise." More laughter. "Well, time to split."

I waited. She sat behind me quietly. A minute. Two. Then, incredibly, she laid her head on my shoulder. Shocked as I was, I didn't stiffen. At least I don't think so.

"You got money, Vance?" she said.

"Some. My bills get paid, and the house isn't mortgaged."

She sat perfectly still, head heavy on my deltoid, her breathing shallow but regular. "Me too. European banks, the islands, here and there. I could retire if I wanted to."

"Why don't you?"

Silence, except for the breathing. And then she said, "I'd give up everything to have a family like yours."

"Me too," I said.

But she was gone.

# Thirty-seven

Heather, pacing and puffing.

Dad, silently sipping Sanka.

Ethyl, stern-faced and uptight.

Dave, half reclining, half asleep.

McElroy, newly released and uncomfortable.

Jason, jittery and unconvinced.

Me, the origin of most of the tension, at least in the view of some of those present.

Heather began. "I cannot, *will* not, believe that you even remotely trust that . . . woman."

"She had him at her mercy, Heather, if you'll pardon the expression," Dave said. "Why would she let him go only to do him in later?"

"Bingo," from McElroy.

"You two are worse than Ty is. How can you trust a, a . . . killer?"

"Heather," I argued, "Dad fought in World War Two and Korea, Dave in Vietnam, McElroy all over the place, and I've seen a little action myself. Last spring Jason, through no fault of his own, killed a man. Last but not least . . ."

"Don't even say it, Tyler Vance! That's not fair. Besides, that was different!"

"How?"

"None of us did it for money!"

"Why, then? Duty? Country?"

Heather lit another cigarette and sat down, fuming. "Come on, Tyler. You know what I'm talking about!"

Dad joined in. "Sure he does. What Ty is sayin' is that there're all kinds of reasons for killin' folks. Just because this Harmony lady does it for green doesn't necessarily mean she won't keep her word. What would she gain by goin' back on it?"

Heather puffed smoke in response.

"More to the point," Dave added, "what does she have to gain if she doesn't go back on her word? A hundred thousand bucks, that's what. As it now stands, she walks away with zilch."

Having none of it, Heather insisted, "That's *her* story, David. And we don't know that she's telling the truth."

"But why would she lie?" I asked. "If she was still under contract to off me, she could have done it right there in Dave's car."

Heather blew a smoke ring, which I hadn't known she could do.

"Perhaps Heather suspects that this Harmony person has a hidden agenda," Jason opined.

Heather yelled "Bingo," and stared defiantly at McElroy.

"Maybe the lady wants all the money," Ethyl added thoughtfully.

Heather came out with "Bingo" again, and another smoke ring. It eddied gently toward the ceiling.

Dad said, "The problem with that reasoning is that she didn't know about the money until Tyler told her."

McElroy shouted "Bingo," and smiled at Heather, who blew smoke at him, dirty pool considering he had a hole in one lung.

"Maybe Har-mon-ee has some other source of information," said Heather, perhaps exhibiting a bit of female rivalry.

"The only other likely source would be Gonzales," I objected, "and how would he benefit from double-crossing me?"

"Well," said Jason, "you already got him out of jail. What binds him to you now, other than his word?"

Heather and McElroy said "Bingo" simultaneously, then erupted with laughter, Heather coughing smoke and the colonel holding his aching side.

"None of this is funny," sniffed Ethyl.

"Or all of it is," I offered.

Dave, as far as I could tell, had fallen asleep.

•　•　•

The Cullen Protection Pact involved the following:

Dave, Dad, Ethyl, McElroy, and I would drive my son to Fort Bragg, never mind which unit. There he would stay, surrounded by the largest military base in the continental U.S., guarded night and day by Special Forces elite, remaining in the constant company of two of his grandparents. Pop would be armed to the teeth and Ethyl could have my mother's lamp, or its military equivalent.

Since Web was not in any danger that we could ascertain—though one never knew—he would stay with his father twenty-four hours a day. Jason had for protection not only the .380 auto I'd lent him, but Adam Colby as well.

McElroy, not exactly in the pink, would act as liaison between his varied official and officious government contacts and one Tyler C. Vance, World's Handsomest Gun Writer.

Heather would fuss and fume and do whatever she could to assist in the narcotics charade.

Dave planned to tag along with me and see I stayed out of trouble. Was I lucky, or what?

• • •

After wending our way to Fort Bragg via Raleigh, Durham, Chapel Hill, Burlington, Lillington, Dunn, and Bonnie Doone, we had long since insured that no one had shadowed our passage.

Ethyl, Dad, and Cullen were then ensconced in a fine, secure barrack, nearly new and made of brick so the big bad wolf could huff and puff all he wanted. Rommel himself couldn't have stormed that place.

Before heading back to Greensboro, I spent a few minutes with Cullen on my knee, outside the barrack watching the moon rise.

Pointing at it, he said, "See the cradles?"

"On the moon?"

"Yes."

"Oh, *craters*. I see 'em, babe." We admired them awhile, until his small head began to nod sleepily.

"Remember, hon, if you need me, just ask Colonel McElroy to call. But I'll phone you every day, no matter what."

Hugging me tightly, he said, "I'll miss you bunches," his mouth to my shirt.

"Me too, sweetheart. When this is over, we'll play Frisbee for a whole hour without stopping."

"Promise?" voice still muffled, not looking at me.

"Promise."

He showed no inclination to turn loose, so I held him until sleep came and Ethyl took him from me.

. . .

Dad gripped my hand, hard. "Take care, you hear?"

"Dave'll look out for me, Pop."

"I want you back here in a week. You ain't, I'll go and have another heart attack. That'll teach you."

I hugged him. Hard.

Then I climbed into Dave's SHO and we motored back to Greensboro.

And more trouble than we could handle.


# Thirty-eight

Jennifer McCurry was manager at the Four Seasons Waldenbooks, where I'd done several signings over the years. As I entered the store, she treated me to a toss of her lovely tresses and a dazzling smile. Her assistant manager, Ron Jackson, was rearranging the magazine display and keeping a surreptitious eye on Ralph Gonzales, who was by the New Arrivals running his good eye over the latest Jack Higgins thriller.

"That's a good one," I said to Ralph in greeting.

"Good as *Storm Warning?*" he replied. An oldie.

"It is in my view."

He put the book down and we walked into the hall, chatting, gazing in store windows; to passersby we were obviously men on a bonding mission, racially diverse, culturally disparate, economically polarized.

Soon, one of us would be basking in the Bahamas with a half-million-dollar nest egg and expanding portfolio.

That someone wouldn't be me.

Business talk: How many large suitcases would I need to hold 264 pounds of fake dope? Who could I get to wrap such a large quantity of baking soda into one-kilo bags, and make it look sufficiently realistic so dopers would kill for the chance to vacuum it right up their nose?

How should I handle the actual buy when it came down? How many vehicles would Diaz have? How many people might I have to shoot? Who looks good for the Super Bowl?

You know. Man stuff.

As I was about to leave, I said, "Diaz in town yet?"

"*Sí.*"

"Where?"

"I don' know. He calls me twice a day, to make arrangements. To-morrow or the nex', he will be ready."

"Don't forget whose side you're on."

"How I'm gonna do that? Hector is expecting lotsa dope. Where I'm gonna find any? Without you, I am fuckin' dead, man. You better know it. Besides,"—he looked at me disdainfully—"I keep my word, you know?"

"How about to Hector?"

He spat, drawing the disgusted attention of a pair of shoppers, who elevated their snoots and walked rapidly away. The quid lay wet on the hard-tiled floor.

*Probably leave a stain,* I thought idly.

Ralph said, "That *puto* Hector lef' me here to rot. I don' owe him nuttin'."

On that happy note, we separated. I went back to Waldenbooks and bought Ethyl a copy of *The Christmas Box.*

I thought she'd like it.

.  .  .

When I got home, I called my Muslim friends. No luck, they said. They'd been following Gonzales everywhere he went, and the only contact he'd had with anyone other than a twenty-dollar hooker was some white guy he spent time with near a bookstore.

I told them to keep watching and hung up.

McElroy next. Everyone was fine. I talked to Cullen for five minutes, then rang off and phoned Heather. Did she have the baking soda? Yes, but it had taken an act of Congress to get that much on short notice. An act of Congress and a large check. I'd pay her back as soon as she came over, I promised.

Dave came into my office and left a carafe of coffee. I was grateful, and showed my gratitude by drinking a cup.

I turned on the AM station, but Limbaugh was too far afield today, so I switched it off and tried twiddling my thumbs.

Forward, backward.

Backward, forward.

This was not as enjoyable as it had been in Mrs. Stewart's second-grade class.

My stomach rumbled, but I didn't feel much like eating.

I sighed several times.

That didn't take long.

One-armed push-ups. Five sets of seventy-five, each arm. I felt like Jack Palance.

Upstairs to the speed bag. Then the heavy. Thirty minutes and a good sweat later, Axel came into the training room and watched me work.

"Stop," he said after fifteen minutes. "You're making me tired."

"You should get back into it," I observed breathlessly.

"I'd lose the belly. Took years to acquire. Besides, you do enough for us both."

Dave came in. After leaning against a wall and watching my frantic pace for a while, he took up a rope and began to jump. Faster and faster he went, looking like a Caucasian Carl Weathers.

Axel sat there looking like Axel.

The phone sounded. "Vance's Gym," said the Ax. Then, handing it to me: "Some broad."

"Hello," I said.

"Tell that beer-bellied son of a bitch I ain't no broad."

"Harmony. How are you?"

"Peachy as all hell. Those fuzzy turds you got shadowing Gonzales?"

"Yeah?"

"They walked right by one of Hector's lieutenants while they were playing hide-and-seek with you and Gonzales at the Forum. Those guys aren't exactly first-team material, Tyler baby."

"Was the splotchy one there?" I asked.

"Not today. Some creep about my size, but uglier." The signature cackle. "Had another jerk along, short, built like a Gummi Bear."

"They don't know who else to look for other than Gonzales, and I put them onto him. They think they're doing me a favor watching Ralph, plus it makes them feel involved."

"Yeah, well, you don't want those cluster-fucks in your corner when the poop hits the Lasko, I'll tell you that."

"Why would I count on them when I got you?"

"Don't butter me up, Sweet Buns. Besides, you have your pal from the electronics place. That guy gives me pause."

"Your instincts are impeccable."

"My end stinks whether I'm impeccable or not." She cackled at me again and hung up.

"Girlfriend?" axed the Ax.

"You bet."

*Ring!*

I jerked up the instrument. "Hello, hello, hello!"

Gonzales said, *"Hola, hola, hola."*

"Everyone's a comedian. What you need, Ralph?"

"Hector wants the dope day after tomorrow. Early. And he plans to have you hit very soon, so he will know for sure it's been done, man. Watch out. *Adiós.*" And he was gone.

"Shit."

"What?" asked Dave.

I told him, and we made plans. Later, he went to the range to implement some of them, while I called Heather.

• • •

"Want to play twinkle toes?"

"No. You always keep your socks on."

She moved sensually, hands reaching and roaming. "Yeah, but that's all I keep on."

"Hussy."

She licked my chest. "That's not what you called me last night."

"I was in the throes of passion."

Another lick. "Me too. Like now."

Lick.

"You're in the throes of passion?"

Lick. "Soon."

•   •   •

Later, much later, we uncoupled and lay side by side, holding hands.

"This is nice," Heather said sultrily.

I breathed slowly. In through the nose; out through the mouth. Willing my pulse back to normal.

"Are you spent?" she said.

"Give me twenty minutes."

Girlish giggle. "More like two hours."

"Hey, I'm not as young as once upon a time."

She traced an ankle up my leg, across, higher, down again, back up. "I am." Higher, then over, in a circular motion. "And I'm ready."

•   •   •

In.

Out.

My breath, not what you're thinking.

Side by side again, holding hands. She was breathing along with me now, sheen of perspiration glistening.

"This is nice," from me.

Breath ragged, she said, "Whew! Maybe I'm not as young as I thought," then rolled onto her side and looked me in the eye. "And you're not as old."

Oh, boy.

•   •   •

Later, I died.

# Thirty-nine

When I came downstairs next morning, my spirits were up, but nothing else was.

Ah, love. Best thing in the world.

Except coffee. I made some, then scrambled a mess of eggs, chopping in mushrooms and peppers. Toast, lightly buttered. Heather waltzed into the kitchen damp and dewy-eyed, and requested her portion of whatever I was having. More eggs and mushrooms, hold the toast. Then in popped Dave—hair freshly blow-dried, redolent of aftershave—to request his fair share of whatever we were having. Eggshells continued to pile up as the world's mushroom supply dwindled. After the troops were sated, discussion ensued.

"I still don't like it," Dave objected. "Not one little bit."

"You've a better idea then," I said.

"You bet I do. Sit tight right here. You got four cops outside, front and back. You think Hector's gunnies will do a drive-by?"

"I certainly do not, and that's the point. I want them to have a clear run at me. Then I can take care of them, not just sit around wondering when they'll strike, or how much longer I have to live like this, or when can I bring Cullen home."

"Tomorrow we nail Diaz," Dave argued. "Cut off the head, kill the snake."

"Maybe not. Harmony says it depends on who took the contract, and whether Hector paid in advance."

Dave had no rebuttal for that.

Heather, from over on the couch, said, "Ty, not to belabor the issue, but I still don't understand why you place so much credence in that woman's opinion."

"Because she's a pro in this line of work, which makes her viewpoint invaluable. Because she's so competent. Because she knows Diaz. Because I owe her the lives of everyone in my family, including mine. Because she's done nothing to undermine my trust."

"Yet," said Heather.

"Acknowledged."

"And the police can't handle this for you, despite the fact that it's their job?"

"We've been over that. The police are quite good at catching folks after a crime is committed, not before. Besides, what could they arrest these people for? It's doubtful they'll have records, at least in this state."

Heather reached for a butt, but stopped when I gave her the Eye, borrowed from Ethyl. She frowned, but pushed it back into the pack.

I looked at Dave. "So. Are we agreed?"

"No, but I give up. Except to restate my concern over being able to run all the way from the chain to the parking area in time to cover your ass."

I patted his muscular, worried back. "Fret not, old friend. I'll be covering it my ownself."

•  •  •

After Heather went home and Dave left to run some errands, I lay on the bed in Cullen's room and stared at the ceiling. Couldn't stand it, so I got up and called him down at Bragg. He was watching Elmer Fudge, he said, mildly distracted. I said I'd let him go and he said okay and we both said I love you and I hung up with my feelings wounded.

I lay on the bed in my bedroom and stared at that ceiling for a while. Then up into my office to triple-check my gear. It was in the exact same state of readiness it had been an hour ago.

Back to the ceiling, guest room this time.

The phone sounded. I jumped up and grabbed it, delighted for something to do.

Some college kid wanted to sell me aluminum siding.

I showed *him*. I didn't buy any.

Downstairs, looping through the living room, dining room, to the kitchen. Repeat in reverse order.

Kitchen. I stood looking at the coffeepot for a couple minutes, but couldn't work up the initiative.

The ceiling over the couch seemed to have deeper stippling than upstairs.

I dozed fitfully.

Finally, time to get dressed.

Cotton underwear and T-shirt, wool socks in case I lay wounded in the woods for hours. Wouldn't want to catch frostbite. Camo pants—blended cotton and synthetic twill with buttoned pockets in both legs as well as the rear; heavy leather belt; lightweight camo shirt; thin olive scarf at my neck to ward off the cold and cover my pale skin; brown wool pullover cap. Into the left front trouser pocket went a folding Gerber, a small tourniquet, several pieces of gauze, a lengthy section of rubber tubing, cherry LifeSavers. Wouldn't want to catch starvation. The right side pocket got a twenty-round magazine for the Colt AR-15 that leaned against the doorjamb, ready for battle. Two other mags rode in a web pouch on my belt. A rear pocket contained my wallet and a rubber vial of iodine. Wouldn't want to catch infection.

In a vertical shoulder holster, I placed a Norinco 1911 .45 automatic, a copy of the venerable military weapon. At my right hip, I wore a Browning Hi-Power, .40 caliber. In a small-of-the-back rig, I secreted a bitty Kahr K9, for insurance. Extra magazines were positioned strategically around my person. Not only was I ready to take on Rambo, but I'd gained 347 pounds in the last five minutes.

Already I was tired.

Somehow I made it downstairs without falling, then sat at the kitchen counter and had a V8. When I heard Dave drive up, I rinsed out the glass, picked up my ditty bag, locked the door, and left.

# Forty
I tooled around for two hours before they picked me up on Lake Brandt Road, just north of the city limit, wheeling in behind me from a side road, dust and gravel flying. Their car was a cream BMW 325i, which had as much horsepower as my Toyota truck and handled better.

Oops.

*David, here I come.*

*I hope.*

Using my rearview mirror, I tried to see who was in the car. I could make out no features, but there were two heads visible.

*Well*, I thought, *let's see if anyone else is tagging along.* I stepped on the gas; the Toyota gathered up its skirt and took off, the BMW roiling in its wake.

We flew north on Lake Brandt Road, negotiating the dips and poorly banked curves at nearly seventy miles an hour. After a few minutes of this, I swung a hard right onto Plainfield Road and turned up the wick. The BMW stayed close. No one else, though. In fact, no one else was even in sight, in either direction. Abruptly, the hardtop ran out and we were skidding too rapidly along a gravel road. I downshifted and cut my speed to fifty. Even at that velocity, I nearly lost the truck's rear end exiting one of the turns. At this point, I couldn't see the Beemer; too much dust. I slowed further, eyes on the rearview, and here came the speedy German car, its color now closer to beige than cream. Reaching a stop sign, I looked both ways—very fast—then spun onto the Church Street tarmac. Still no other cars in sight. Good thing it wasn't rush hour.

A quarter of a mile north, I turned right onto Archergate Road. Before my truck had fully straightened, I rammed the shifter into first gear and double-clutched, slamming my go foot to the firewall. For a few precarious seconds, I feared I'd overcooked it. The Toyota fishtailed all over the road—clawing for grip, leaving rubber in zigzag patterns—then the tires took a bite at last and I left the BMW wallowing on its overtaxed suspension. (It had, after all, multiple passengers.) The next curve, a mild right-hander, I took at sixty, slowed a little for the second, a less gentle twist to the left, then blasted into a long straight, grabbing third, clipping right along, then popped the clutch, stabbed the brake, downshifted, checking the mirror for the BMW—now exiting the second curve, leaning on its springs and coming hard.

I wheeled onto the range road with a spray of dirt—making certain they saw the move, not wanting to lose them now—and Dave was there, holding the chain in one hand, gesturing frantically with the other for me to hurry. I dipped my head at him as I roared past, caught a glimpse of him jerking the chain into place as I poured on the coal, saw him diving into the weeds for cover.

The low bright winter sun forced my eyes nearly shut as I hustled down the dirt road, dragging a tail of dust behind. My palms were sweating.

Forty seconds later, I nearly fell out of the truck in my haste to gather up gear and sprint the eighty yards to an Enfield .30–06 which Dave had hidden the day before. I managed to grab everything and was just beginning my run when I heard a shot in the distance, muffled, as if fired at a downward angle. *There went the lock,* I thought, which meant guests would arrive in less than a minute.

*Move your ass, Vance.*

Skirting the left end of the fifty-yard bank, I dumped my plunder in a pile at its back side and scrambled up the slope. My breath was rasping more from excitement than fatigue as I dug at the branches hiding the rifle. Then it was in my hands and I was clearing off pine needles, peering through its scope, working the bolt to chamber a round, flopping on my belly, clearing my field of fire. For the first time, I glanced at the entrance road. A smokelike cloud dissipated in the slight breeze, not far on this side of the chain. That would place them alongside the stand of mature pines to my right front, shielded from sight. What if they stopped there? And came forward on foot, or through the trees?

*Can't control that. Pay attention.*

I strained my ears, caught a faint crunch of gravel. As the sound grew louder, I could tell it was that of a car rolling very, very slowly— not footsteps. The BMW gradually came into full view, made the turn into the parking area, crept up behind my Toyota, stopped. There it sat, engine idling.

There were now four men visible in the car. Obviously, a couple of them had been scrunched down in the back seat; somewhere between here and the paved road they'd popped up. Well, now.

My plan had worked just fine so far. Here they were, all in a bunch. Now to make sure they stayed here.

I centered the cross wires on the driver's ear, knowing I'd have to go through glass, took a shallow breath, held it, began a gentle squeeze on the trigger. The rifle slammed back against my shoulder and I lost my view through the scope. Pulling the muzzle down out of recoil, I worked the bolt without thought while recentering the car in the scope's field of view. The driver's-side window had disintegrated; the driver was slumped forward against the steering wheel, facing down, part of his head gone.

I put another shot into the interior of the car just as the three remaining passengers were making a hasty exit from its lee side. The shot drew a surprised yell but no blood. Scattering for the sheltering stand of pines, the trio split off on varying tangents, dodging and weaving as they ran. I fired several shots at the fleeing figures, succeeding only in hastening their departure. They disappeared into the treeline.

Shoveling more cartridges into the Enfield, I went to work on the BMW. Two rounds into the engine compartment effectively killed the motor. My reward for such nasty and perhaps unexpected tactics was twofold: one of the hoods opened up on my allegiant Toyota; another opened up on me. Several rapid shotgun blasts brought dozens of buckshot pellets whistling angrily, thwacking into my escarpment, showering me with debris. I ducked. More whirring pellets splattered into the sheltering bank.

Time to move.

I removed the bolt from the Enfield—shoving it under my belt—and left the heavy rifle beneath the bush. That way, even if they found it, they wouldn't be able to use it. I slid down the bank, scooped up my gear, grabbed the AR-15, and retreated into the hardwoods.

Round one was mine.

And where was Dave?

# Forty-one

For nearly an hour I'd been seated, propped against a tree trunk, screened by bushes and a lightning-killed sapling, listening to my stomach rumble. What I wouldn't have given for some of Ethyl's blueberry cheesecake; a succulent brownie from Boston Market, a warm cup of Dad's spiced pumpkin custard . . .

A squirrel ran by; stopped twenty feet away; started digging for dinner, a handful of nuts.

Occasionally, a crow would caw raucously to one of its fellows, breaking my reverie and reminding me that I should be doing more watching and listening, less thinking and salivating.

I had been going over my opponents' options mentally, trying to anticipate their moves before they made them. My current position was roughly sixty yards from my original ambush site, in the fringe areas of the woods southeast of the shooting range perimeter. I was scrutinizing the forest to the south and west of my current position, the directions from which I thought attack most likely.

The bad guys had no way of knowing for sure whether I'd vacated my sheltering dirt bank, or whether, like Brer Fox, I lay low, hiding in the bushes atop the bank to scan the stand of pines into which they'd scattered. If the latter, it would be exceedingly dangerous and foolhardy for them to attempt a wide-swinging stalk from the north—which would require someone's hotfooting it across an open section of rye grass, then into an even less protected cow pasture. Anyone trying that approach would be a sitting duck for a couple hundred yards. So I had ruled it out, and hoped they had as well.

Because I wasn't watching it.

Dave was supposed to cover that approach, anyway.

By similar reasoning, no one would approach the fifty-yard bank—assuming they thought I was still there—from its front, or west, side. Whoever did so would have to cross the entire parking lot and then the additional fifty yards to the bank.

Imprudent.

In order to approach from the northeast side, a stalk of nearly a mile would be dictated by the layout of the open fields and pastureland that dominated the terrain all the way out to the chain gate. The only heavily wooded areas surrounding the range were to the south, southeast, and of course the pine thicket on the west, where the merry band had taken refuge. And thus did I reason that my hidey-hole in the southeastern quadrant must face south and west. It did.

The move expected from the opposing camp was a wide southeasterly loop from that western pine thicket, skirting the hundred-yard rifle bank at its western end, swinging due east into the hardwoods, then circling northeast in an effort to come up behind me and the dirt bank, where I may or may not still be. In an effort to thwart such a move, I'd been sitting here stewing, guessing, watching for someone to come slinking by. No one had.

Except the squirrel, the thought of which made me hungry again.

Shifting my feet quietly, I crossed my legs at the ankles, then scanned the forest with the binoculars, searching for movement. A blue jay flitted across my field of view and landed on a cedar stump. A sharp rustling caught my ear and I quickly swung the glasses to my right . . . just a field mouse, seeking sustenance.

Though it was by no means warm, I felt itchy and damp. My rapid descent from the dirt bank had showered my upper body with pine needles, some of which had found their way down my shirt collar and were irritating both skin and nerves. I resisted the almost overwhelming impulse to remove my scarf and shake the hell out of it; I couldn't risk the movement.

Hearing the mouse again, I lifted the glasses to spy on him. He wasn't there. I swung to the stump, looking for the jay. Nowhere in sight. I stopped breathing, just slowly panned the woods, searching for anything out of place. An oddly shaped tree trunk caught my attention, curiously void of branches. Tension plucked at my nerve endings like a harper.

The tree trunk stirred slightly, took a cautious step forward, became a man's leg. Through the binoculars, I examined the rest of him. He was wearing a khaki long-sleeved shirt open at the throat, baggy brown cotton slacks, brogans, and an ammo belt slung over one shoulder. Standing in the shadows of a white oak, he peered warily around. At his waist was a black synthetic holster; in his hand was a Casull .454 revolver. He didn't look particularly comfortable with it. I didn't blame him. The .454 kicks harder than Jean-Claude Van Damme. One thing was for sure; if he didn't get me with his first shot, it would take him forever to get off a second.

Very slowly, I put down my binoculars, lifted the AR-15 from my lap, eased it into firing position, all the while staring a hole through the khaki shirt. The meshuggener took another slow step, swiveling his head from side to side like an owl. I judged the range between forty and fifty yards. He had moved in too close, too quietly. Which made me nervous. If this city slicker had stalked so near, one of his cronies might be equally close, watching over the front sight of a shotgun for me to make a move. I fought the impulse to spin around and try to look in all directions at once.

With considerable effort, I reminded myself to stick to the original game plan of dealing with one man at a time and to hell with what his compadres were doing. If they succeeded in dividing my attention, I'd be in serious trouble. I took a shaky breath and laid the front sight blade against the khaki shirt. The safety I'd released just after seating myself—to avoid a telltale click when my quarry came into view—so all I had to do now was take up the slack in the military-type trigger and fire. I did, three times, very fast.

The first bullet staggered him a little, the second a little more, the third blew off his jaw hinge. He slumped at the base of the oak, unmoving.

I sat quite still for maybe ten minutes, watching the body. It never twitched. There was no sound except for the faraway buzz of a power saw. I lifted the binoculars and studied my victim for five more minutes. No breathing; no other signs of life. At length I mentally declared him a corpse—no longer a threat—and decided to move.

That decision nearly got me killed.

•  •  •

I stood up, slowly, carefully, and scanned the woods. Nothing. I slipped on my cap, snapped a fresh twenty-round magazine into the AR-15, put the one from the rifle—now holding eighteen cartridges—into the pouch from which I had drawn the replacement magazine. The AR-15 was back up to full capacity, twenty-one rounds.

I looked around. More nothing. The stiff was still leaning against his tree, looking pretty bored except for the hole in his jaw. My stomach was knotted, the back of my neck alive with electricity. All was not right in the forest.

Rotating slowly on the balls of my feet, I surveyed all around me. Just a mellow afternoon woodlot, basking in the late-autumn sun.

Where were the others? Where was Dave? If I shot him by mistake, he'd never let me live it down.

Had to shift my location; my shots would have located me. I knew it, but my feet didn't. They wouldn't budge. Some primordial instinct rooted them to the spot. I should have obeyed my senses and stayed put.

I didn't.

A dozen quiet steps to my left carried me to a dogwood. Stopped, scanned the trees. Nothing. Ten more steps; I knelt beside a cedar stump. The corpse was now to my right front, thirty yards distant. Its open eyes stared at me accusingly. I moved again, forward, slowly, moving my eyes more than my feet. Pausing at a blowdown, I knelt, rested my elbows on the now horizontal trunk, and studied the forest with my binoculars.

I was making a second sweep, panning left to right, when the heavy branch I'd propped my elbows on shuddered, splintered, erupting moss and rotted bark into my face. More pellets cracked simultaneously into adjacent logs and branches, missing by scant inches. Throwing myself back and left, I hit the ground so hard the breath was pounded from my lungs. I grabbed for the AR-15, found it, rolled to my right, then again. The shotgun was still blasting, the nasty whirring balls fragmenting the fallen tree.

Suddenly, the roaring ceased. *Out of ammo*, I thought. Scrambling to my feet, I cut loose with the rifle, fanning my shots from left to right, two per second, not aiming but firing from the hip, charging forward as I fired. My bullets were having little positive effect that I could see, but I just kept pulling the trigger, pounding the turf, grating for breath. I had covered about thirty yards, dodging trees, jumping logs, spraying lead, when the well ran dry, the bolt locked back on an empty magazine. Diving to my belly, I ejected the spent mag and rammed home a loaded one, released the bolt, looked for a target.

I'd probably covered half the distance to the shotgun; I saw neither it nor its wielder, but knew they were near. *Is he completely out of shells?* I thought, doubting it. As if in answer to my question, a beefy man in red suspenders stepped from behind a sycamore twenty yards away and aimed his shotgun at my face. I moved and he fired, filling the air with buckshot where I'd just been, me falling and firing five shots back at him as fast as I could jerk the trigger. He ducked behind his tree. Wiping dirt from my eyes with my left hand, I watched the tree through the aperture sight of the Colt. *Come out either side and I'll nail you, dickhead.*

He didn't. For several minutes I lay staring at the sycamore. While I watched, I cogitated.

This clever fellow had likely been following the first guy at a distance, probably just barely within sight, using him as bait to set me up. If I ambushed Gunny Number One, I'd give my position away to the second man, who would promptly perforate me repeatedly with the scattergun. Besides, there was always a chance the first hombre might get lucky and bust me himself. Either way, the backup guy came up smelling of rose. Pretty damn sneaky. Pretty damn smart.

And where did the fourth player lurk? Nearby as well? Behind me perhaps—a sobering thought that brought on the familiar compulsion to look in every direction at once.

Where was Dave?

Something showed over by the beefy guy's tree. At first I thought it was a stick and wondered just what the shifty bastard was up to now. No stick; half the length of a shotgun barrel. I aimed carefully and put a hole in it. The force of impact flung the gun away, where it clattered noisily to the ground, several feet from the sheltering sycamore. I shot the gun again where it lay, this time aiming at the action area. It spun away, thoroughly, unfixably, unusably broken. Old Beef was out of the shotgun business.

*Does he have a sidearm?* I wondered. *Have to find out.* I climbed to my feet, partially protected by the trunk of a sizable pine, withdrew the full magazine from my right front pants pocket, switched it with the depleted but not entirely empty one from the rifle. That—now containing ten cartridges—went into the empty pouch at my belt. Stepping out from behind my pine, I advanced on the sycamore, holding my rifle at chest level, its muzzle trained on the tree, crunching my feet in the leaves and twigs of the forest floor, hoping to make Beefy nervous. It worked. He appeared around the side of the tree that I wasn't watching as closely as I should have been and tossed a shot off at me just as I reacted and fired at him. His bullet chipped a branch off a spindly shrub at my right; I've no idea where mine went.

Refuge again, this time behind a more substantial tree on my left. Roughly forty feet separated us. He had gained the move on me; I was now the one hiding behind a tree with him looking through his sights, awaiting my pleasure.

*Shit.*

Had I never played this game before? My stomach knotted again.

I thought up several maneuvers, most of which would end with a similar conclusion: my body bleeding a lot. I discarded those. One idea offered a glimmer of hope. I went over it again; it seemed reasonably sound. Besides, I couldn't come up with anything better and I had to do something; it would be but a matter of time before Nasty Number Four showed up to put in his two cents. Then I'd be caught between them.

My plan was simple. I'd make a noisy feint to my left, showing myself to El Beefo, then spin adroitly around and jump out from the other side of the tree. If it worked properly, I'd catch him as he was lining his gun up on the wrong side of the tree. My stomach flip-flopped and I made my move, springing away from the shelter of the tree, pirouetting beautifully backward, passing the tree again as I skipped lightly to its right, all done rapidly and with flawless timing. Unfortunately, it didn't fool the guy with the red suspenders.

When I made my perfect swing out from the right side of the tree, he was waiting, pistol in firing position—held in both hands like he knew what he was doing—less than fifteen yards away.

Uh-oh.

We were both fully in the open when he started blasting. His first slug burned a furrow across my left shoulder. His second shot whispered past my ear but by then I'd found him in my sights and we were both firing frantically. My second or third shot clipped him in the body—I saw his shirt jump—but he didn't even grimace. I fired again, then felt a smashing blow to the pit of my stomach that staggered me backward. My next several shots were not aimed, just pumped at him hoping to destroy his accuracy, or send him diving for cover. Didn't work. One of his bullets slammed my left wrist, slicing across it to whap into the extended magazine of my rifle, twisting the gun in my hands. My wrist went numb, useless. I let go with it and fired the rifle with my right, one-handed, still holding the butt at my shoulder. After one shot, it jammed.

Beefy stopped firing. I watched him eject an empty magazine with his right hand, reach into his coat pocket with his left—going for a loaded one—staring at me all the while, his movements taking on a slow-motion, surrealistic quality. I felt nauseous. Looked stupidly at my useless AR-15—at its bent magazine filled with impotent cartridges—back up at the man in red suspenders, blood running from his chest even as he shoved home the fresh mag. I thought that this couldn't be happening; I wouldn't let it happen.

I roared out in defiance, flung the battered rifle from me, reached for the autopistol at my hip. My fingers closed on its butt as he finished recharging his own piece and began lifting it back into firing position; I thumbed off the holster's retaining strap as he extended his arms and fumbled for his slide release, to snap a round into battery; I snatched my gun clear of the holster as his pistol jerked in recoil, *Don't give a shit, taking him with me!* I thought as my Browning came to eye level, me thumbing its safety on the rise, him firing again, missing, and then my gun talking back, bucking in my hand, once, twice, again, four times, all the while with me striding forward, yelling in the intensity of battle, "SHOOT AGAIN, YOU SON OF A BITCH!" even as I saw my first bullet strike him, and the second, and the third twist him half around, and he was staggering backward while still I yelled, "DON'T QUIT ON ME!" shooting again, his head snapping from the impact, and then he turned and fired back, trying to live, not quitting despite the pain and anger and frustration, his slug finding my leg, dropping me to one knee so close we were nearly touching each other, and he tried to yell at me like I was screeching at him, but he had a hole in his face and couldn't, so he spat at me instead, a bloody froth, until I shot him once more and he fell heavily and died.

I knelt there for a while, exhausted, then went off to lick my wounds.

# Forty-two

The pain was bad but the blood was worse. I couldn't stop it completely; it oozed from the hole in my leg like the juice from an overripe tomato, thick and red. I'd somehow managed to get a tourniquet in place—despite the wound in my wrist, and pretty tightly at that—but the blood still seeped, clotting my trousers. The leg ached throbbingly and no amount of cussing helped. Neither the wrist nor the superficial tear in my left shoulder bled appreciably; they merely provided extra discomfort. I wasn't sure how much ground I'd covered before settling in under a deadfall, hands and knees into its center, brushing away leaves and twigs to make a crunch-free mat to lie on—probably less than the length of a football field. By the time I'd begun to survey the damage, my elevated supply of adrenaline deserted and waves of pain and nausea washed over me.

Despite my racked condition, I was relieved to discover that my assailant had shot me with full-jacketed ammo, not the more devastating hollow-point stuff I'd used in return; the hole in my leg went straight through, and the damage to the major thigh muscles appeared minimal.

Further good news: I'd not been shot in the body, despite my vague recollection of having received a wound there. The awesome blow I'd felt to my stomach had been a bullet smashing into my belt buckle, deflecting to my left, burrowing a course along the upper edge of my gun belt, then plowing into the lower end of my shoulder holster. I twisted the slug out with my fingers. Had I taken that bullet amidships, the dance would have been over.

I packed every bloody hole in sight with gauze, after first dabbing each gingerly with iodine. Tightening my Velcro watchband served admirably at holding the wrist gauze in place, although the increased pressure upped the pain a notch. Maybe I'd pass out. Or throw up. Or both.

I did neither. After patching myself up, I reloaded the Browning and held it in my lap. And waited, starving. Where's a hot dog vendor when you really need one? Despite effort to the contrary, I dozed, chin heavy on my chest, until a sharp noise or stab of pain would awaken me and I'd jerk my head up and stare wildly around.

Repeat.

If I kept that up, I'd get whiplash.

The fourth man came from the north on the cool evening air. I saw him long before I heard him. He advanced slowly, taking a step, then eyeballing the terrain in a circle before moving again. At times I'd see him clearly, too far for a shot; other times he'd disappear completely for several minutes. After what seemed an interminable wait, he drew close enough for me to essay a try. Fifty, fifty-five yards; maybe a bit farther. Risky for a handgun under these conditions.

I considered waiting for a surer opportunity, but realized that if he spotted me before I brought off my little surprise, Social Security might not figure in my future. I raised the Browning to arm's length, surprised at how heavy it felt; focused on the sight picture, surprised at how blurred it looked; began the trigger squeeze, surprised at how my hand quaked. The gun snapped upward in recoil; the fourth man appeared to spin and fall at the same time.

Or maybe he had just turned and dived.

I waited—leg throbbing, wrist aching, shoulder burning, stomach rumbling, head swimming—for five minutes. Ten. And then he was coming, pounding, twigs cracking underfoot in his haste, charging from the right where he wasn't supposed to be, where he must have crawled. Then I was firing and so was he, neither of us connecting until I rolled twice and rose to my good knee and fired again. I saw my first slug strike him, then the second, the third, and he was falling back, shooting into the ground, then wheeling and tossing one more bullet at me, the white heat of its passage hornetlike as I shot into him again and he stopped, depleted, nothing left, and slipped to the forest floor.

And lay still.

Me too.

•   •   •

"You gonna lie there all day?" said Dave.

I one-eyed him from the ground. "I will if I feel like it. Where the hell you been?"

He sat down beside me. "Looking for you."

"Find me?"

"Most of you." He tried to examine my wounds. I slapped his hand away.

"Leave me alone," I demanded.

"Right, be testy. That'll do you a lot of good." He paused, then added, "They dead?"

I nodded, then stopped nodding because it hurt. "Every mother's son."

"Can you stand up?"

"Stand up? Hell, I can whip you a game of tennis."

"Let's see," he said.

"See what?"

"You stand up."

"Go away. I want to rest."

"You can rest later. How many times were you hit?"

I didn't answer. I was starting to dream. He brought me back by yelling into my face, "How many times were you hit?"

"How the hell do I know?" I slurred. Speaking required great effort. I preferred sleeping.

"Open your eyes!"

"Fuck you," weakly. Very weakly.

"That's better." He looked me over, then put a bottle to my lips and told me to drink. I did. Big mistake. Then he put something against the hole in my leg and I hollered awhile and passed out.

Unfortunately, he brought me around once more with a sniff of ammonia. He said, "Can you focus on me?"

"Who'd want to focus on that ugly puss?"

"You patched yourself up pretty well, and I augmented. I put another tourniquet on your leaky leg, higher up, which stopped the blood flow. For now. But I have to get you to a hospital pretty quick, before it starts again. If you won't walk, I'll have to carry you."

"Up yours."

"Right," he said, and picked me up fireman fashion. I yelled and kicked some; he told me to quit bellyaching and just faint again.

So that's what I did.

# Forty-three

"I'm not staying," I said.

"Oh yes you are," Heather objected.

"Oh no I'm not," I insisted.

"You'll stay until I'm through with my questions," argued Sergeant Carl McDuffy.

"Like hell," I demurred.

"How about if I arrest you?" said McDuffy.

"What for?" asked Rufus E. McElroy, Colonel, United States Army, from a chair over in the corner. I had a private room.

"I'll think of something," answered the McDuff.

A nurse came in, gave me a shot that hurt like the dickens, patted me near the offended spot and said, "You're staying."

"Like hell," I disagreed.

"Why don't you want to stay, Daddy?" from my child, freshly scrubbed and fresh from Bragg.

"The food is lousy, son," I informed.

"You're staying," reiterated McDuffy, "until I say different."

"And the company is worse than the food," I told my boy, looking pointedly at McDuffy.

"The hospital can't hold you," from McElroy, "against your will."

"Don't encourage him," Heather admonished the colonel.

"I'm leaving now," I insisted, then rubbed my backside, still smarting from the nurse's ministrations. "Well, in a couple minutes."

"Your father's a jerk," an irate McDuffy told my child.

"Well, sir," replied my boy, "one of you sure is."

• • •

The scene was:

Everyone at my house, in the living room, with its eggshell walls and carpeting, Vermeer print, framed photo of my great-grandmother when she was with the Follies, antique three-leg in the corner with Christmas skaters on top, surrounded by cotton bunting (ersatz snow, courtesy of Cullen), the second Fraser fir, all white of lights to keep our neighbors from lynching us.

Ethyl sat in my golf-motif armchair, feet crossed on the matching ottoman, hot tea at her elbow on the cherry side table.

Dad reclined in the big leather chair he loves so dearly, an empty milk glass on one of its arms.

Dave was in a corner leaning against the wall, arms folded.

Heather and Jason and McElroy, all in a row, were warming chairs borrowed from the dining room suite.

I sat on the fleur-de-lised couch, sideways, gimpy left leg extended straight out.

The conversation began with Heather. "Surely you don't plan to go through with this charade tomorrow."

"I doubt Diaz would agree to put it off," said Jason. "Even if he could be persuaded, since he doesn't have any idea Tyler is involved, what excuse might he accept?"

McElroy said "Bingo."

Heather, looking at McElroy, ordered, "Don't start with that 'Bingo' crap."

McElroy just smiled.

Dave said, "Heather, the dope deal is coming off as planned. Diaz might or might not know about the situation at the range. Fanner agreed to keep it off the news for twenty-four hours. As soon as Hector finds out about it, he might send another group after Ty and Odie. Or Cullen. We don't want that, now do we?"

"Of course not," Heather snapped. "Don't patronize me. The problem is that, like it or not, Ty isn't in shape to take on the Latin monster and whoever he has with him. Not with a bullet hole in his leg, and a wrist and shoulder that aren't one hundred percent."

"I'll be fine," I proffered.

"Sure you will. And after, we can go skiing."

McElroy said "Bingo."

Heather just glared at him.

From upstairs we heard Cullen cry, "Candy on the loose!" and a quantity of hard, marble-sized peppermints tumbled down the stairs to strike the floor, rolling this way and that. In three seconds flat, our two boys were scooping them up.

Web said, "Sorry," somewhat sheepishly and with his mouth full.

The scene ended on that sugary note.

# Forty-four

Ear to the phone, I heard, "Council of war concluded?"

"You seem to know everything that goes on," I said.

Soft chuckle. "I didn't, I'd have been dead years ago. Still going through with it tomorrow, bum leg and all, ain'tcha?"

"Yep."

"Not 'yep,' 'yup.' Didn't you ever see *High Noon*?"

"Yup."

"That's better. You know, the mention of *High Noon* is not remiss here. I knew Hector growing up. He was—"

"You grew up in Mexico?"

"Mexico, Shmexico. Hector grew up in El Paso, dearie, right along with me and one of them boys you greased out there in that rural woodlot. And don't interrupt, this is *muy importante*.

"Being a Marshal Dillon fan, Hector grew up with a Mattel Fanner-50 in his big hand. Then in high school, he read Ed McGivern's book and switched over to double-action gunplay. Never a Cooper disciple, more into Bill Jordan and his border patrol exploits, Hector refused to abandon his revolver in favor of an autoloader. He totes a Smith Model 58 four-inch, nickel. You familiar with it?"

"Sure. Nonadjustable-sight N-frame, .41 Magnum."

"You betcha. And he can make it prance. He runs only semi-wadcutters through it for practice. The important thing is that he switches to Mag-Safe prefragmented for social purposes. He tags you with one of those and it's all over but the dying. He's quick as a sidewinder, my friend, so don't let him start the play. Preemptive strike is your ticket. *Comprende?*"

"Yup."

"And Ty. Don't second-guess me here. Take a chance with Hector and you'll wind up kitty litter. I know you're good. Those four stiffs at the range prove that. But Diaz is beyond good, he's magic. I had to kill him, I'd deck him with a sniper rifle from four hundred meters," Harmony concluded.

"I'll remember that."

She paused for a count of ten. "The hell you will, you sap. You intend to go head-on with him."

I didn't answer.

"Don't you?"

More not answering.

"Why, you dumb schmuck?" she pressed.

"I have something to say to him."

"Could be the last thing you say to anybody."

"Who knows?"

"Well, ace, don't say I never warned you."

"I won't. And don't think I don't appreciate it."

"Now go play patty-cake with your sweetie. Might be your last chance."

"Will do."

She chuckled. Then: "Oh, one more thing. When you open the ball, keep your weight on your good leg."

"Thanks, doc. I've been shot before. By the way, you were bleeding pretty good at the school. Didn't seem to hamper you at my house shortly after."

"Superficial stuff. Only one was even worth antiseptic. You think I'm a pussy, that you're the only one can function with fresh bullet wounds, you chauvinistic asshole?"

"Sorry, Eloise. No slight intended."

She chuckled again, then waxed silent. "Ty?" she said after a moment.

"Yes?"

*"Focus* on Hector. Don't take chances, don't try to be fancy. Just get it done."

"I will."

"And don't call me Eloise." Then she was gone.

# Forty-five

Before getting around to patty-cake I had to deal with Lieutenant John T. Fanner and his brummagem sidekick, McDuffy. There they were on my doorstep, despite the late hour, so I invited them in. To the den; the living room was for company. We all found seats.

Fanner first. "We have identified all four of your, ah, attackers."

"Why do you say 'ah, attackers,' as opposed to simply 'attackers'?"

"He means we're not so sure you didn't set them up," McDuffy yipped, Chihuahua-like.

I looked to the lieutenant. "He right? That what you mean?"

Fanner cleared his throat.

"Okay. You got me." I stood and held out my hands, painful though it was to my shoulder. "I lured four armed men to a secluded area, then ambushed them. All by myself. Cuff me. I'll go quietly."

"Sit down!" McDuffy barked.

Still standing, I said, "Don't tell me to sit down in my own house, Sergeant. You want to boss me around, arrest me. Otherwise, shut your petty little yap."

And then McDuff was on his feet, in my face, ready to square off right there.

Me too.

Fanner intervened. "McDuffy!" he growled.

"But, Lieutenant . . ." McDuffy whined.

"McDuffy!" Louder growl.

"Yes, sir."

"Sit *down!*"

Like a moderately obedient puppy, McDuffy sat. I hoped he was house-trained.

"I must apologize for the sergeant's behavior. He does not seem to like you."

I eased back into my favorite rocker. "How can you tell?"

"May we return to the subject of your assailants?"

"Please do."

"Three of them are from the Southwest, one from North Dakota. All have lengthy records of violent crimes."

"So what's the problem?" I asked.

"The problem is what they were doing here."

"I think they were after me."

"Why?"

"Because Hector Diaz put out a contract. Or three."

"You know that for a fact?"

I looked at him incredulously. "Well, Lieutenant, I can't prove it in a court of law, but due to three recent attempts on my or someone in my immediate family's lives, I have a strong suspicion."

Fanner concurred by nodding unhappily. "Might we expect a continuation of hostilities?"

"Not if you snare Hector Diaz."

"We have no idea where he is."

"Well, then. I doubt you'll be able to do me much good. As usual."

Fanner had the good manners not to ask for coffee, so I showed them the front door. They recognized its purpose and used it.

I went upstairs to see if the boys were asleep.

They were. I switched off the lights on Cullen's tiny personal Christmas tree, prodded Mannheim Steamroller out of his personal tape deck, kissed him, and whispered "I love you" into his personal ear.

Then I went to seek patty-cake material.

• • •

Lawrence Goodall came to me in the night.

"Hiya, Spud," he said.

"Mr. Goodall," I said back to him.

He wore sandals instead of his shoes with the holes cut out to allevi-ate pain from his corns—sandals and a fuchsia T-shirt with tobacco stains and Garfield on the front. No halo in evidence, but I was confi-dent he had one.

"How you getting along?" I said to him.

"Fine as goose hair," he said back to me.

I was wearing red athletic shorts and saddle oxfords and my dark green shirt with *GUILFORD COLLEGE YMCA—YOUTH SPORTS COACH* on the front and a cowboy hat I'd had when I was seven.

"Where's your boy?" he said to me.

"At the pool with his mom," I said back to him.

He nodded placidly and smiled.

"Are you sorry to be gone?" I said to him.

"Gone where?" he said back to me.

He began to shift a little sideways with no apparent effort or move-ment from his legs.

"I'm visiting with Hector Diaz tomorrow," I said to him quickly, be-fore he could go. It seemed important to me.

"Tell him hello," he said back, and licked my face. Only he was Lucky and it was dawn.

I put the dog out and went back to bed, but sleep eluded.

# Forty-six Preparations.

Decisions to be made: Logistics, tactics, troop dispersement, armaments. Sustenance. Then we got down to business.

"Here's the plan," I began. And laid it out for them.

"You think it's a good idea bringing McElroy in? After all, he has a hole in his lung," Pop queried.

"He got that hole trying to help you, plus he lost a man on our ac-count. You think I should leave him out?"

"Besides," prodded David, "you had a heart attack, and maybe a brain-damaging stroke."

"First you have to have a brain to damage," Ethyl mumbled. Then: "What about the police?" with a crumb of toast at one corner of her mouth.

Axel harrumphed, "They'd just fu—foul things up."

Cullen's mouth flew open. "I know what *you* almost said."

Axel got the Eye from Ethyl. Better him than me.

"I tend to agree with Ax," I said. "Once the whole thing is over, we'll let Fanner handle it."

"Why not simply have him arrest Diaz in the act?" Ethyl asked.

"The act of what?" asked Dave. "Buying a large quantity of baking soda for an obscene amount of money?"

"Well, if no law is being broken," continued Ethyl, "how are you going to explain why you went after the man in the first place?"

"I probably won't. I'll say he jumped me."

"Will they believe you?"

"If I work it right, and there are no witnesses, and I'm lucky. Otherwise, you'll have to take care of Cullen by yourself for a few years. The rest of us will be in jail."

Cullen looked up in alarm, a crumb matching Grandma's in evidence. I winked at him. Relieved, he winked back and bit off a mouthful of cinnamon toast.

Propitiously, the phone rang. Around a mouthful of blueberry bagel, I said, "Hello."

"Diaz is here," said Ralph Gonzales.

"With you now?"

"In town, not with me."

"He have instructions for me?"

"*Sí.*"

"Let's hear them."

For about a minute, I did.

•  •  •

Cullen and the Ax took Dave on in basketball. Twenty minutes later, Cullen stomped in to sit down in a blue funk.

"Yes?" I said.

Lower lip you could perch a brick on. "We lost!"

"So?"

"I wish I was so jumpative that I could slam-dunk, like Dave."

Jumpative? Good adjective.

"Shug, the reason Dave can slam-dunk is that your goal is only eight feet high. Can any of the kids on your team dunk the ball?"

Head shake.

"Of course not. And did I not see you score two points night before last?"

Head nod.

"And did I not see my only son steal the ball from Landon, drive the length of the court—dribbling all the while, mind you—and lay the ball up?"

Another nod.

"Any other kid on your team ever do that?"

Slow headshake.

"And what's all this attention you're paying to winning lately?"

"Well, Web beats me all the time at Chinese checkerds, and our basketball team has lost three straight, and Paw-paw . . ."

"Cullen?"

"Yes."

"Who beat Gran'ma at Monopoly last night?"

"Me."

"And who got a 'superior' rating at his first piano recital?"

"Me."

"And what is the object of sports and games and music?"

In a singsong litany: "To do my best and have fun."

"It's when you forget those two things that problems arise."

"Like now?"

"Like now."

"I'm being a poor sport?"

"You think so?"

The lip again, sneaking out. "Am I being bad?"

I made as if to sit on his lap. "Arrgh, you'll squish me," he protested, pushing at my hindquarters with his tennis shoes.

"No, babe, not bad. Little selfish, maybe."

He locked his legs onto my upper arm, the dreaded scissors hold.

"How do you think Dave and Axel feel right now?" I said.

He relaxed the hold. "Not good."

"And whose fault is that?"

Three seconds' hesitation, then "Excuse me" and outside he went.

# Forty-seven

Lucky was chewing on a rawhide bone at my feet when Gonzales called again. I leaned forward in my rocker and snatched up the phone.

"Drugstore."

"You are very funny."

"Riot, ain't I."

"Do you know the pay telephone at the corner of West Market and Stage Coach Trail?"

"Diaz with you now?"

"*Sí*, 'cross from the bank that wen' broke." Ah, code.

"Is it just the two of you?"

"No, the phone on the corner, not in the store."

"How many more, besides you and Hector?"

"No, three o'clock is too early."

"The two of you and three more?"

"*Sí*, four-thirty is good."

"Now we really are talking about the time, right?"

"Of course we have the money. You jus' have the stuff, *pendejo*."

"Can I get away with having someone with me?"

"No, man. Nobody. An' we will check out the car. No bugs, no wires, no *nada* but produc', *gringo*."

"Your name is Ralph, and you're calling me *gringo*?"

He laughed.

"I'll be in a red Dodge pickup," I said. "Make sure someone other than Diaz checks out my truck. He sees me and the party will start right there."

"Is fuckin' for sure. Remember, four-thirty. Beat the rush hour, man."

We hung up without saying goodbye.

•  •  •

Dave's truck was a four-wheel drive Dodge Ram with blackout windows, covered cargo bed, and an engine as big as Kansas. "Try not to wreck it. It's no dainty thing like that tin can Toyota of yours," he advised.

"Don't remind me of my poor defunct Tacoma. Ah, well . . . Diaz picked a good spot. For him, not us. He'll likely have enough men to spot a tail, so each of you will have to park not only within eyeshot of the pay phone but in an out-of-the-way place. Dad, I want you out West Market away from town, with Axel back the other way, probably near Swing Road. Pick a good vantage point that you can leave quickly but unnoticeably."

"Thanks for the tip," said the Ax, who had done more surveillance in his life than Spenser.

"Dave'll park in the Barn Dinner Theater lot. That early in the evening, the supper crowd shouldn't be a problem. It's a good thing Stage Coach doesn't go all the way across at Market. We'd need a fourth man to cover that way."

Dad said, "Only one of us'll be able to see you leave."

"Right. But McElroy'll be roaming. He'll do what he can."

"What are the rest of us supposed to do if we miss you?"

"Come back here to help Jason and Heather and Thurman cover the boys."

"I mean about you, son."

I cupped his shoulders in my hands. "I know what you mean, Pop. It can't be helped. This is the only way, given the hand we've been dealt."

"You said there was goin' to be five of them."

"Four. Gonzales will opt out."

"So he says. What if he double-crosses you the way he's claimin' he'll do Diaz?"

"Have to play it as it falls. Besides, you and me can handle five of these slimeballs easy."

"I know that," he said testily. "I'm worried about them two." He indicated Dave and the Ax with a thumb.

"By the way," I said, to shift his attention. "Why don't you carry my Galil?"

"Toted an M-1 carbine all over the Pacific, not to mention the Chosin Reservoir. I reckon it'll do for Market Street, too."

"Dave?" I said.

"Yo."

"What're you taking?"

He shifted his bulk on the couch, opening his jacket to show me the blued Smith & Wesson .44 mag in its shoulder rig. He let the coat flop back.

Axel said to him, "When you gonna buy a real gun?"

"You mean one that fires six hundred times?"

Axel grinned. "Yeah, like my SIG."

"Quick to reload, too?"

Axel opened his sports coat, exposing the ends of two thirty-round magazines. "You bet."

Dave just smiled. "No thanks. Six for sure, says McClure."

"Who the hell is McClure?"

Dave shrugged. "I dunno, but it rhymes."

"Let's go load up our baking soda . . . excuse me, dope . . . then have lunch," I suggested.

"Knew food would come in somewhere soon," Dave said, getting to his feet.

Gimping along beside him on the way out to his Dodge, a heavy suitcase in one hand, I said, "What you got loaded in the Smith?"

"Cor-Bon 180s, the midrange stuff."

I nodded my appreciation of his choice while I stacked the suitcases onto the front seat, then we went to chow down.

A man needs his strength.

•　•　•

He was holding on tightly, very tightly, tears hot against my cheek. A bit unexpected, this. So I kissed his head and hugged him back, Heather standing in the front doorway watching in amazement, with Cullen beside her.

"He's a very bad man," Web cried, my chest muffling his voice.

"I know, hon. That's why I have to go after him. So he won't show up sometime when we don't expect it and take us by surprise."

Little shoulders quivering from fear, he said, "I watched him shoot Mr. Goodall like he was a . . . a worm or something. Then he laughed after." Horrible memories, haunting, repressed, bubbling unbidden to the surface.

I held him a moment longer, then gently pried him loose to get his eye. "Web? He won't shoot me like he did Mr. Goodall."

"How do you know?"

"I won't let him."

"But he's so big and so mean."

"You ever hear of Wyatt Earp?"

"No."

"He was an old-timey gunfighter, a policeman some of the time. He was in many fights with guns."

The tears had run their course. Heather and Cullen were listening closely, obviously harboring fears of their own.

"This man, Wyatt Earp," I continued, "despite all his battles, was never shot once. Not once."

Interested, incredulous, inquisitive, Web pursued. "Not even snibbed?"

"Not even. Never."

"How come?"

"That's a good question. For one thing, he was very good at fighting with a gun. For another, he knew tactics, how to play the game, like you know Chinese checkers. Maybe God was on his side, or perhaps he was just lucky. But he never got shot. He lived to be an old man."

"Are you very good at fighting with a gun?"

"Yes."

"Can you do tactics?"

"You bet."

"Is God on your side?"

I squeezed him hard. "I hope so, Web."

He squeezed back, more for me this time than himself. "Me too."

Then Heather took Web inside and Cullen came over. "Was all that true?"

"What I told Web? Yes, according to history books."

"But you've already been shot. More than once."

"Let's not dwell on that."

"So I shouldn't worry about you at all?"

"Don't worry, just be glad to see me when it's over. And expect to."

"See you?"

"Yes."

"I will."

A kiss and he was gone, not wanting me to see him fail at not worrying. His heart has always been in the right place.

Then Heather was back, and in front of me, but no hug or kiss. She just said, "Come back to us, Wyatt," and went inside.

And I went to see the elephant.

Again.

# Forty-eight
It was a bright day, cold though, and I was splendidly dressed in an old Army fatigue jacket. The idea was not to impress Hector Diaz (assuming that's who I was actually going to meet, and not yet another cousin), but to secrete in a roomy outer pocket my little Airweight snub-nosed .38 revolver. And despite Smith & Wesson's stated admonition that such would void any warranty, either expressed or implied, I had the gun stuffed to the gills with lead hollow-point Plus-P ammo. Stuffed to the gills in this case meant five cartridges. Not many, huh?

I didn't think so either; for insurance I wore on my left hip—butt forward—my Browning .40 in Condition One. That's cocked-and-locked to the nongunnies among you, and it translates to quick as hell to whip out and cut loose a barrage. The Browning held eleven rounds, much more comforting than five, especially when you might have to take on a quartet of meanies by yourself. Last time I did that, I barely came through it. And those meanies did *not* include Hector Diaz.

Driving to the meeting place, I observed that while Dave's truck had more power than a locomotive, it was only half as heavy. My sore left shoulder was grateful for power steering as I pulled into the designated parking lot, drove up to the designated phone, parked with the motor running, glanced at the clock on the dash—4:29—and waited, George Strait serenading me robustly through six speakers.

A brown Chevy Suburban with mud flaps and three antennas pulled into the parking lot, stopping about ten yards in front of me, engine idling.

Then a Sedan De Ville, green, Northstar engine, pulled up behind me.

Boxed.

Was I smart, or what? If this shindig was about to go down, I was in big trouble.

A very non-Hispanic gentleman stepped from the Caddy, walked around to the passenger side of Dave's Dodge, and opened the door.

"Hi, Freckles," I greeted.

He didn't say "Hi" back.

"I'm going to search your truck," he informed me. "If there's anything or anyone in it but you and the shit, we leave."

"That's only fair."

"Other guy in the Cad's gonna run a bug hunt on your undercarriage, then check you for a wire. Got a problem with that?"

"Not so long as I don't have to get out of the truck."

"Your legs broke?"

"You brain-dead?"

He liked that even less than being called Freckles, but he motioned with a pale, spotted hand and another non-Hispanic gentleman quit the De Ville, some pretty sophisticated-looking equipment in hand, and bent to his task.

Me and Mr. Strait kept on groovin'.

Freckles searched the Dodge Ram, studiously avoiding the stack of suitcases on the seat beside me as George sang, me joining in on the last refrain, my rich baritone melodious and *loud*.

Freckles liked that even less than being called brain-dead.

Abruptly, my door opened, causing my elbow to slip off the armrest. At my shoulder stood the man with all the sophisticated equipment. As he started to lift the lapel of my spiffy jacket, I said, "There's a gun on my hip, left side. Touch it and your remains will fit into an aspirin tin."

"Guy's a riot, ain't he, Antonio?" said Equipment Man. "Gonzales said he was a riot."

Tough guy, trying to impress. Nonetheless, he rushed the frisk and missed my little snub, as I'd intended. He stepped back and slammed the door and gathered his sophisticated-looking equipment and tossed same in the Caddy and slid in behind the wheel, just as Shania Twain burst forth with "Any Man of Mine."

Freckles grimaced. "You got to play that redneck crap so loud?" he bitched, reaching for the suitcase on top.

I snaked the Browning out kind of slow like—say about a quarter of a second—and put the muzzle so close to his forehead he had to cross his eyes to focus on it. "You're about to receive a lobotomy," I said conversationally.

He liked that even less than my singing.

"I need to see the shit," he said, standing very still.

"Got the money on you?"

"It's in the Chevy." Eyes still crossed, examining the black hole at his end of the Browning.

"Then that's where you need to be. Getting it."

"I ain't flashing three mil in cash in this fucking parking lot!"

"Then you ain't checking no shit, commode lips."

"Who you calling com—"

"Let us be reasonable, Tony my man. I'll follow you to a secluded rendezvous where we can play show-and-share unobserved and uninterrupted. Agreed?"

He nodded. As well he should. It's what he'd planned to do all along. I wasn't supposed to know it, though. He was holding up his act quite well, even breaking out a little bead of perspiration on his philtrum, just as if he were really nervous. Oscar material, old Freckles.

Or maybe he just hated country music, in which case he needed shooting.

Continuing to play his role to the hilt, he closed the passenger door carefully, signaled to the Suburban, walked around the front of Dave's Dodge, got into the De Ville. The car squatted slightly as Equipment Man put the big Caddy in gear and backed it up. Shania and I followed along out of the lot, the Suburban falling in behind.

We were heading Dave's way.

# Forty-nine

There he was, Mr. Michaels himself, his SHO backed into a parking slot beside the Barn's white board fence, head lolled back, mouth open, sound asleep.

Sure he was.

We motored on past, our little caravan, bristling with guns and ersatz narcotics, five rough characters and me. And Shania Twain.

Nunn Pools and Spas was coming up on the right, then Sherwin Williams to my left, and Southeastern Freight Lines with its long row of diesel rigs beside the building. Priba Furniture's big red brick building, then a house or two, woodlots, the entrance to Guilford Primary School. We kept on, the Caddy in front crossing West Friendly, staying straight on Stage Coach, then more houses, the topography gently rolling now, a couple of open fields on each side, bordered by tall evergreens. We doglegged to starboard at Ballinger, a pair of neglected silos silently monitoring our progress. Golf course on the right; a mule on the left, inside a fence. The Caddy slowed at the corner of the fence then turned onto Breezewood—a short stretch of gravel that meandered north over a small rise and disappeared. I followed suit.

The plot thickened. If I only had my phone, I could call Dave and tell him: "Turn right at the silos, then hang a left at the mule."

If I was so damn funny, why was there a knot in my stomach?

So what if Dave couldn't find me, like out at the range?

So what if he missed the turn?

So what if I developed a few extra navels?

Not much point in defeatist thinking. I remembered my advice to Cullen: The object is to do your best and have fun.

Well, I was doing my best.

When would the fun start?

Soon. We were approaching a hand-lettered sign hanging from a wire suspended across the road. It read:


CLOSED
FOR THE
WINTER
REOPEN
APRIL 1±


Oddly, the sign lifted my spirits. I'd been alone many times before, and against worse odds than these. Like Tuesdays at the washerette.

"Let's see what these bad boys are made of," I said to Shania.

But she was gone.

.  .  .

The Cad had circled and stopped near the hand-lettered sign; the Suburban had parked athwart the gravel road, to hem me in.

I don't respond well to hemming.

Me and Dave's big red Ram, all four wheels a'churning, took off across a narrow but deep ditch, bottoming out on the bump stops but still moving, bouncing, tires spinning and slinging mud high in the air, a few sodden clods whapping onto the Suburban's windshield—*splat*—like oversized guano.

Hey, this *was* fun!

I did a horseshoe in the middle of the semi-grassy field, and stopped with my engine running.

The Suburban backed up slowly, coming to a stop on the road directly in front of me and maybe forty yards distant. The De Ville nosed up to its bumper.

And waited.

Three minutes.

Five.

Seven . . .

Maybe they were lighting up, talking ACC basketball: Hey, how 'bout that Tim Duncan?

Nope. Here they came.

Out of the Chevy stepped Hector Diaz (I assumed), so big he barely fit through the doorway. Behind him from the right rear exited a Latino about half Hector's size. Which still made him above average. He looked like a fox about to invade the henhouse, grin of malicious humor pasted on his face. *We'll see about that*, I thought.

Gonzales came around the back of the Suburban just as Freckles and the equipment man egressed the De Ville. From under a lab coat, Foxface withdrew a short, stubby machine pistol, its make indistinct from where I stood. The high-capacity magazine protruding from its belly was not indistinct.

I'd need to take him first.

While I was considering how best to accomplish that, Dave stepped out of a copse thirty yards to my left, carrying a Savage twelve-bore double as negligently as if it were part of his arm. I'd seen him shoot that gun often; it *was* a part of his arm. He said to the group spread out in front of me, "And why wasn't I invited?"

Diaz just looked at him, then at me. Back to Dave. Like someone watching a tennis match. All the while he said nothing, just stood there as big as Mount Rainier.

Gonzales moved toward Dave, as if preparing to brace this unexpected challenger. Diaz would have none of it. He growled something in Spanish. Gonzales slowed, but didn't stop. Quick as an adder, a gun appeared in Hector's hand, aimed at Gonzales. More Spanish, too rapid to follow, but Gonzales gave as good as he got until Hector suddenly shot him in his good eye, *BAM!*—just like that, with no warning at all. The remains of Ralph Gonzales crumpled to the ground, lay twitching spasmodically, blood pooling under the head.

Diaz turned to me. I was about to start the ball when a Mercury Topaz careened onto the gravel road, rear end slewing around, and slid noisily to a halt not far behind the Suburban. Out of it popped the big bearded Muslim and his little splotchy pal, Karl.

The unexpected troops unnerved Foxface. He upped the machine pistol and hosed down the Topaz and everything near it, including Dave, but excluding Karl and the big Bosnian, who wisely sought the ditch beside the road. Dave fell to one knee, hit somewhere belowdeck. When Foxface ran dry and reached under his coat for another mag, Dave gave him both barrels. Down the man went, machine pistol plopping benignly in a puddle.

The two non-Hispanics had stood as if mesmerized, but now joined the fray. They ran into an obstacle. Karl had obviously found another gun since I bent his Frommer—a bigger one at that—and he rose out of the ditch like Lazarus, splotches of mud on his face, and employed it well. He shot Freckles in the side, then the arm, then the knee, then the chest, all in the span of two heartbeats. Freckles fell back against the Caddy, tried briefly to hold on to the antenna, then sank.

Meanwhile, the equipment man used a stainless-steel something-or-other to blast away at Karl. Ineffectually; his bullets kicked up divots while Karl was attending to Freckles. Then Karl turned his attention to this current threat and four more shots rang out, very rapidly. Only one struck home. One was enough. Adam's-apple-less, Equipment Man stumbled aimlessly in a circle for a few seconds, gasping and grasping at his neck, then seemed to implode.

The bearded one was up now, beside Karl, a long-barreled revolver aimed at Hector, who'd remained unmoving during the carnage, all of which had taken place in maybe ten seconds.

Dave reloaded his shotgun from an elastic shell holder on its stock, then he too covered Diaz. Karl dropped the mag from his pistol, replaced it with a fresh one, tripped the slide release—*clack!*—and went to check the four men down, feeling for the carotid pulse. No dice; a shake of his head, once, twice, thrice, four times. Only a coroner needed.

Diaz stood looking at me.

I could feel the heat. The hate. The desire.

*You came here to finish this*, I said to me. *Go do it.*

With Dave hopping along at my shoulder, I limped the forty-odd paces with my hands in the pockets of my jacket, to confront Hector Diaz at long last, up close and personal.

• • •

To Dave, I said: "Take no part in this."

"Who, me?"

"Tell the others."

He stepped aside to do so.

Then there was Hector, ten feet away, his gun hanging at arm's length beside his right knee. He smelled like a basketful of unwashed athletic supporters. His teeth were few and far between, his breath noticeably fetid even at this distance.

"You and that one,"—he inclined his head toward Gonzales's body— "sucker me here good, you know? But I was gon' to kill you anyway, sooner or later."

"Lawrence Goodall came to me in a dream. Said to tell you hello," I replied.

Blank stare for a moment, then the light of comprehension. Snapping the sausagelike thumb and middle finger of his left hand, he said, "He was nothing, that ol' man. I kill him quick."

Hector was so blindingly fast that his gun was almost up, almost pointed at my face before I could react and poke my jacket pocket forward, gun tight in my fist. I knew it was hopeless, that I'd started too late, but tried anyway, intending to take him with me, waiting for the wicked blow of his bullet, when suddenly his jaw eructed blood and teeth, one of his incisors smacking into my cheek, adhering wetly as he staggered from the impact, but still getting off his shot despite the awful gaping wound, his bullet sailing away, the blast from his big magnum revolver at such close range rending my eardrums as I fired through my pocket, *BOOM!BOOM!BOOM!BOOM!BOOM!* in one long muffled roll of thunder, point-blank, all five slugs striking his barrel chest, punching through the enormous rib cage, expanding, ripping, spinning, shredding, blowing holes into his lungs and heart and dumping him in the mud.

Like he'd dumped Lawrence Goodall.

For no reason except pure, undiluted meanness.

Well. He was mean no more.

• • •

"That was the stupidest thing I ever saw you do!" Dave yelled, hobbling over to me. "And I've seen you pull some boners!"

I made no reply. Because he was right.

"What the hell were you thinking about!" Grabbing me, turning me to face him. "It sure as hell wasn't Cullen," so mad he was quivering. Suddenly he pulled me to him, hugging tightly until he'd regained some composure. "You scared me to death," he said into my ear. "You ever do that again and *I'll* shoot you!"

"And I'll deserve it." I looked down at what was left of Hector Diaz and shivered. "He had me nailed."

"You're damned right he did. Why the hell did you wait? Why didn't you just shoot him through the coat when you walked up to him?"

"Had something to tell him."

"Something to . . . What the hell is this, amateur night?" Starting to quiver again.

"It was about Lawrence."

That stopped him. His face showed understanding, and remembrance. With a big hand on my shoulder, he said, "I know, bud. But you almost bought it there. Diaz took you by surprise, and you flat never would have caught up."

"Don't I know." I shivered again. "It was foolish."

"Thank goodness one of the Muslims bought in," said Dave.

I looked up, startled. "One of the Muslims? I thought you . . ."

"Not I. That sneaky Mexican snake had too much of a head start for me, too, though I was trying to make it up."

Glancing at the Muslim duo, busy with their own agenda at the moment, I said, "Which one?"

He looked where I was looking. "Are you kidding? Neither one of them. Shot came from across the paved road, near the golf course."

"The hell you say," from me, squinting into the distance. "That's a quarter of a mile. Maybe better."

He shrugged. "All I know is I heard the shot and it came from there."

I mulled things over. "What makes you so sure it was a member of the Muslim faction?"

"Who else? If it was Odie or the Ax, they'd have come in by now, don't you think?"

He chewed on it a moment, continuing with, "It couldn't have been your dad. His old carbine doesn't have that kind of reach. Well, whoever it was, they were either very good or very lucky."

"Or both," I said.

"Right, and we'll probably never know for certain," he ventured, prodding the body at our feet with his boot. "That you, Hector? Don't want you popping up again, you nine-lived son of a bitch."

Abruptly Dave sagged against me. "My leg hurts," through his teeth.

"Let's go sit down," I said, and we did.

# Fifty

While I was applying a tourniquet to Dave's thigh, the big bearded Bosnian and his splotchy sidekick searched the Caddy and the Suburban. They found more guns, plus boxes of ammunition, a carton of Luckies, a Zippo, and two Harley-Davidson buckles.

No money.

One gym bag in the Caddy's trunk. Inside was a pack of Trojans, unsullied. Thank goodness.

No money.

Then, hidden in a compartment in the undercarriage of the Suburban, eureka. Money. In copious quantity.

The large fellow brought his foliated bulk over to stand beside Dave, who was now sitting with his back against the Topaz, wounded leg straight out in front of him. "Is leg okay?" he queried solicitously.

"Never better. The look of pain on my face is to gain sympathy," Dave answered.

The big man frowned, then brightened. "You pull my rope, eh?"

"Chain," Dave and I said in unison.

Everybody laughed, easing accumulated tensions. We'd all had a stressful afternoon.

"We must leave," said our Muslim pal. "Police are on the way. We have police band monitored, and all routes watched, so we know this by telephone."

"Do you have a sharpshooter across the road?" I asked.

"Sharpshooter? Oh, with a rifle. No, we do not. Why?"

"Just checking."

The big Muslim prepared to leave. "We will abide by our agreement, and make the money drop as planned."

I nodded. "Never doubted it. Thanks for the help."

"Yours too," extending a paw the size of a fruit platter. Ever adventurous, I shook it. Dave did, as well. Then the two of them drove off in David's backrest.

"Could you call me an ambulance, now?" said my pal, my bosom buddy, the guy at my feet with a hole in his thigh not terribly unlike the one in mine, except mine wasn't bleeding and his was.

"Sure. You're an ambul—"

He tried to kick me with his good leg.

# Fifty-one

The sheriff's homicide man was a dapper dude, a haberdasher's dream; his raiment and ancillary items probably cost as much as Diaz's Suburban. Hair clipped tight to his ebony skull, he was too short for an NBA center. Maybe a power forward. Strong grip, long, tapered fingers enclosing mine when we shook. Gold cuff links; heavy college ring; Baume & Mercier Riviera two-tone, champagne face. Probably had a matching Walther P-88 in a calfskin Gucci shoulder holster.

Over a leather-bound legal pad he poised a Cross pen, ready to depose me. "So what happened here, sir?"

Mr. Polite Interrogator. In a backroom downtown, he'd probably use a truncheon.

"Those gentlemem"—I waved inclusively at the bodies lying in the sun—"started shooting at me and my cohort."

"Yes, sir. And why did they do that, do you think?"

"I haven't a clue."

He nodded to my jacket pocket, bullet-riddled and scorched from powder burns. "What happened to your jacket?"

"Some of their shots came pretty close."

He arched a skeptical brow.

"What were the two of you doing here?"

"Showing some foreigners around. They were thinking about buying land."

He looked around. "I don't see any Land For Sale signs."

"You neither? It's why we were turning around to leave, just when those maniacs came zooming in here and started blasting away."

Again the arch, other brow. Ambidextrous. I couldn't do that.

"And you have no idea why."

"Nope."

"Where are these foreigners?"

"They were scared off."

He arched both brows. That I could do.

"Who were they?"

"The foreigners?"

"Yes, sir."

"Some folks from Bosnia. Never caught any names."

He scribbled on his pad.

"How did you know them?" *Skritch, skritch.*

"They were recommended to me by an associate."

He stopped writing. "You're shuckin' and jivin', my man."

"What does that mean?"

"Telling me what you think I want to hear."

Seeing the conversation was heading south, I said, "How about calling an ambulance for my friend?"

"In a minute." Scribble, scribble.

I said, "He's bleeding. Do it now."

More scribbling.

I jerked the pen out of his hand. He was deciding what to do about that when Fanner arrived. I tossed the deputy his Cross and went to greet the lieutenant.

•  •  •

"What happened to your jacket?" Fanner said as salutation.

"Boll weevils."

"You mean moths?"

"Jacket's cotton."

Dave snorted.

Fanner smiled. "Everything we say to one another for the next few minutes will be off the record. Otherwise, you will simply lie."

I nodded my acceptance.

"Tell me."

I did, most of it.

"So that is the real Hector Diaz," he said, pointing at the real Hector Diaz.

"Take his prints, then *you* tell me," I suggested.

Dave snorted again, this time painfully.

"How's the leg?" I asked him.

"Still there." He loosened the tourniquet a little.

"An ambulance is on the way," said Fanner.

"From Baltimore?"

"Did your Muslim friends take part in this?"

"It's mostly their handiwork. One of them, dude named Karl, is a wizard with a shortgun. He nailed those two Irish in half a tick."

"Who did that one?" Fanner indicated the machine pistol wielder.

"I must confess," spoke Dave, as he retightened the tourniquet, grimacing as he did so.

"Don't make a face. The lieutenant'll think you're a sissy."

Fanner gave me a look of censure. Lately, more and more people did that. "And Gonzales?" he said.

"He was first to go. Diaz."

"Hector must have surmised a double cross," Fanner conjectured.

"Or maybe there was a falling-out among thieves. Gonzales may have been doing the Curly shuffle, trying to scam us both."

"Then where would he stand in future deals?" Dave objected.

"Perhaps his intent was to desert our clime for good after the score," said Fanner.

"We'll never know. Not now," from me.

Fanner nodded. "Who did Diaz?"

"Me."

"The coat?"

"Yes."

"Why through the pocket? You might have missed."

"Second rule of gunfighting."

"Second? What is the first?"

"Have a gun."

"Oh. Right. And the second?"

"Have it in your hand."

"Ah. And was Diaz aware of that rule?"

"You betcha, and his hand wasn't in his pocket, and his gun was much bigger than mine."

"And he may have suspected you of violating both rules."

I smiled.

"Little did he know," Fanner concluded.

And then the ambulance came.

• • •

Heather and I visited Dave in the hospital next morning. She carried a foot-tall decorated tree; I took along a book.

Jason and the Ax were about to leave when we walked in. Dad sat over in a chair by the window, saying, "If I'd a been there instead of himself"—he stabbed a thumb at me—"you wouldn't be in here now."

"Don't I know it," Dave agreed. He turned to me. "Why is it that when you and I both get shot, my wound is more serious?"

"Because he's Wyatt Earp," said Heather.

"Come again?" from Axel.

"Never mind," I said, then to Dave: "How's the gam?"

"No jogging this week."

"How's the nurse?"

"She's a he."

"Jason offer to take your place?"

"Ha-ha," said Jason. "We in the gay community don't make fun of you straights."

"Like hell," laughed Ax. "You call us breeders."

Jason, suddenly serious, objected, "I'd never say that."

I touched his shoulder. "We know. It's why we tolerate you."

"Tolerate. Gee, thanks."

The atmosphere cleared. Somewhat. I glared at Ax. He turned palms up, as if saying, "What?"

In popped Dave's nurse, who looked like Erik Estrada on eight hundred calories a day. "Enough, already. Shoo, shoo. Mr. Michaels needs his rest. He has an extra hole in him."

I mouthed, *Mr. Michaels?* to Dave, who shrugged and mouthed, *Kiss my ass,* back at me. I reached over to hand him the book I'd brought. He took it, then read the title aloud: *"Pain: The Gift Nobody Wants."*

"Great. This'll get me through the night," he said dryly.

"Don't mention it. I've got one at home entitled *Pain: Hanging Around with Tyler Vance."*

Nobody laughed.

"Humor-impaired, all of you," I complained, as we left en masse, the nurse shoo-shooing us along.

Dave gave me a thumbs-up from the bed. He was my friend and he was going to be okay.

# Fifty-two

It was blustery and cold and leaden outside the Vance ancestral home, warm and potato-soupy inside, the odor of homemade yeast rolls and rum balls in the air. Pop was at the kitchen counter, up to his elbows in flour, Web nearby trying to crack eggs without getting pieces of shell in the bowl. Cullen was helping Heather decorate Dad's tree, a stately pine just this morning plucked from its secluded moorings and carried to the house in the bed of Dave's Dodge—with him driving, of course, injured leg and all.

McElroy and I sat in the living room quaffing eggnog and lapping up the ambience. He was saying, "Word I get is that the Mexican authorities have taken advantage of Diaz's absence to shake up what was left of his organization south of the border. Actually, with Resovic out of the picture for so long, Hector'd let things pretty much go to seed. He was more into fuddling and partying than fiscal management. And he was a mean bastard. Not much loyalty amongst his employees and associates."

"They scattered?"

"Like banty hens after a handful of corn."

Cullen came through in search of a specific box of ornaments, which I disclaimed knowledge of. He was dressed in trousers that had fit him perfectly. When he was four. They now ended somewhat north of his ankles.

"Son, those pants are cut for high water, aren't they?"

Putting his quest on hold momentarily, he paused, looking quizzically at me as he ran the unfamiliar southernism through his mind. Couldn't put it together.

"It means they're a bit short for you."

"Oh." He brightened, looking down. "Yep. Reckon so. But they got lotsa pockets." Off he went.

McElroy was chuckling to himself between sips. "Haven't heard that expression."

"Got it from Ethyl. One of my favorites," I said between sips.

Dave came in, peg-legged and hangdog, crutch under one arm, and parked in a wing chair near the fire. Reached for my eggnog.

"You'll draw back a nub," I warned. He took it anyway.

"How about I go get you some?" I asked.

"This is fine," he said between sips.

I went to fetch me another cup. Returning, I told Dave, "The colonel thinks things will quiet down, now. Means you can stop hanging around all the time. Stay home more. Maybe move to Buffalo."

We sallied thus until well into the gloaming, the air thick with contentment, bonhomie, and Christmas.

• • •

Lucky 32 isn't only for rich folks, they just make you feel rich when you dine there. The decor is mostly wood and red vinyl; mahogany paneling, square cherry-rimmed tables inset with grey Formica, a fire tulip at each table in a simple glass bud vase. A spotlight is affixed high overhead, aimed at the center of each table, with red floodlamps suffusing the room with a merry glow.

For the season, a huge wreath was attached to the wall in the bar/ dining area. Pierre did me a favor and seated me under it. I'd've tipped him a nickel if I'd had the change.

Why was I alone? you ask, two days before Christmas, with a houseful of family just a few miles away. Because my Dad had said: "Heather's office assistant called. Heather wants you to meet her at Lucky 32 tonight around sixish." And I had said back to him: "Melinda actually said 'sixish'?" And Dad said: "Don't know Melinda, just passin' on the message. You plan to meet her or not?" And I said, "I thought Heather went to Charlotte to see her parents." And he said: "Well, she must be back, son." And I said, "Will you keep Cullen?"

So here I was, and it was sixish, and Heather wasn't.

I looked at my watch, an exquisite Timex with digital readout and a band that matched the holster under my jacket. It was twenty after six.

If I didn't eat something soon, Pierre would have to prop me up in my seat.

At six-thirty, out of sheer desperation I ordered the baked artichoke dip. In a jiffy there it was. Mayo base, Parmesan cheese, a little sour cream, parsley—you probably know it well. Round Carr's crackers on the side, and little slabs of toast. I dipped and ate and refrained from making a yummy sound, which would have been inappropriate in a place that tony.

Six forty-five came, and with it a tall blonde to the bar. Male heads swiveled.

No Heather.

Boredom is a terrible thing. For want of something better to do, and since VH1 was blaring on all three TV sets spotted about the room, I went back to the blonde. Others, equally beguiled, joined me in surreptitious scrutiny.

Maybe five six or seven, hard to tell with her seated on a barstool. Gorgeous hair, thickly gleaming and piled high, secured I had no idea how but adding to the overall impression of loftiness. High cheekbones, satiny skin, eyes bluer than blue. Mae West figure; maybe not quite as much frontage but ample from the rear without apparent necessity for artificial restraint.

Voluptuous.

She caught me watching, in the mirror. And watched back. Not brazen, but not coy either.

Ahem. Where was Heather?

Our eyes met once again, briefly, then hers slid away. But not before the smile, lopsided and offbeat.

I felt like I knew her. Or should know her. Or once had known her.

Only I hadn't. I'd never examined that face before; I would have remembered. It was that kind of face.

Seven oh-one. No Heather.

At the bar, no blonde either.

Ah, well.

Now what to keep me occupied?

VH1? Better to slash my wrists and write my name on the tabletop in blood.

"Mr. Vance?" A server I didn't know approached.

"I confess."

"You have a call, sir." He handed me a phone and I told him thanks.

"Why aren't you here yet? I'm starving and the dip has disappeared," I began.

Soft chuckle. Not Heather's.

"Harmony?"

"Hiya, sport."

"You still in town?"

"Leaving tonight. How's the leg?"

"Good. Listen, I'm glad you called. I wanted to be sure that you got your money."

"Indeedamundo. And there's lots more than a hundred grand here."

"You deserve it. If it hadn't been for you, who knows what would have happened to my family."

No sound for a few seconds, then: "Did you tell Hector hey for me?"

"No, but I gave him a message from someone else."

Longer pause.

"You still there?" I said.

"Yes. For some odd reason I'm reluctant to ring off."

"Me too. Eloise?"

Chuckle. "Hmm?"

"If you ever need anything . . ."

"I can count on you?"

"You bet."

Another long pause.

"You know the really, really sad thing?"

"What?"

"I believe I can. And Tyler . . . don't ogle blondes in bars. Heather wouldn't like it."

Then she was gone.

I leaped up and ran to the bank of pay phones near the bathrooms. One of the phones was hanging by its cord amid the cloying but not unpleasant essence of Joy.

Back to my table. And there was a box, gift-wrapped, bright paper and a red bow.

I sat down. Looked at the package.

Finally opened it.

Inside, nestled in a wad of tissue paper, was an empty cartridge case. A *fired* empty cartridge case. Long and sleek, brightly gleaming. Its headstamp read ".308 Norma Magnum." Just the cartridge for long-range precision shooting . . . for winning at Camp Perry . . .

For taking a man out at a quarter-mile.

"Well, I'll be damned," I said to me.

A hand-lettered note read:

> I told you not to take any chances
> with that big galloot. Hardhead.
>
> HC

I looked at the note and the cartridge case for a very long time, and left the restaurant in a disquieting spirit of felicity and melancholy.

# Epilogue

Cullen and I, sitting on the couch before a dwindling but cheerful fire, watching light dance in the eaves, bulbs winking and blinking like fireflies on the tree. Dad and Ethyl this Christmas Eve have wrapped gifts and placed them around the manger at the foot of the tree. All are festively colorful, ribboned with gay yarn, some bedecked with holly sprigs or mistletoe. Santa Claus artistically depicted; and cherubs; Madonna and Child; Rudolph with his consorts; snow, snow, snow.

Christmas.

How I love it.

Cullen does, too. He sits beside me—leaning against my arm—freshly scrubbed, still warm from the shower, a poinsettia bloom to his cheeks, eyes half lidded. Sleepy; soon visions of sugarplums . . .

For now, he's watching tiny skaters on our plastic pond, swirling and twirling, the tracks of their skates making broad figure eights. His gaze swings back to the tree, then up to the angel, down to the Babe.

"Daddy?"

"Hmmm?"

"Are you *sure* there's no Santa?"

"Yes."

"But are you sure there is a Jesus?"

"Yes."

His eyes seek mine.

"Positive?"

"Yes."

"You promise?"

"I promise."

Smiling, he says, "That's good, isn't it?"

"The best."

Holding my forefinger with all of his, trusting little head sinking slowly down my arm, he reaches for sleep. Where his mother dwells.

They celebrate there, together.